MW01124256

Dragon Dojo Brotherhood

Reign of Dragons

Fate of Dragons

Blood of Dragons

Age of Dragons

Fall of Dragons

Death of Dragons

Queen of Dragons

A Legend Among Dragons

Blackbriar Academy

The Trials of Blackbriar Academy

The Shadows of Blackbriar Academy

The Hex of Blackbriar Academy

The Blood Oath of Blackbriar Academy

The Battle of Blackbriar Academy

The Nighthelm Guardian Series

City of the Sleeping Gods

City of Fractured Souls

City of the Enchanted Queen

Demon Queen Saga

Princes of the Underworld

Wars of the Underworld

Sentinel Saga

By Dahlia Leigh and Olivia Ash

The Shadow Shifter

exclusive bonus novella from the Nighthelm Guardian series, *City of the Rebel Runes*, the prequel to *City of Sleeping Gods* only available to subscribers.

https://wispvine.com/newsletter/olivia-ash-email-signup/

Enjoying the series? Awesome! Help others discover the Dragon Dojo Brotherhood by leaving a review at Amazon.

A LEGEND AMONG DRAGONS

Book Eight of the Dragon Dojo Brotherhood

OLIVIA ASH

The end game is here. Come hell or high water, I *will* win.

War is coming—one I didn't start, but I can damn sure finish.

As I gather my allies and put the final touches on my massive dragon army, there is one last thing I want.

The lords orb is within reach, and I need its power.

The men I love stand with me in this fight, but we're facing ancient gods and savage dragon Bosses who destroy everything in their path.

The fabled orb can imbue my men with my power and protect them as we march into battle. But even then, it's a gamble, because we're up against forces we've never seen before.

My nemesis makes a pact with the dragon gods—and the dead awaken.

As Kinsley Vaer uses innocent humans as bait, I swoop in to save them from her clutches.

But when she triggers the gods and aim them in my direction, I use all my magic and wit to fend off chaos, deception, and an army of the dead.

Let them come. They're about to know my true strength.

I'm a warrior, the only white diamond dragon in existence, and most of all a protector.

Anyone foolish enough to attack my home and those I love will regret it.

I've finally accepted my destiny as a hero and queen.

And once I vanquish the gods and their monsters, I'll become a legend.

CONTENTS

Important Characters & Terms   XV

Chapter One   1
Chapter Two   11
Chapter Three   21
Chapter Four   27
Chapter Five   35
Chapter Six   43
Chapter Seven   49
Chapter Eight   67
Chapter Nine   77
Chapter Ten   89
Chapter Eleven   97
Chapter Twelve   105
Chapter Thirteen   121
Chapter Fourteen   129
Chapter Fifteen   139
Chapter Sixteen   149
Chapter Seventeen   157
Chapter Eighteen   171
Chapter Nineteen   179
Chapter Twenty   187
Chapter Twenty-One   205
Chapter Twenty-Two   219
Chapter Twenty-Three   227
Chapter Twenty-Four   237
Chapter Twenty-Five   247
Chapter Twenty-Six   257
Chapter Twenty-Seven   267
Chapter Twenty-Eight   275

Chapter Twenty-Nine   285
Chapter Thirty   299
Chapter Thirty-One   307
Chapter Thirty-Two   317
Chapter Thirty-Three   331
Chapter Thirty-Four   337
Chapter Thirty-Five   345
Chapter Thirty-Six   353
Chapter Thirty-Seven   363

Author Notes   381
Books by Olivia Ash   387
About the Author   389

IMPORTANT CHARACTERS & TERMS

CHARACTERS

Rory Quinn: a former Spectre and the current dragon vessel. Rory was raised as a brutal assassin by her mentor Zurie, but escaped that life. When Zurie tried to force Rory to return, Rory was forced to kill her former mentor. Rory's newfound magic is constantly evolving and changing, and now that she has shifted, her magic continues to defy all known limits. Her diamond dragon is the only one of its kind, and the only other diamond dragons known to exist were the fabled dragon gods themselves. But Rory was born a human, so she can't be a *goddess*... can she?

Andrew Darrington (Drew): a fire dragon shifter. Drew is one of the heirs to the Darrington dragon family. With no real regard for rules or the law in general, Drew tends to know things he shouldn't and isn't fond of sharing that intel with just anyone. Though he originally intended to kidnap Rory and use her power for his own means, her tenacity and strength enchanted him. They have a pact: if he doesn't try to control her, she won't try to control him. Drew sees her as an equal in a world where he's stronger, smarter, and faster than nearly everyone else.

Tucker Chase: a weapons expert and former Knight. Tucker's a loveable goofball who treats every day like it's his last—because it very well might be. He was forced to kill his father, the General of the now-defunct Knights anti-dragon terrorist organization, when the man brought a war to Rory's door. Tucker was originally assigned to hunt Rory down and turn her in to his father, but as he spent more time with her, she became the true family he'd never had. To protect her, Tucker fed his father false intel about her abilities—and gave up his old life to stay at her side.

Levi Sloane: an ice dragon shifter and former Vaer soldier who went feral when his commander killed his very ill little sister. When he was feral, Rory saved him from a snare trap on the edge of the Vaer lands, and he has been by her side ever since. Feral dragons slowly lose touch with their human selves, but Rory helped bring him back from the brink. Though all dragons can communicate telepathically when they touch, Levi and Rory can also communicate this way in human form. To save Rory's life, he and his dragon healed their relationship, and Levi can once again shift and retain full control. He's the only dragon to ever come back from being feral.

Jace Goodwin: a thunderbird dragon shifter and former Master of the Fairfax Dragon Dojo. Jace grew up in high society and has the vast network to prove it. A warrior, he used to operate as the General of the Fairfax army—and his only soft spot is for Rory. He gave up his position at the dojo to take her as his mate, and now his full attention is devoted to her. As Rory's mate, he is deeply connected to her and her magic, and he's the only person who can soothe her wild power. If she dies, his dragon will go feral, so he has quite a bit at stake if one of Rory's many enemies comes after her.

Irena Quinn: Rory's sister and former heir to the Spectre organization. She betrayed Zurie when she discovered her former mentor wanted to sell Rory as an assassin-for-hire, which would mean they would never see each other again. A brutal fighter, Irena's only purpose in life is to keep her sister safe and destroy the Spectres organization that almost killed them both. A powerful bio-weapon created by the Vaer gave Irena strange super-strength and bright green eyes that are eerily similar to Kinsley Vaer. Irena might develop magic or even a dragon of her own, though no one knows for sure what Kinsley's experiments have done to her.

Zurie Bronwen (deceased): former leader of the Spectres and former mentor to Rory and Irena. Zurie was a brutal assassin and held the title of the Ghost. Cold-hearted, calculating, and clever, Zurie considered both Rory and Irena as failed experiments—and she was determined to kill them both. The war she started between the Fairfax family, the Vaer family, and the Knights will have lasting consequences, and it's unclear if Zurie realized just how terrible the outcome would be.

Diesel Richards: a former Knight turned Spectre.

With Zurie dead, Rory out of the picture, and Irena excommunicated for her betrayal, Diesel is now the Ghost. His incentive is to kill both Irena and Rory to ensure no one threatens his rule. He's helped Rory once and tried to kill her on other occasions, so Rory isn't sure what Diesel really wants or what game he's playing with her life.

Harper Fairfax: a thunderbird, the Boss of the Fairfax dragon family, and Jace's cousin. Harper is friendly and bubbly, full of life and joy, but Rory knows a fighter when she sees one. The young woman is smart and cunning. As Rory's first friend, Harper has a special place in Rory's life. She will do anything to protect her friend—including going to war to protect her.

Russell Kane: a thunderbird and new Master of the Fairfax Dojo now that Jace has stepped down. He endured brutal trials to earn his place as the new dojo master. He grew up with Jace and Harper in the dojo and has a deep love for both the castle itself and the people within it. He will do anything to protect the Fairfax dragons—and Harper, for whom he seems to have a soft spot.

Eric Dunn (deceased): a fire dragon and part of the Fairfax family, Eric was the one man Irena was beginning to let herself love. After a betrayal by someone she adored, Irena had shut down. Eric's death broke her, and she left Rory's side shortly after.

Brett Clarke: a former Knight and once the General's second-in-command. With the General still out of commission after his last run-in with Rory, Brett led the Knights' charge against the Fairfax Dojo. When the Knights lost, Brett was captured, and he realized everything he knew about dragons was wrong. He helped Rory defeat the Knights, but they're still not sure if he's trustworthy.

William Chase (deceased): mostly referred to as the General. William is a former military man who was discharged from the army in disgrace for his terrorist connections to the Knights. He now runs them in a brutal regime that kills defectors, and he now has his sights set on his son Tucker.

Guy Durand (deceased): an ice dragon and former second-in-command to Jace Goodwin at the dragon dojo. Guy always wanted power. When he lost the challenge to Jace for control of the dojo, he joined the Vaer and gave over top-secret intel about Rory and the dojo itself. He was killed by Jace after he tried to kidnap Rory and return her to Kinsley.

Ian Rixer (deceased): a fire dragon, Kinsley Vaer's half-brother, and a master manipulator. Ian was smarmy, elitist, and arrogant. He was often referred to as honey-coated evil for his ability to speak so calmly and kindly, even while torturing his prey. He treated everything like a game, and playing that game with Rory cost him his life. He tried to control her and Jace's magic with specially designed iron cuffs to block their power, but Rory's magic can't be contained. She destroyed the cuffs—and him.

Mason Greene (deceased): a fire dragon and sadistic Vaer lord tasked with dismantling the Spectre organization. Irena gave him access to their sensitive Spectre intel in exchange for giving her and Rory a fresh start, but he betrayed them both. His attempt to kill Rory backfired massively and ultimately cost him his life.

Kinsley Vaer: an ice dragon shifter and the Boss of the Vaer family. Her power and cruelty make most grown men tremble in fear. She's utterly ruthless, cruel, vindictive, and vengeful... the sort to kill the messenger just because she's angry. She's increasingly frustrated that Rory has slipped through her fingers so often, and she's done giving her minions chances to redeem themselves. Now, it's personal—and Kinsley is coming after everything Rory loves.

Jett Darrington: a fire dragon, the Boss of the Darrington family, and Drew's father. He wants Rory for reasons not even Drew fully knows, but everyone's certain it can't be good. He disowned his son when Drew wouldn't hand Rory over, but he promised Drew everything he could ever dream of—including ruling the Darrington family—if he betrays her.

Milo Darrington: a fire dragon, Drew's brother, and current heir to the Darrington family line purely because he's older than Drew. Not much of a fighter, but an excellent politician and master manipulator. He's been growing increasingly resentful of his younger brother's skill and charm. When he tried to kidnap Rory and blackmail Drew into doing his bidding, she shifted into her dragon to beat him into submission. He knows her secret, but he's too terrified of her to tell a soul. Probably.

Isaac Palarne: a fire dragon and the Boss of the Palarne family. A skilled warrior and empowering speaker, Isaac can rally almost anyone to his cause. He's a deeply noble man, but there's something unnerving about his eagerness to get Rory to come to the Palarne capital.

Elizabeth Andusk: a golden fire dragon and Boss of the Andusk family. Vain and materialistic, Elizabeth can command attention without even a word. She exudes power mainly through her beauty and has a knack for getting people to share secrets they wouldn't have shared otherwise. She's determined to obtain Rory and considers the girl to be nothing more than another object to control and display.

Victor Bane: a fire dragon and Boss of the Bane family. He's a brutal fighter, excellent negotiator, and never gets caught in his many illicit dealings. With his hot temper, he picks fights whenever he can. He has very little direction and purpose, as he is merely looking for the next thing—or person—he can steal.

Natasha Bane: a fire dragon and Victor's sister, Natasha has almost as much influence and control over the Bane family as her brother does. She's smart, clever, and cunning. A sultry temptress, she enjoys bending men to her whims. Though both demanding and entitled, she knows when to keep her mouth shut to get her way.

Aki Nabal: an ice dragon and Boss of the Nabal family. He's excellent with money and can always see three moves ahead in any dealings—both financial and political. Clever and observant, he can pinpoint a fighter's weaknesses fairly quickly, though he's not an exceptional fighter himself. He believes money is power—and that you can never have enough of either.

Jade Nabal: an ice dragon and Aki's daughter, Jade is young and not much one for words. As a silent observer who prefers to watch rather than engage, little is known about Jade. She and Rory have met once, only briefly, and Rory knows there's far more to Jade than meets the eye.

Other Terms

The Dragon Gods: the origin of all dragon power. The three Dragon Gods are mostly just lore, nowadays. No one even remembers their names. But with the dragon vessel showing up in the world, everyone is beginning to wonder if perhaps they're a bit more than legend...

Dragon Vessel: According to myth, the dragon vessel is the one living creature powerful and worthy enough to possess the magic of the dragon gods. Rory Quinn was kicked into an ancient ceremony pit—the one Mason Greene didn't know was used to judge the worthiness of those who entered. With that ritual, Rory unknowingly brought the immense power of legend back to the world.

Castle Ashgrave: the legendary home of the dragon gods, said to be nothing more than ruin and myth. Drew believes he's found the location, but he's not yet sure.

Mate-bond: the connection only thunderbirds can share that connects two souls. The mate-bond is not finalized until the pair make love for the first time.

Even before it's finalized, however, the mate-bond is powerful. The duo can vaguely feel each other's whereabouts and, if one should die, the other would go feral.

Magical cuffs: complex handcuffs that cover the entirety of a shifter's hands when they're in human form. These cuffs are designed to keep thunderbird magic at bay. The Vaer have designed special cuffs just for Rory, with the ability to block her magic. These cuffs come with a remote that allows the captor to electrocute their captive to help subdue them, as thunderbirds are notoriously powerful.

Spectres: a cruel and heartless organization that raises brutal assassins and hates dragonkind. The Spectres specialize in killing dragons and are known as some of the fiercest murderers on the planet, in part thanks to their highly advanced tech that no one else has yet to duplicate. They're a spider web network that spans the globe, all run by the Ghost. Often, Spectres are raised from birth within the organization and are never given the choice to join. Once a Spectre, always a Spectre—quitting comes with a death sentence.

Override Device: Spectre tech. Very frail and easy to break, it fits into USB ports and can grant access to sensitive files. Though imperfect and obscenely expensive to create, it *usually* works.

Voids: Spectre tech. Fired from a gun with special attachments, a void can force a camera to loop the last 10 seconds and allow for unseen access to secured locations.

The Knights: an international anti-dragon terrorist organization bent on eradicating dragons from the world. Run by General William Chase, they'll do anything and kill anyone it takes to further their mission. There are some rebel Knights organizations that think the current General is too soft, despite his brutal rampage against dragons and his willingness to kill his own family should the need arise.

Fire Dragons: the most common type of dragon shifter. Fire dragons breathe fire and smoke in their dragon forms. They're found in a wide array of colors.

Ice Dragons: uncommon dragons that can freeze others on contact and breathe icy blasts. Usually, ice dragons are white, pale blue, or royal blue. The only known black ice dragons belong to the Vaer family.

Thunderbirds: dragon shifters that glow in their dragon forms and possess the magic of electricity and lightning in both their dragon and human forms. They're the most feared dragons in the world, and also the rarest.

The Seven Dragon Families: the seven dragon organizations that are run like the mob. Each family values different things, from wealth to power to adrenaline. Usually, a dragon is born into a dragon family and never leaves, but there are some who betray their family of origin for the promise of a better life.

Andusk Family: sun dragons who prefer warm climates, almost all of which are golden or orange fire dragons. They're notoriously vain, focused on beauty and being adored. Fairly materialistic, the Andusk dragons hoard wealth and gems and exploit those in less favorable positions.

Bane Family: ambitious fire dragons who deal mainly in illegal activities. They view laws as guidelines that hold others back, while they aren't stupid enough to follow others' rules. They like to see what they can get away with and push the limits.

Darrington Family: the oldest and most powerful family. Darringtons are mostly fire dragons, and angering them is considered a death sentence. They're well situated financially, with a vast network of natural resources, governments, and businesses across the globe. They're notorious for thinking they're above the rules and can get away with anything… because they usually do.

Fairfax Family: a magical family known as the only one to have thunderbird dragons. They have innate magic and talent, but sometimes lack the drive it takes to use those abilities to obtain greater power. They prefer to think of life as a game, and the only winners are those who have fun. To the Fairfax dragons, adrenaline is more important than money, but protecting each other is most important of all.

Nabal Family: wealthy fire and ice dragons. Money and information are most important to the Nabal, and they have an eerie ability to get access to even the most secured intel. Calculating and cunning, the Nabal weigh every risk before taking any action.

Palarne Family: noble fire and ice dragons known for their honor and war skill. Ruled by their ancient dragon code of ethics, the Palarne family operate as a cohesive military unit. Their skills in war are unparalleled by any other family.

Vaer Family: a secretive family of fire and ice dragons, they're known to be behind many conspiracies and dirty dealings in the world. Some see them as brutal savages, but most fear them because they have no ethics or morals, even among themselves.

CHAPTER ONE

I have to tame this wild magic. No matter the cost.

If I don't learn to control this magic soon, I could lose everything and everyone I care about. I won't let that happen.

I will learn to control the dragon gods' magic. I have to.

As I silently stalk through the hills and valleys near Castle Ashgrave, the sun's rays wash the early January morning orange. I search the area for the fighting dummies that my mate and Flynn have placed throughout the area.

I walk around a small copse of evergreen trees and spot one. This dummy is out in the open, and I can feel the weight of eyes on me. It's a heavy tension that sits between my shoulder blades. Jace and Flynn are close.

Then I spy him. The person responsible for the heavy weight. His little metallic body sits across from me on a boulder, watching me. Ashgrave. He never leaves my side lately. But there's someone else. I search the area around my evil butler and spy Jade sitting on a smaller rock behind Ashgrave. Great, now I have a watching party. I suck in a deep breath and shake out my arms to remove the tension.

Time to do this. I stride up to the fighting dummy. It's unlike any type of dummy I've seen before—two burlap bags sewn together and stuffed with rice. The bags are propped up by a wooden stand that resembles a coat rack. The burlap has a big red "X" at its center.

Jace and Flynn want me to control my magic enough to only blast a small hole through the center of the "X." If I can shoot with that type of precision, it means I'm one step closer to fully owning this power. This is the fifth dummy I've come across this morning. The other four are piles of debris that are spread across the valley floor.

I shake my head to get rid of the images of the other four dummies exploding as I concentrate on where I want my magic to go and what I want it to do. As I pool my power in my hands, I see it. I focus my blue magic into a narrow stream and shoot it through the center of the red "X." I did it.

Wings flapping against the air has me searching the sky for the two thunderbirds responsible for my early morning training. I spot them. Jace and Flynn fly toward me. Jace comes in from the west and Flynn from the east.

My dragon purrs at me. She wants to fly—I give in and shift.

As I take to the air, Flynn fires his magic at me. I roll to the left and dodge his blast. I can feel Jade's chest puff up with pride and admiration as she watches from the rock below. I still haven't figured out how her odd connection to my power works. I steal a glance and notice her eyes narrow in concern.

Jace, my mate, circles me and shoots quick short bursts of his magic at me. I pool my magic in my throat. *I need your help,* I ask my dragon.

As I fire at Jace, my power burns hot then turns cold, and spots swim in my vision as I struggle with my power. Jace turns at a quick angle to avoid the blast. My stomach tightens as another nearly uncontrollable surge of power grows within me, begging to be released. I fight against the surge, and it's like trying to tame a wild beast. It takes all my strength to pull my magic back into my body then direct the next blast to hit my mate in the left leg rather than his head. My general rolls to the right and fires back at me with his blue thunderbird magic, hitting me in the chest and sucking all of the air from my lungs. As I fall through the sky, I struggle to catch my breath. I roll over onto my back so my hardened hide will take the brunt of the impact. My head slams into the ground, and I fight the darkness that tries to pull me under.

The last time I was almost knocked unconscious was when I battled Kinsley. If it wasn't for my sister, I might not be here.

As I lie on the hard ground, I search the sky for my mate. It doesn't take long before I spot Jace circling above me. I focus my magic, and as I'm about to fire at my mate, my head swims with dizziness and my power burns hot—so hot that I feel like I'm going to burst into flames at any moment. My body turns ice cold as my ears ring. Damn it! I have to learn to control this wild magic.

My magic isn't purely physical. It can't be. This power of mine has to be a mind-body connection. If I connect my mind and body, I'll be able to master the power of the gods. The next time I meet the Vaer Boss in battle—only I will walk away. The safety of my loved ones depends on it. The world depends on it.

I press my hand against a downed tree and use it as leverage to pull myself up and stand. I shake my head to remove the black spots dancing in my vision.

The whir of Ashgrave's metal wings has me searching the sky above as a burst of confusion and concern comes to me from Jade through our connection. *I'm okay,* I tell Jade, and she nods to let my vengeful castle know that I'm fine.

I use the powerful muscles in my legs to push off from the ground and take to the sky again. Jace scored a point with that hit, but the game isn't over yet.

As I search the surrounding area for the two thunderbirds who are training me, I spy another training dummy. I pool my power into my throat, and I concentrate it into a stream that burns a hole through the middle of the "X" in its chest.

Good job. Let's do it again, my dragon tells me with a toothy grin.

The flap of wings has me flipping onto my back and firing at the thunderbird behind me. I hit Flynn in the chest, and he plummets from the sky and falls to the valley below with a growl.

A change in the air current tells me Jace is close—

too close. As I hover in the air, I tuck my wings and suddenly drop in altitude. I turn my head and notice Jace was beside me when I dropped. As I gather my magic in my throat, I concentrate on knocking the air from my mate's chest as I look into his glowing blue eyes. I focus on shooting a small stream of magic, and it hits my mate in the chest.

As I tuck my wings close to my side and angle my head toward my falling mate, I know he's fine. My dragon is laughing at the fact that he allowed us to actually hit him. Silly mate.

Jace lands on his back, digging a deep gouge into the ground beneath him.

I land on my back claws next to him as he sucks in deep breaths of air. Smoke rises from his chest, and I touch it with the tip of my wing. *I did it. I finally downed the great Jace Goodwin,* I tell him through our bond.

Ha ha, very funny. Are you going to help me up? He asks.

Nah! I shake my head. *I think you look sexy on the ground.*

Really? He grabs me with his front claws and pulls me down on top of him.

My beautiful diamond dragon coos with anticipation at the way our mate's body feels against ours.

No way. Not now, I tell her. *We still have to learn to control this magic. We need to make sure there won't be any more power surges or wild fluctuations.* She sighs her frustration but lets me pull out of our mate's grasp.

Let's go practice on the dummies before we have fun time, I tell my mate as I pull away from him. *I need to make sure I can control this magic. Our family's safety depends on it.*

Fine, he growls at me.

I look up into the sky at the sound of wings flapping. Flynn is hovering about twenty yards away, swiveling his head like he's a bobble head doll as he attempts to hide that he was watching us. The whirring of Ashgrave's wings has me watching for him as Jade lands silently next to me and my mate.

Jade extends her wing, and I brush the tip of mine against it as I stand up. *That was kick-ass, Rory. Seriously. The way you knocked out Flynn and Jace —awesome.*

I'm going to practice with the rest of the dummies. Do you want to join me? I ask her.

She nods her beautiful white head in agreement.

You ready? Or do you need more rest? I brush my wing tip across my mate's chest and wink.

After you, my queen. He pulls himself up to stand.

I push off the ground and take to the sky, still amazed at the beauty of my castle and its surrounding area as I search the vast landscape for the rest of the fighting dummies. My party does the same.

Jade flanks my left side and extends her wing. *There are two dummies in the grove to the right.*

Thanks, I tell her as I bank to the right.

My magic pools into my throat and concentrate it on making a small stream as I fire at the dummy on the right and then the one on the left. I let out a victorious roar as both streams of magic burn small holes through the center of the red "X's" on their middles. Only four dummies left.

As I search for the remaining dummies, I notice Flynn and Jace are hanging back. They're gliding and touching each other's wings. Jace won't meet my eyes and every time I try to catch Flynn's gaze he looks away. The thunderbirds are planning something.

I spy another dummy in the middle of a clearing and bank to the left to land and burn a hole into it. Jace lets out an earsplitting roar as he and Flynn land on either side of the dummy. He's challenging me. My mate knows that I'm still struggling with the surges and now he's pushing me to finally take control. If I launch an attack on the dummy with Jace and Flynn standing on either side of it, I had better hit my target, or I'll incinerate them. I focus my power into a single stream and fire it at the red "X," but at the last second my vision starts to swim and my magic swerves to the right and strikes Flynn in the upper leg.

Flynn groans and quickly jumps out of the way. Jace rushes to his side, but Flynn shakes his massive black head at him. I know the wound will heal.

I roar an order for us all to return to the castle. I can burn holes in the dummies another time. We need to tend to Flynn's wound.

This can't keep happening. I have to be more careful—more in control, because on the battlefield, when I have to deal a deadly blow, I can't afford to accidentally hit my men or my allies.

My wild magic is finally bending to my will, the way I need it to. I still need practice, but I can tell that I'm beginning to master my power. I'll use the magic of the gods to take down the Vaer and step into the role I'm meant to fulfill.

CHAPTER TWO

As we fly through the chilly midmorning sky, I fall behind Jace, Flynn, and Ashgrave to spend some time with Jade. I brush my wing against the tip of hers. *Jade, you look amazing. It's almost like you're glowing.*

Thanks, Rory. I think it might have something to do with how much I've learned since working side-by-side with Brett.

Her eyes turn downward, and I can tell there's something she's not saying. *But?* I nudge her wing with mine.

But... deep at heart, I'm a warrior, she admits. *I'm itching to get back into battle.*

You'll have your chance soon enough, I promise. *Does the connection we share bother you?*

Not at all, Jade responds. *It makes me feel close to you. You're my mentor, Rory, and my new family.*

I just wanted to make sure you're okay with it. I kinda like it too, I admit. *We're connected, like a true family like sisters.*

Jace roars as he lands in the front courtyard of the castle. Brett rushes through the front doors carrying a medical kit while Ashgrave hovers around his general's head. Flynn's large black thunderbird body lands and collapses into his human form.

Damn it. I hurt Flynn.

Jade and I tuck our wings and dive for the courtyard. I shift on the fly and roll to my human feet next to Jace. I place my hand on my mate's big black leg. *Did I really hurt him that bad? I thought it was just a flesh wound.*

He will be okay in a couple of hours. You nicked a bone, but thunderbirds heal quickly, my mate reassures me.

I rush to Flynn's side, and Jade joins me. "I'm sorry, Flynn."

"Don't you dare apologize for a righteous hit, Rory," he says with sweat dripping down his face. "I'll be good as new in a few hours."

"Ashgrave, please make Flynn comfortable in his

room and ask the doctors and nurses to care for him there."

"AT ONCE, MY QUEEN," my little steampunk castle booms as he disappears.

A few moments later, a doctor and two nurses approach. They take over Flynn's care from Brett and wrap his injured thigh with gauze. They help him up to his room to rest.

I meet Brett's gaze. "Where are Levi and Tucker?" I ask.

"Levi is on patrol, and Tucker is off adding the anti-dragon gun to his jet." He shakes his head. "I still can't believe you let him rebuild one of the massive guns that was abandoned during the last battle."

"My weapons expert has a way with guns," I say. "Plus, rebuilding guns makes him happy. Leave it alone, Brett."

Jace shifts back to his human form. He walks up to me and wraps his arm around my shoulders, making my dragon coo with desire. *Hussy, calm down,* I tell her. *We need to eat.*

"Ashgrave, can you please dress Jade, Jace, and me?" I ask. "I need something to eat."

'RIGHT AWAY, MISTRESS." My murderous castle wraps us in his blue magic.

We are instantly dressed in black jeans and black

sweatshirts that fit us all perfectly. We even have matching black combat boots on our feet.

My castle amazes me at how he is learning to dress me. He used to place me and the other women in gorgeous gowns that we couldn't fight in. But now, it seems that he's learning my style.

"I'm going to train with some of our soldiers. I'll see you later, okay?" Jace kisses my forehead then heads into the castle.

"Yep. Have fun," I reply to his back.

I love that he has an army to train and care for. Jace is a true general at heart. It's who he is.

"I'm going to the surveillance room to check on any chatter on the networks about Kinsley's movements," Jade says, heading into our home.

"A few things came up that I'd like to discuss with you, Boss." Brett catches my gaze.

"Let me eat first," I tell my public relations expert. "Then, I'm all yours."

I turn away from Brett and head for the doors of the castle. Once I pass the threshold, I take my time to admire the new tapestries. They are truly beautifully woven images of everything I love about Castle Ashgrave. My family. My *home.*

As I travel the elaborate hallways toward the kitchen, I'm overcome with gratefulness. I'm grateful for my castle, for my family—for our safety.

I enter the empty kitchen and stroll over to the large stainless steel refrigerator, and open the door. A salad with grilled chicken, cheese, tomatoes, and croutons on a bed of romaine lettuce already awaits me. Ashgrave must have made it for me. He knows this is my favorite.

I grab the bottle of ranch dressing from the door of the refrigerator and the bowl of salad, and head to the table with my lunch.

A cup of the anti-pregnancy tea appears next to me as I pour ranch dressing onto my salad. "Thank you, Ashgrave."

"IT IS MY HONOR, MY QUEEN," my castle's voice booms.

I eat my salad and drink my tea quietly as I sit at the little breakfast nook in the empty kitchen, thanking the gods for this moment of peace.

As I put my empty bowl and cup in the sink, Brett walks through the door. "I timed that perfectly, didn't I?"

I rub the wrinkle that's forming between my eyebrows. "Brett, why do I want to punch you?"

"Probably because you know that I have bad news. Well, sort of," he answers.

"Nope. I think it's because I have a feeling you want to talk to me about the public opinion war." I shake my head. "You know I'd much rather fight in a physical battle than to try and sway people's opinions of me by telling them what I'm doing, rather than showing them."

"Just listen for one minute, then you can go and blow something up, okay?"

I slump my shoulders and stare at the marble floor. "Tell me what's going on."

"The good news is that there are pro-Rory fan clubs in every country of the world." He smiles.

I narrow my eyes as I stare at his face. "And the bad news?"

Brett's smile fades, and his shoulders and gaze drop. "Kinsley is drumming up some negative press. She's blaming you for food shortages and blackouts in Los Angeles, Las Vegas, New York, Beijing, Paris, London, Shanghai, Mexico City, and Cairo."

"Why?" I ask. "What does she gain by doing that to those people?"

My public relations expert lets out a deep sigh. "She wants people to think twice about siding with you or becoming your ally by raising questions about your loyalty to the human population of the world."

"Is it working?"

He shakes his head. "It's all crap, and most people don't believe it. There are a few protestors against you, but the pro-Rory marches far exceed the negative protests, and I intend to keep it that way. Unless there's some catastrophe, I really don't think you should worry about this, Boss."

"Thanks for telling me," I tell him. "Let's keep an eye on Kinsley, though. It sounds like her stirring up people could be a problem down the road."

"Will do, Boss." He leaves the room with a quick salute.

I head out of the kitchen and straight for the surveillance room. I need to check on Drew.

As I open the door to Drew's favorite room of the castle, I spy my fire dragon sitting in front of one of the dual monitor computers, typing away. I run my fingers through his messy black hair and give it a little tug to get his attention.

Drew's eyes meet mine, and my dragon purrs from the heat in his eyes. "Hi. I thought you'd be training with Flynn and Jace until nightfall."

My gaze lowers. "Yeah, well I kinda nicked Flynn's femur with my magic, and he won't be healed until this afternoon."

My fire dragon lifts my chin with his finger.

"You're growing stronger. Don't be ashamed of that. We all know you didn't try to hurt him." He wraps his arms around me and pulls me close. "You do know that he's going to be fine, right?"

"I know he will." I nod against his hard chest.

He tilts my chin upward and looks into my eyes. "I'm having a hard time tracking Kinsley's movements since we got shut out of the Vaer intelligence network."

"We need to find a way to draw Kinsley out and end this once and for all. The Vaer have caused more damage and bad press for me since we destroyed the bio-weapon. They still want their war—and they're willing to take out innocents to get it. Do you think Jett would be open to join us?" I ask.

"I honestly don't know." Drew shakes his head. "I do know from the bug we planted that my father has learned of Milo's excursion into L.A. and that my brother helped us. He didn't seem pleased, but he didn't reprimand or punish Milo either."

"That's good news, right?" I ask, searching his black eyes.

"It seems like it is. But, Jett still wants to keep an eye on how things go. At least he's still withholding any support or favor toward the Vaer."

"So the Darrington Boss could join us like the Palarne, if we play our cards right."

"IRENA IS APPROACHNG THE SOUTHERN BORDER IN DRAGON FORM, MY QUEEN." Ashgrave's voice thunders in the small surveillance room, making the computer monitors rattle.

"It's just my sister alone?" I ask, wondering what happened to her small group of former Spectres.

"SHE IS BEING FOLLOWED CLOSELY BY A GROUP OF VAER DRAGONS AND A FEW JETS, MY QUEEN."

Drew and I exchange a knowing look. "Something must've gone terribly wrong," I say.

CHAPTER THREE

"Ashgrave, please tell Jace, Levi, and Tucker to join us in protecting my sister."

"AT ONCE, MY QUEEN."

Drew and I rush outside, closely followed by a limping Flynn and his rebels. Jace and his dojo soldiers waste no time in joining us.

Jade rushes after us. "Rory, do you want me to fight?"

"Yes, can you take a few of the soldiers and cover Ash Town for me, please?" I ask her.

Jade rounds up fifty dojo soldiers and they shift and fly off to protect the little village on our western border.

I give a quick nod in greeting to Levi, who's already hovering in the air. I shift and roar into the sky. I'm ready to tear into the dragons who foolishly thought it was a good idea to chase my sister this close to my home. Jace, Drew, Flynn and his rebels, and the remaining dojo soldiers shift and join Levi in the air. As I take off from the front courtyard, Ashgrave's cat-sized steampunk body rushes to my side.

I flap my wings as hard as I can and join Jace at the front of our army. A pang of dread makes my heart feel like it has frozen solid in my chest. If something happens to Irena, I will destroy every last Vaer dragon, starting with Kinsley.

The scream of a jet draws my attention to my weapons expert who is advancing on us from behind. I let out a chuckle that sounds like sandpaper rubbing together at the sight of the sleek fighter jet with a giant anti-dragon gun on top of it.

A spray of bullets from one of the Vaer jets whiz past my head, and I pool my magic in my throat. *You're going to have to try harder than that,* I think as I release a steady stream of magic at the jet that fired at me. My power cuts a hole from the nose to the tail of the plane, then it flows wildly, cutting the wings off of two of the jets that were following it in a "V" formation. The lead jet plummets like a rock toward the ground and explodes on impact. The other two damaged planes spiral toward the ground, but they crash into each other and a fireball erupts, sending pieces of metal to the valley floor.

Irena roars in pain as one of the Vaer dragons hit her with a blast of fire magic. Flynn rushes ahead of me, sending a silver stream of lightning into the dragon who is blasting my sister, making the burnt-orange fire dragon's chest erupt with electricity. The Vaer dragon falls to the now cluttered valley below, dead.

Two of the black Vaer ice dragons separate from the group and try to force Tucker to land. Levi silently stalks the black dragons as they pool their magic in their throats to blast my weapons expert. Levi unleashes his magic and freezes their wings. Both black dragons fall into a heap on the valley floor, sending their fire magic over their wings to thaw them. As Levi flies toward them, aiming his ice magic toward them for a deadly blow, they take to the sky and split up. My ice dragon lets them go and heads back into the fray.

Flynn lets out an ordering roar. The colonel and his rebels, and the remaining dojo dragons chase the remaining Vaer stragglers toward the border and to ensure there are no more Vaer coming our way.

The high-pitched whistle of a rocket firing has me searching for Tucker and Levi. I shake my head at them. They're playing a game of chicken with the two remaining Vaer jets. The jet that fired at Tucker is on a collision course toward the mountain to our left with two frozen engines, and Tucker's favorite toy is barreling toward the last remaining jet with no sign of slowing down or pulling up. If they collide, Tucker is dead. But I know better, my weapons expert has this. He loves to play chicken with his brothers. As Tucker's jet and the Vaer jet get closer to collision, the Vaer jet pulls up and loops back toward our southern border, giving up. Levi roars into the sky to let everyone know that Tucker won.

My general roars a victory cry into the air, and I join him. But our celebration is short-lived when I spot Irena's bronze dragon, with glowing green eyes, flying next to Flynn's black, silver striped thunderbird. Flynn's rebels surround them in a protective formation. Tucker screams past us in his jet, while Drew and Levi join me and Jace on our flight back toward our home.

As we sail through the air back toward the castle, I can't help but think about how I just focused my god power enough to turn another dragon to ash. Now that I can control this magic, anyone foolish enough to attack my family or my home will regret it. My dragon and I are improving—growing together. And soon, we'll be unstoppable.

CHAPTER FOUR

Even with the wind in my face and my wings beating against the air, I detect my sister's whimper, and it cuts through me like a knife. I know she was hurt by that fire dragon before Flynn took him out. I turn my head mid-flight and spot her at the center of Flynn's rebels, and she catches my gaze. Irena looks at her side, which oozes blood, then back at me. She shakes her big bronze head, telling me not to worry, and it will heal.

As I touch down at Castle Ashgrave, I shift to my human form and run toward my sister as soon as she lands and shifts. She's so banged up that she leans on Flynn's large dragon leg for support.

"Irena, let me see," I demand, pushing her bloody hand out of the way so I can see her injury.

My sister slaps my hand out of the way. "Rory, calm down. It's only a flesh wound. I'll be fine."

"I'd feel better if you'd come with me to the infirmary to get it checked out," I tell her.

Jace, Levi, and Drew land and shift to their human forms.

"Go and retrieve Jade and the other soldiers from Ash Town," Jace orders Flynn.

The rest of the rebels and dojo soldiers stand at attention in their dragon forms, awaiting my general's orders. "The rest of you may retire until our training session. Dismissed." With that, the courtyard is free of dragons.

"Can someone help me get Irena to the infirmary?" I ask my men and my little metal castle. "Ashgrave, if you could let the doctors know we're on our way, that would be great." Gods only know how he would take my injured sister to the castle infirmary.

"AT ONCE, MY QUEEN," my little metallic evil butler booms before disappearing.

Drew approaches Irena and lifts her with a hand around her back and his other arm cradling her legs. "I got her."

Irena's face screws up in a scowl. "Put me down! I can walk."

"Just let him carry you," I tell my sister. "I don't

want your blood dripping all over the halls of my castle."

I catch Irena's gaze and she lets out a deep sigh as she lays back into my fire dragon's strong arms, giving in and allowing herself to be carried.

"I'll meet up with you guys later. Tell Tucker I said great flying out there," I say to Jace and Levi.

Heavy breathing and the thud of Drew's footsteps on the tile floor is the only sound in my beautiful castle's hallways as we head to the infirmary.

I open the door to our infirmary, and I'm greeted by the blonde nurse. "Hello, my queen." She bows her head toward me. "The castle has informed us of your sister's injury." She points Drew to the closest bed so he can lay Irena on it for her examination.

Drew gently places my sister on the bed then approaches me, planting a kiss on my forehead. "I'll see you later, love." My sexy fire dragon walks out of the infirmary, giving me and my sister some time to talk.

I sit in a wooden chair next to my sister's bed as the nurse starts prodding my sister's wound, examining her bleeding stomach.

"Is that really necessary?" Irena questions.

"Just be still and let her do her job, please." I roll my eyes.

The bald fifty-something doctor walks in, shrugging his white coat on. "What do we have here?"

"It appears a few stitches and a good cleaning should help her heal, doctor," the blonde nurse says.

"Please irrigate the wound with saline, and I'll put in five stitches," he tells his nurse. "I'll grab the suture kit from the supply closet and be right back." The doctor heads over to the far corner of the room and opens a door I never paid attention to. He rummages through it.

"Shit! That's cold. And I'm a fucking ice dragon, so I know cold," Irena yells, drawing my attention to her.

I shake my head and roll my eyes at my sister's outburst. Since when has she become so dramatic?

"I'm sorry, but I have to wash out your wound so it will heal properly and quickly." The nurse pours a couple of bottles of what looks like water over my sister's stomach. "You might be a dragon, but an infection will slow down your healing time."

"Wait a minute. I didn't think we could get infections?" I ask.

The nurse shakes her head. "You, my queen, probably can't. The rest of us can get an infection that won't kill us, but it will most definitely slow our healing time. I'm trying to make sure Ms. Irena has the fastest healing time possible. The saline and sutures will cut her healing time down to hours. We did the same thing to Mr. Flynn earlier."

The doctor approaches the bed with a blue wrapped package. "Are you finished, Miriam?"

"Yes, Doctor." She sets the empty bottles on the bedside table and assists the doctor with placing five stitches in my sister's stomach.

As he ties the last stitch, the doctor catches my sister's gaze with his. "I'll have Miriam dress your wound, but you need to rest for at least two hours to make sure it heals properly. Your muscle tissue was cut also, so you have to allow them to heal. Okay?"

Irena gives the doctor a short nod of her head. "Got it. Rest for a couple of hours, then I'm good to go."

The doctor carefully scoops up the needle he used to stich my sister, a set of tweezers, his used gloves, and the empty bottles, and wraps them all in the blue wrapping then carries the bundle to the trash. The nurse joins us with a roll of gauze and some paper tape. Within moments, my sister's new stitches are covered by a fresh dressing.

Miriam hands my sister a fresh pair of scrubs to put on. "Do you want me to help you dress?"

"I'll help her. Thank you," I tell the nurse.

I pull on my sister's left arm until she's sitting up on the bed. Irena lifts her arms with a wince of pain as I help her put on the scrub top. I put each of her legs through the holes of the pants, and my sister leans on my shoulders as she stands, pulling the scrub pants up and then tying them.

"It's going to take me some time to get used to this whole naked thing." Irena sits on the edge of the bed.

"That's the least of your worries. Am I right?" I quirk a questioning eyebrow at her.

"What are you trying to ask me, little sister?"

"Didn't you leave with a small group of former Spectres to gather supplies and intel a few days ago, sis?" I stand with my hands on my hips, demanding an answer.

Irena's eyes narrow. Her face turns red, and the deepest scowl I've ever seen takes root on her beautiful face. "We were actually on a sabotage mission against a Vaer facility that was being used as a weapons cache. I'm the only one who survived. I had to shift last minute to make it back to Ashgrave's borders." She shakes her head and looks at me as a frown replaces her scowl. "I lost some good and loyal fighters."

I put my hand on my sister's elbow and help her lay down. "I know I'm the younger sister, but I feel like I have to watch out for you. And sis, if you're going to lead anyone, you have to start weighing the risks more." I brush a stray hair from her face as I help her settle into the pillow behind her head. "Your Spectres may be willing to die for you, but it doesn't mean you should let them rush into it. I figure your rebels still have some Spectre training ingrained in them, but that training is contrary to what I've learned about being a leader."

"What do you expect me to do?" Irena retorts. "Sit around this castle combing over surveillance or watching the news? I need something to do." She shakes her head. "Some of my rebels have remained at the castle, vowing to stay with me and fight in their own ways."

"Be careful, sis. It may be an ego boost and temporary high to run head first into these sabotage missions, but Kinsley is no fool, and she knows that you can shift now." I search my sister's face for any sign of reaction. "Why are you doing this, Irena? I need to know the *real* reason."

Irena gazes at her hands on her stomach and lets out a deep sigh. "I do it because every time I do something to hurt Kinsley or destroy her resources, it makes me feel like I'm rejecting Kinsley's blood and any connection that I have to her."

I pull the wooden chair up to the bed and slide onto the seat. I place my hands over my sister's, drawing her gaze to mine. "The best way to get back at Kinsley and show the world that you're nothing like her, is to become the best version of *yourself*."

CHAPTER FIVE

The early morning sun washes the jewels and precious metals in my treasury beautiful hues of yellow, orange, and red. I sit with my legs crossed beneath me, reading Clara Astor's diary.

The ancient protected book spells out the locations where the orbs were hidden after being taken from the magical castle. However, the book doesn't list current landmarks or boundaries, since it was written almost three thousand years ago. The maps have changed many times since then. But there are hand-drawn images of natural landmarks in Clara's diary that I'm hoping will help us locate what we need.

There's one more orb out there, but I can't feel it. The orb could possibly be destroyed or damaged. I need to find it, even if it's in pieces. As long as there's a possibility of repairing it, I'll retrieve it. I figure like my magic, the orb will play an important role in defeating Kinsley. I'll use the orb, and every other tool in my arsenal to end the brewing war before the human population and all of dragonkind are damaged beyond repair.

"Ashgrave, can you feel if the gods are stirring?" I let out a deep sigh. "I've had what I think are visions of them. The first time I touched Morgana's dragon armor, I saw her stunningly beautiful green diamond dragon battling a fearsome red warrior in black armor. The next time I touched her armor, the world shimmered with blue and white light while the dragon gods threatened me. It felt so real, like they were standing in front of me." I shake my head wearily. "And let's not forget that I had visions of you, before I found you."

"I CAN FEEL THEM, THOUGH THEY HAVE NOT FULLY AWAKENED, MY QUEEN."

A pang of cold dread washes over me as I wonder if or when Morgana returns, will Ashgrave's loyalty lie with the dragon goddess or me?

My beautiful, murderous castle owns a special part of my heart, and it will hurt if he turns on me. Especially if I put the last orb in its domain and give him his full power. It could mean the end of not only me, but my men—and my family also.

I brush the thought from my mind. I can't think about what-ifs right now. I need a plan to find the last orb.

My mind wanders as I remember the room of memories that Ashgrave showed me when I first arrived here at the castle.

"Ashgrave, can you take me to the mural room, please?"

"RIGHT AWAY, MY QUEEN," he booms as the wall next to me slides open.

I step into the tunnel and a stairway appears. As I follow it upward, my heart leaps with joy. He's never refused a request of mine, which is a positive. I'm thankful that I have his loyalty—for now. The wall slides open in front of me and I exit into the hallway and walk through a familiar arched doorway. The room is massive in height. The ceiling stretches above me like it goes on forever. Shadows above me start to turn darker and thicker as they wrap themselves around each other and pull on the darkness around them until they change into massive black storm clouds that are dancing. As the dark clouds bump against each other, they set off sparks and give off a small golden glow.

Like the first time I was in this room, a bolt of lightning brightens it with white light as the wall across from me shimmers with a golden glow and ripples like water. Murky images arise with people lying in pools of their own blood. The scene shifts, and Morgana is in her green diamond dragon form as she leads the charge, dressed in her intricately-carved gold and white armor. With little effort, she casts her chaos magic on those closest to her, making them turn on their allies and cutting down anyone close to them, including their wives and children.

The image ripples and shifts to Razorus who infiltrates soldiers' minds with his trickster magic. The troops in front of him fall under his illusion and they rip their helmets off and tear the skin off their own faces. The golden glow fades then ripples like water as the image changes to a different area of the battle. Smoke rises from a burning town as Caelan touches the villagers, and they turn a sickly grey color as they fall dead at the death god's feet. He kicks the dead bodies out of his way, and they turn into a grey filmy ash that sticks to his boots as he crushes their remains beneath his feet.

The images are gruesome, and I turn my gaze downward, unable to watch the horror anymore.

The dragon gods killed without caring who they hurt. Soldiers, women, children—it didn't matter to them as long as they got what they wanted. Chaos, manipulation, and death was all they strived for.

It takes me two tries to swallow the hard lump that instantly forms in my throat as I watch the images of the dragon gods. I know I possess their magic, and it bothers me that I have the potential to do the things I just witnessed. But I've used my powers to defend and save people, so far, at least. I saved a plane full of humans when Kinsley used them as fodder in our battle. I've saved innocents, where the dragon gods or Kinsley wouldn't care.

I may have their power, but I am not like them.

I will never be like them.

One thing I've learned is magic is a sliding scale. A single power can have multiple applications, and powers that were once used for evil can also be used for good. It's the person who wields the power that decides how it will be used.

Kinsley chooses to use her power to manipulate and control those she was chosen to lead. She uses her brilliant brain to hurt others instead of helping them. I don't understand how she can continually hurt those she's responsible for, but I do know that I can never lead that way.

My whole life I was controlled and made to submit to Zurie, and I will never do that to anyone else. I refuse to lead through fear and control. My power will not be used as a weapon against those who follow me. Instead, it will be used to bring about peace.

I'm not Morgana, thank the gods. I refuse to hurt or kill people just because I can. I've been forced to kill in the past, and I will not take someone's life just because I can. *Not anymore.* A good leader makes others better by being with their people and standing by their side. A true leader doesn't make others bend to their will like a tyrant.

My heart bangs hard in my chest as I realize that I don't have to follow in anyone's footsteps. I can forge my own way with my powers. But first, I have to learn to tame my wild magic because I want to use it in the right way at the right time. I need to make sure that no more innocent lives suffer because this magic exists. I'll control it. Change it from chaos, manipulation, and death to something that gives unity, peace, and life. The key to controlling my magic is all in the implementation.

I need Ashgrave back to his former glory if I'll have any chance of defeating Kinsley and the dragon gods. And to do that, I have to find the last orb.

According to Clara's diary, it was taken to the Americas, but the ancient book doesn't say exactly where. I gathered enough from the history and images in the diary to figure out that it's somewhere in the U.S., but that's still a whole lot of land to cover.

I shake out my arms and roll my shoulders then concentrate my mind and my magic on the last glowing crystal orb needed to power my castle. The more power I call forth, the more my mind races, causing me to fall to the hard stone floor with a massive headache. Wherever the last orb is, I can't find it. Not like this, anyway.

"ARE YOU ALL RIGHT, MY QUEEN?" Ashgrave's voice thunders, making me grab my aching head.

"I have a headache, Ashgrave. Please be quiet," I whisper.

A metal hand extends up through the stone floor and deposits two white pills that I assume are aspirin and a glass of water.

"Thank you," I say quietly, taking the pills and swallowing them down with the water and forcing myself to my feet.

I can't continue to search blindly. And I can't force a vision of the missing orb, because I don't think my brain can handle it. I give my head a small shake and regret the way the movement sends spots dancing in my vision.

Maybe Drew will have better luck. He does seem to have contacts everywhere. One of them may be able to help us pinpoint a location, or perhaps Drew can check for any movement on the black market.

My mind tumbles as I think of a plan for Kinsley. It will be best if I lure the Vaer Boss away from the incredibly vulnerable human cities. The humans have armies, sure, but once they're deployed, innocent bloodshed will be inevitable. I can't let that happen. Kinsley has already taken too many innocent lives.

I wonder if Kinsley will come back to Castle Ashgrave or its surrounding area. The only population that we would need to defend is that of Ash Town. We defeated her the last time she came here, but maybe if I lure her here with something that the Vaer Boss wants, it could work. But what does Kinsley want besides my sister? *Me*—my power.

CHAPTER SIX

I walk under the large archway and notice the ornate molding and fleur-de-lis designs that decorate the outside of the mural room. This castle of mine is a true work of art—it's gorgeous. As I follow the hallway around a curve, I realize that I'm close to the surveillance room and that my headache is going away. Thank the gods.

As I approach the door to Drew's favorite room, I notice a loud tapping coming from inside. I stroll through the open door, expecting to find Drew typing away at the keyboard of his preferred computer, but instead I find Tucker sitting in front of the dual monitor desktop. He's busy with something, and as I walk up behind him, my weapons expert turns around in his over-stuffed chair and meets my gaze with an adorable goofy grin that is all Tucker.

"Why are you sneaking up on me, babe?" He grabs my hand.

"I'm not sneaking. I'm walking." I shake my head to remove the naked image of Tucker from my mind as my dragon coos with desire. "I figured Drew would be here. Do you know where he is?"

"He's out with Jace, training the army and bolstering the area's defenses," Tucker tells me.

It seems my men are of the same mind that our final showdown with the Vaer forces will be here.

Tucker stands and places his hands on my shoulders, making small circles with his thumbs as he meets my gaze with his green eyes. "What's the matter? I can tell something is on your mind."

"Oh, really. How?" I ask.

He removes one of his hands and pokes me in the middle of my forehead. "This vein right here turns a deeper blue when you are thinking too hard. It actually turns the same sapphire blue of your magic."

I brush his hand away from my face. "That's not true."

"It is," he confesses. "Rory, you and I have trained our expressions to mask emotion our whole lives. It makes sense that I'm the only person you know who can read your emotionless face. We look for little things, like the color of veins to tell how the person is actually feeling. You and I notice the tells that no one else in the world would care to note."

"You're right." I grab the hand I pushed away and hold it while his other hand still massages my shoulder.

"Do you want to tell me what's bothering you, or should I torture it out of you?" he asks, wiggling his eyebrows up and down.

I shake my head, not wanting to burden Tucker with all of my thoughts and concerns.

"You do realize the world is too heavy for one person to carry alone, right babe?" he asks. "So stop trying. Family is all about sharing, or at least this one is. So, spill, babe. What has my beautiful queen turning an adorable shade of blue this morning?"

A chuckle escapes my lips and I plant a kiss on the palm of the hand I'm holding. Leave it to Tucker to make a joke to lighten the mood.

"Your heart is what counts. And you have the biggest and best heart in the world that I know of." Tucker pulls me into his arms and plants a kiss on the offending vein in the middle of my forehead.

I wrap my arms around my weapons expert and

hold him tight. "I'll feel a lot better if I could get eyes and ears on Kinsley.

A throat clearing has me turning out of Tucker's arms and coming face-to-face with my sister.

Irena is standing in the middle of the surveillance room's doorway, dressed in a pair of black jeans, a dark forest green sweatshirt, and black combat boots. Her upper lip twitches upward, giving me a smirk as her gaze meets mine.

"I have something for you, little sister. But if I'm intruding, I can come back later," Irena says, wiggling her eyebrows.

I give her a curt nod. "Or, you could tell me now."

"I didn't want to mention it unless it actually worked." She drops her gaze to the floor. "I'm not in the mood to hear another lecture from you, if my plan fails."

"What did you do?" I ask my sister.

"Tucker, can you adjust the frequency of the bug I planted yesterday to 23.6?"

"Sure thing, Irena." He makes his way to the computer that he was sitting in front of when I walked in and hits a few keys on the keyboard.

"…does everyone understand where they need to be for the mission tomorrow?" A familiar voice asks over the computer speakers. "Remember, we're going to a research facility in the state of Washington to retrieve an important artifact. All of you will be punished severely if we don't return with it. The artifact we're going to retrieve is very important to the Vaer Boss. Is that understood?" the speaker demands as the clothing of the people in the room with him rub together and chairs creak. I can picture them all squirming while being threatened with Kinsley's wrath.

My stomach churns as my instinct tells me the Vaer general I met in Chinatown is going after the last orb.

"We have to beat them to it," I say. "It has to be the last orb."

"See, little sister?" Irena's voice cracks, and just like Tucker said, I can detect the little signs in her face. She's getting emotional.

"Is this what you were doing when you were on your sabotage mission?" I ask in a soft voice.

My sister sniffs and nods her head. "This and a few other things."

"Like?"

"Destroying a weapons cache," Tucker interjects, shaking his head.

"And forcing Kinsley into action, like going after the orb," Irena says with tears in her eyes. "I had a plan before I went in. It just didn't end exactly how I planned it. I didn't plan on losing my whole team and barley escaping with my life."

I wrap my arms around my sister, holding her tightly against me. It hurts to lose people who follow you. My heart aches at the loss of Jakobe, our driver in Reims, the soldiers who lost their lives when Kinsley attacked Castle Ashgrave, and now for my sister, who lost a group of her best soldiers.

Kinsley will pay for the deaths of Irena's rebels.

She will suffer for the losses she's caused. All of them. For every life Kinsley Vaer has taken, I'll make sure she feels their pain before I wipe her off the face of this earth.

"My fighters' deaths weren't futile. I'll make sure of it," Irena announces.

"We both will, sis," I say.

And retribution can't arrive fast enough.

CHAPTER SEVEN

A change in the whir of the chopper blades has me gauging my surroundings. The silvery light of the setting moon filters in through the chopper's windows as I watch Jade and Irena leaning on Drew, who's sitting in between them. They're nestled in the seats across from me. Their eyes are closed and they're breathing steadily. I don't blame them for taking a quick rest during this helicopter ride. The sun has yet to rise as we travel across the pre-dawn morning sky.

Levi stirs to my left, accidentally kicking Ashgrave's little steampunk body by our feet, making my castle's metal wings click as he rights himself, while Jace's body stiffens on my other side. My mate is always ready for battle.

"Thank you, tower. Preparing to land." Tucker's voice pierces the darkness, and the chopper starts its descent.

My weapons expert lands the chopper on a helipad on a private mountain airstrip that sits at the summit of a huge hill about ten miles away from the secret United States government's research facility. I rub the sleep from my eyes as my team starts to stretch their tired arm muscles while we wait for the go ahead to unbuckle from Tucker.

We found out the exact location of the orb from Milo just as the sun was setting last night, and none of us has slept except for the catnap we caught during the flight to Washington. We're all tired, but this has to be done. We have to get in, get the orb, and get out before the Vaer suspect a thing.

The only animals awake this early in the morning are the owls hooting in the cold Washington mountains while they search for a last-minute meal. My team and I prepare to retrieve the last orb that will give my evil butler his full strength.

Thanks to Milo, we know exactly where we're going, but I still wonder what shape the orb's going to be in, because I can't feel it at all. The orb is here. It has to be.

As I think about Milo and his willingness to

help, I figure the Darringtons should just make it official already. The powerful dragon family should declare their alliance with me and my family and get it over with. The world knows that Drew is a Darrington heir, and Jett realizes that Milo will back up his little brother. Jett's just being stubborn at this point.

Jade, Irena, Drew, and Jace all unbuckle as Tucker turns the whirring blades off and searches my eyes with his, rewarding me with a wink. A small grunt turns my attention to Levi's face as he unlatches himself from the five-point harness and reaches over to unbuckle me. Jace stands and starts grabbing backpacks that hang over our heads.

Levi brushes my hand with his, opening our connection. *Are you sure bringing Jade is a good idea?* he asks.

I give my ice dragon a nod. *I'm sure,* I reply. *She's an excellent fighter, and we share a magical connection not only with each other but to the orb too. She's earned it, Levi. Jade is a brilliant fighter, and she will be able to tell you when I've located the last orb and what kind of shape it's in. She will also be able to keep in contact with me in case something goes wrong with the comms.*

You have very valid points, he confesses as his eyes drift toward our feet. *I didn't know that your connec-*

tion to her was changing. It used to be that you could only locate her.

As my magic grows, so does our connection, I admit. *It's kinda nice knowing that not only my magic and my dragon are growing, but so is Jade's connection to me. It's like we're becoming a real family.*

We are a real family, Rory. He gives me a heat-filled kissed. *We're a chosen family. A family of our hearts, not our blood.*

Ashgrave in his little metallic body flutters from the floor by my feet with his head swiveling around. "THERE ARE NO VEHICLES HERE TO MEET US, MY QUEEN." My castle's voice booms, making us all cover our ears.

"Yes there are, silly castle." Tucker stands and stretches his legs, chuckling. "There are four snow-mobiles waiting for us," he says, pointing out the window behind me, drawing the eyes of my family members outside to stare wide eyed and open mouthed at the sight.

"Great job, Drew," Irena says, beaming. "I love driving snowmobiles. They're so much fun."

"Right on, sis." Tucker gives my big sister a high five.

As I look around the chopper I know in my heart that Levi's words are spot on. We are a chosen family. My men, Irena, Jade, Ashgrave, me, and hell even Brett are becoming a family of the heart. Where we came from doesn't matter. We're a family that chose each other. They will do anything for me, and I'm willing to do anything for them, because of how we feel about each other.

Drew clears his throat and pulls a map from one of the backpacks that Jace pulled down. He spreads the map of the secret facility out in the middle of the floor of the chopper and we gather around and study it.

My fire dragon hands me a lanyard with a keycard on it, and I slide it over my head and tuck it into my black jacket. "Okay. Once you get in through the glass double doors, there are two hallways. The one to the left goes toward the chemical labs while the one on the right leads to storage and containment facilities. Milo has assured me the orb is being held in one of these two rooms. The government locks all of its extremely confidential experiments in there." Drew points at me and Irena and then to the two "X's" written in black ink on the map. "You two will search these two rooms here for the orb. Remember, we don't know what kind of shape the artifact is in, so keep your eyes open." He taps my chest. "That keycard will allow you to open any of the doors you need access to."

I give him a salute. "Aye aye, captain," I say with my lips turned up.

Drew chuckles. "You've been hanging around with Tucker lately, haven't you?"

"Don't be jealous, big guy," Tucker interjects, slapping Drew on the back. "She loves us all equally. But I'm her favorite," he adds, wagging his eyebrows up and down and making me hide a chuckle with my hand.

My fire dragon stares at Tucker. "You and I will stay here with the chopper to make sure we can take off at a moment's notice as we hack into the facility's computer system. The cameras will be shut down, and her keycard should open any of the security doors. We will watch and make sure she can get wherever she needs to go. You and I will also take care of anything else that comes up," Drew says, making sure to meet my eyes with his.

"While Jade, Levi, and I act as a distraction and draw attention away from Rory and Irena," Jace adds. "Jade, you'll be able to tell how Rory's feeling and can tell us if something unexpected comes up, right?"

Jade's eyes meet mine, and her lips quirk upward

into a dazzling smile. "Yes. I'll be able to let you know if we need to help. But where is Ashgrave going to be?"

"I WILL BE PERCHED IN A TREE NEAR THE ENTRY OF THE FACILITY, MISS JADE." My steampunk castle's voice thunders through the interior of the chopper.

The young Nabal's eyes drift downward to the floor.

"Remember, Ashgrave, you're going to be quiet. You can't talk while you're keeping watch," I tell my castle.

"We can't shift. We don't want the humans to know who we are," I remind everyone. "Not unless it's absolutely necessary. It will get tough when the Vaer arrive, but we need to remain anonymous." I pull my black ski mask over my face and stand, making sure not to step on the map.

Drew takes the map off the floor and folds it. "We all know what to do?" He pulls two laptop cases out from under the seat across from mine.

Jade, Jace, and Levi pull their masks over their faces as I open the chopper door, and the stairs lower.

Irena approaches me, pulling her mask down

over her face. "Ready to get Ashgrave his last orb, little sis?"

"You know it," I say through a toothy grin.

Irena approaches the first sleek black snowmobile and sits at the front, patting the seat behind her. She slides a black helmet off the handle bar and places it on her head. She offers me the second helmet just as I take the seat behind her. I slide it over my ski mask and buckle it under my chin. The loud purring of the engine has me searching for the rest of my family.

Jace, Levi, and Jade get on their own snowmobiles, slide on their helmets, and start the machines. They give me a nod before starting down the mountain.

Irena follows Jade down the hillside. Ashgrave hovers near my head as the snow weighs the branches of the trees down in the low light of the setting moon.

We travel through a beautiful scene of darkness and shadows as we approach the secret government facility. I tap my sister's helmet, letting her know to slow down. We need to take a right at the fork in the trail and park the snowmobile in the woods close to the entrance.

My sister nods her helmeted head as she slows

the machine and takes the turn. The machine decelerates to a crawl as my sister searches the dark forest for a good hiding place for our snowmobile. We duck our heads as she pulls under the low lying branches of an evergreen tree and turns the machine off.

My sister and I pull our helmets off and perk our ears to the noises of the early morning forest, searching for something that doesn't belong. The whir of Ashgrave's metallic wings has me watching him lead the way through the dark and cold forest toward the facility.

His head swivels to look at me as Drew's voice comes in through my comm. "Give me a couple minutes to turn the cameras off and for Jace, Levi, and Jade to get into position. I'll let you know when everything is set."

Irena stalks silently around my hovering castle and keeps walking until a light pierces our shadowy surrounding. We head to the edge of the woods, coming to a dirt road with the government facility sitting on the other side of it. I point to a tall tree to my left, giving my murderous castle a silent command, and Ashgrave flutters to a branch near its top to keep watch.

I'm grateful that Ashgrave doesn't need me to tell

him what to do. A simple point of my finger was all he needed.

"Jace. Go," Drew says over the comm, and gunfire erupts from the rear of the facility. I take a deep breath. I know my men and Jade will be okay they're all soldiers.

"Once Jade is clear from the front of the building, you're good to go, Rory," Drew informs me over the comm.

Waves of joy and happiness come to me from Jade as she whizzes on her vehicle around the corner of the nondescript building, pulling along a large chunk of chain link fence with two guards holding onto it. Her snowmobile engine screams as she bounces the piece of fence off the surrounding trees. One of the guard's heads collides with a large white birch tree and he falls off the fence, unconscious. The other guard must have his glove wrapped in the fencing. He pulls at the offending glove with his free hand. Jade rattles the fencing as she bounces it off two more trees before the last man's body dangles unconscious on the chunk of fencing.

A sense of pride washes over me as I watch Jade unhook the chunk of fence from behind her snowmobile and waves at me. She gets back onto the vehicle and heads toward the rear of the facility.

I scan the grounds of the top-secret government facility and notice that I'd never be able to spot this place if I didn't know it was here. There are no signs, no bright lights, and no military guarding it. There are only a handful of guards who were behind the facility, like the important things were in the chemical lab portion of the building. I figure the government didn't realize that it's holding a piece of the dragon gods' magic in its walls.

Irena and I stalk silently toward the front of the building, keeping our heads continually moving, looking for danger as we approach the glass doors. We position our bodies flat against the building and peer around the corner to peer inside of the square nondescript building. Drew's map is right, once you enter the building, there is a big window covered by a metal roll-down shade with a scanner attached to its counter. I figure depending on your security clearance, you can either go right or left. The orb is in one of the rooms to the right.

I take the keycard Drew gave me out of my jacket and slide it through the scanner of the silver box with a keypad and card scanner. The little red light on top of it turns green, and the glass doors slide open automatically.

Once inside the building, Irena turns her back to

me and keeps watch to ensure we aren't surprised as I scan the keycard in the scanner attached to the counter. The red light turns green, and the next set of doors to our right slide open.

This place seems dull—there are no decorations, no art of any kind, or any plants. The walls inside are painted an off-white with grey linoleum tile flooring, and the internal doors remind me of a rainy day grey. Boring.

My sister and I search for the rooms that Drew pointed out to us as we stalk through the drab hallway with our ears perked to hear anything out of the ordinary.

Irena taps my shoulder, indicating the room on our left is the first one we need to search. I scan the key card on the scanner outside the door, and once again the little red light on top turns green. I don't know where Drew got this keycard, but I'm thankful for it. The little plastic card is allowing us access to everywhere we need to go.

My sister opens the door to what appears to be a storage room with shelves of wooden boxes. She pulls her little flashlight from her pocket and searches the labels on the boxes on the far wall. I pull my flashlight from my pocket and start searching the boxes on the left side of the room. As I move to the corner, I feel a tug in my soul. The orb is close but not in this room.

I hope we find the orb soon. If the Vaer show up while my sister and I are in here, it could go south quickly.

I touch Irena's shoulder and tap my elbow then point to the door. She gives me a quick nod and follows me out of the storage room and back into the bland hallway.

This is the first mission Irena and I have done relatively alone together since our time in the Spectres. I'm thankful she's by my side and watching my back, like it's supposed to be. My sister stands guard, watching my back as I scan the keycard in the scanner of the next room.

When the red light turns green, Irena pushes the door open, and I walk into a dark room with a single light bulb hanging over a Lucite box sitting on a small metal table. My heartbeat races as both my soul and dragon start to hum a now-familiar vibrating song. I move to examine the contents of the clear plastic box.

The orb. We found it. It isn't whole, though.

No wonder it took me getting this close to feel it. It's been broken into over a dozen pieces, and its shards lie on a red velvet cushion that sits in the clear plastic box.

Irena waves a hand in my face before I grab the box from the table and I let out a frustrated sigh. My sister points to a laser that's aimed at a small opaque square on the back of the box of the fragmented orb.

She takes a piece of gum from her pocket and unwraps it, putting the gum in her mouth and chewing it while she hands me the silver foiled wrapper. I pull and tug on the wrapper, getting all of the creases out of it, and I walk over and place it in front of the red laser beam at the back wall that's aimed at the pad on the back of the clear box.

Zurie used to stage little scavenger hunts for us while we were growing up. One of my ex-mentor's favorite booby traps was laser-triggered bombs and guns. If you break the laser's connection, you get a nasty surprise, but I figured out when I was about ten years old that the silver foil of a gum wrapper would fool the laser. The laser sending the beam could be "tricked" into still reading the connection, and I could access whatever Zurie put the booby trap on. In those days it was usually a map, gun, or item that we needed to continue our search, but those little tricks trained my sister and I for what to do in a lot of situations. If I didn't hate the ex-Ghost for killing my mother and making my life hell, I might thank her for teaching us to fool a laser today.

I search my sister's face and hold up my right hand, silently counting down to five by rolling down a finger a second. She nods as my hand forms a fist, and I grab the box from the table. My muscles tense as we both search the room for anything out of the ordinary. When nothing happens and all is silent, we head out of the room, making sure to walk slowly as to not draw attention in case someone besides Drew is watching.

I scan the keycard at the double metal doors, and the doors open. As we make our way to the shutter covered window, Drew's voice comes in over the comm. "We have company, everyone."

"On it," Levi replies in the little device in my ear.

Irena scans the area outside the glass doors as the red light turns green and the doors slide open. We exit the facility with the fragmented orb that's locked safely in its clear plastic box.

A blond man wearing all black stands with his back to us in the middle of the road. He has his hands placed on his hips as he searches the woods in front of him. By the way he stands, the width of his shoulders, and the way my dragon is urging me to jump his bones, I can tell it's Jace.

Irena and I approach him, and as my eyes meet his stormy grey ones, I can tell he's pissed. A feeling of dread and excitement washes over me as Jade and Levi come to stand behind me and my sister. I look over my shoulder at the youngest member of our team and offer her a smile of encouragement. The Vaer are coming. Time to take them out and then get home as quickly as possible.

The crunching of snow beneath boots has my head swiveling to see who is coming and from where. Eight Vaer step into view and surround us. They are dressed in all black with a green cursive script letter "V" stitched onto the right shoulders of their jackets. Each of them drags a bloody, broken body behind them, like the people they killed were nothing but trash.

I didn't see or hear them coming until they were on top of us. Either my intuition is failing or they're just that good. I'm betting on the latter being true.

I peek over my shoulder at my ice dragon, and his eyes narrow and his lips become a thin straight line at the "V" on these soldiers' shoulders. He shakes his head and tightens both of his hands into fists like he wants to rip the offending letter off their shoulders. It's clear Levi recognizes it, and he wants to destroy these shifters because of their uniforms.

These assholes think they can just kill innocent people without any consequences. I'm done with the Vaer. This is exactly why I need to fight Kinsley on my terms and away from human cities. This shit needs to end. Soon.

CHAPTER EIGHT

I search the Vaer fighters' faces, looking for the new general we met in Chinatown. But he's not here. I've never seen these men before, but by the way Levi tenses his muscles and chews on the inside of his cheek, he knows who they are and what they represent.

A blond man who stands over six feet tall steps forward, dropping the broken body of a man that's wearing a white lab coat. "Give us the box and no one has to get hurt."

"It looks like you've already killed these people, so getting hurt isn't really an option for us," Jace growls in a voice that doesn't even sound like him. "You're going to get more than hurt if you don't allow us to pass."

"I was hoping you'd say that." The tall blond soldier nods his head.

Two of the fighters in the rear of their formation step to the side, and they drop two more bloody bodies to the snow-covered ground. They suddenly shift into orange fire dragons.

The dragons take to the sky, and I spy Ashgrave's throat glow. I shake my head at my evil butler, and the blue sparks building in his mouth disappear.

I can't let the Vaer know it's us. We need to remain anonymous. If Ashgrave makes himself known, our anonymity is gone. I want Kinsley to think anyone can outsmart her and rattle her feeling of superiority.

The shifted dragons fly to opposite sides of the building and blast it with their magic, and two different fires begin to smolder, spewing smoke and flames into the air. The fire dragons blast the building again, and smoke erupts from the back of the building.

These assholes are going to burn this building to the ground if we don't stop them.

I place my hand on Jace's back and whisper into the comm. "Drew, are there any survivors in the building?"

"Yes. There are five people in the rear near the

maintenance room, trying to escape the flames," Drew's voice responds from the little device in my ear.

"We gotta get them out. These assholes have already killed eight people that we know of. We can't let them kill anymore," I say quietly, and my team nods in agreement.

"Just stay safe, and don't let them get that orb," Drew commands.

"Kick some Vaer ass, babe," Tucker adds.

My gaze meets Jade's, and I can sense her worry and excitement battling, and I give her a wink and mouth, "You've got this." She rewards me with one of her dazzling smiles, and my heart pangs with pride at how far she's come since she came to live at Castle Ashgrave. She really is blossoming into a beautiful, smart, and lovely young woman.

Levi puts his hand on my neck, opening our connection. *Jade and I will save the people in the rear of the building. You kick their asses.*

I'll also keep the orb safe, I reassure him through our bond.

Levi blows me a kiss as he and Jade race toward the back of the building.

My muscles tense as the five Vaer who are still holding broken bodies, drop them from their hands.

Three of the Vaer make a point of stepping on and digging their heels into the corpses at their feet.

My lip curls up in a sneer at the audacity of their lack of concern for human life.

The Vaer need to go down. Soon.

The tall blond lunges at Jace with an outstretched arm, and my mate grabs his arm, rotating the man and pulling his arm up behind the man's back with a sickening crunch of bone and cartilage as another soldier punches Jace in the head, making him drop the blond man's mangled arm.

Four of the soldiers approach me and my sister. "Just hand over the box," the soldier on my right says, and I raise my eyebrow at him.

Does he seriously think it's going to be that easy?

Irena circles around behind the two Vaer closest to her and gives me a nod.

Here we go again. Time for another game that we played when we were younger. I return my sister's nod as I toss the clear plastic box up into the sky and my sister places her hands in the middle of both Vaer soldiers' backs and pushes them forward with all her strength and I do the same to the soldiers near me. All four Vaer stumble into each other, and I catch the clear box with both of my hands.

One of the dragons roars into the sky, and I

search the area for Levi and Jade. I spot them as they assist the five human survivors toward the surrounding woods. Jade has her arms locked around two women and Levi lifts the men off of the ground as they continue to slip and fall as they race across the snow and icy ground.

A Vaer soldier grabs the box in my arms, and I jerk the box toward me and head butt the soldier, knocking him unconscious at my feet.

Silly Vaer, don't touch my box.

A loud grunt has me searching for my sister. I spot her lying on her back, struggling against two soldiers trying to take her ski mask off.

My dragon roars in defiance. I send a blast of magic at the Vaer with his back to me, creating a hole through his chest, and he falls down dead.

Irena pulls the remaining soldier's shoulders down toward her and kicks him between his legs. He falls down on the ground next to her. She leans on his back and pushes herself to her feet and gives me a wink as she throws a handful of snow into the eyes of a soldier behind me.

Jace kicks the knee of the soldier who hit him in the head and the man falls to the ground, and the tall blond soldier keeps ramming his wrecked shoulder into the tree that Ashgrave is perched in.

The soldier Irena threw snow at is on his feet and stalking her. I spy a glint of metal in the low light of the rising sun in the soldier's hand and silently approach him. As I hold the box by its handle, I call on my magic in my free hand. The soldier raises his knife over his head to strike my sister, and I blast him with my full power, turning him to ash instantly. I kick the ashes out of my way as I throw my free arm around her.

"Thanks, lil sis," Irena says into my hair.

"You'd do the same for me."

"Ready to go?" Jace shouts from near the entrance of the facility. Two Vaer soldiers lie at his feet, rolling around and moaning.

The feeling of accomplishment washes over me, and I know that Jade and Levi have gotten the humans to safety as they rush toward us.

"Do you need me to pick you up, or can you make it back to the chopper?" Tucker asks over the comm.

I search the eyes of my family. "We can make it to you. Ashgrave can watch our backs."

Jace, Jade, and Levi rush toward their snowmobiles near the side of the building, and Irena and I follow them. Jace pats the back of his machine, and I hop on while Irena hops on the back of Jade's vehicle. Levi leads the way back to the chopper while all three machines race through the early morning light with a hovering Ashgrave behind us.

The flap of dragon wings has me turning around to find an orange dragon flying above us. The whirring of Ashgrave's wings gets louder as he flaps them to get closer to the offending dragon and takes on a blue glow. My murderous steampunk castle blasts the fire dragon and instantly turns him to ash as we continue to race toward our other family members and the chopper.

As we round the bend, we spy our chopper with its blades turning and ready to go.

The bang of guns being fired echoes as we pull our snowmobiles onto the small private air strip. I search the area and find three Vaer soldiers on snowmobiles aiming handguns at us as we get off of our machines and race toward the chopper. Jace, Levi, Jade, and Irena surround me and the orb as Ashgrave blasts the Vaer soldiers with his magic.

As we approach Tucker's second favorite toy, Drew extends his hand to help me into the chopper. I hand him the clear plastic box and jump in. Ashgrave continues blasting the Vaer with his magic, hitting the tall blond man and turning him to ash as the other two soldiers fall back into the woods surrounding the air strip. Jace lifts Jade into the chopper, and Levi gives Irena a strong hand to hold while she lifts herself inside. As Levi and Jace pull their strong bodies into the chopper, I let a wolf whistle escape my lips to tell Ashgrave that it's time to go.

The remaining Vaer will serve as witnesses that they were beaten. Kinsley was beaten. We have the artifact that she wants so badly. I figure the Vaer Boss will put two and two together to find out it was us who took the orb, especially since they saw Ashgrave. But I'm not worried, I've defeated her before. The next time we meet will be the last, though. The world will be much better off without the Vaer Boss in it.

We buckle ourselves into our seats as Drew examines the outside of the clear plastic box. "It's like it's fused closed. There is no place for a key to even be inserted." He shakes his head.

"Let's worry about opening it once we're home," I say. "I have the last orb, and we can read Clara's diary to figure out how to repair it once we get it home safe."

Drew leans over and hands me the clear plastic box after I'm finished buckling in. I cradle it in my arms as the yellow-orange light of dawn washes through the chopper's windows.

As I look at the pieces of broken orb, I hope that my words ring true—that between the diary and Ashgrave's mural room, I'll be able to put it back together and use it to bring Ashgrave back to his full power and share my magic and my soul with my men.

A sigh escapes my lips as I lean my head back against the wall and tell myself that bringing Ashgrave to full power will be for the best. But still, the nagging question of my castle's loyalty buzzes around inside my brain like a gnat. Will Ashgrave choose to be loyal to me or Morgana, his creator? I figure time will tell since the dragon gods are stirring from their sleep.

CHAPTER NINE

The bright mid-morning sun glimmers off the different treasures in my castle's treasury as I stand observing the Lucite case that holds the broken orb.

For over twenty-four hours, I've been trying to open this box with hammers, chisels, putty knives, and screwdrivers. Hell, I even tried a small amount of plastic explosives. But I still can't figure out how to gain access to the broken orb inside. The orb I need to fix to bring my vengeful castle back to his full strength.

A knock on the closed double doors has me leaving the frustrating case on the small table and approaching the doors.

I need to get this case open if I'm ever going to fix the orb, but how?

A sigh escapes my lips as I shake my head to clear my thoughts and open the doors.

Tucker rushes in and picks me up, twirling me around in a circle. "Did you get it open yet, babe?"

"Not yet." My gaze drops to the gold coins at my feet.

"Don't worry, beautiful. Your favorite man is here to help you." A goofy grin on my weapons expert's face has me returning his smile.

Tucker's faith in me and his joy for life, no matter what's going on around him, has me treasuring his personality and love for me. I'm also grateful for the fact that he's got skills I don't, and if anyone can open this clear plastic box, it'll be my weapons expert and resident goofball.

He approaches the clear plastic box and wipes the soot from where I tried to blow its hinges open. "You tried plastic explosives, I see."

"I've tried just about everything but the kitchen sink." My eyes drop to his black boots as I approach my weapons expert's side.

"I have an idea how to get it open. Do you want me to try?" he asks.

I knew he could figure out this clear plastic

puzzle. Tucker has seen and ruined things I've only dreamed of.

He grabs a tiny fat head screwdriver off the table next to the orb's see-thru plastic cage and sets the tip of it into a non-existent groove that separates the top from the bottom of the box.

"Tucker, what do you think about becoming one of my lords?"

"I'm yours, babe. No matter what." He continues to run the small screwdriver around the box by walking around it as it lies on the table.

"You do realize that you'll be receiving a piece of my power and my soul, right?"

My weapons expert stops working on the clear heavy-duty plastic box, and his gaze meets mine. "Becoming your lord, my queen, will make my life complete."

As I stare at his handsome face, I search for any signs of a smile or smirk, but there's nothing there. Tucker is serious.

"Are you sure you want to be stuck with all of us, forever?" he asks. "Maybe you should think about it. It'll give you some time to thin the herd." Tucker gives me a wink.

He's such a jokester. I truly love that my adorable goof can still show me his tenderness and devotion, even after everything we've gone through.

The doors swing open and Brett suddenly drops Jade's hand as they walk into the treasury. My top lip curls into a smirk at the fact that he's still trying to hide their relationship from me. My eyes meet Brett's, and I figure he's here to update me on another PR issue, and by the look in his eye, it's probably negative.

"Hey, Boss," Brett greets me as Jade's feelings of pride and joy leak to me through our connection.

"Good morning." I flash them both a toothy smile.

"I'm sorry to interrupt you. I know you're working on getting the orb out of the case, but you need to know that there's a caravan of people approaching the castle and they're coming from the East, so they aren't from Ash Town." Brett's eyes glance to Jade's beautiful face.

"How do we know?" I tense, getting ready for a fight. "Ashgrave hasn't informed me of an invasion."

"The bees roam the area surrounding the borders. That's how we were able to see the caravan before they entered our borders." Brett's gaze meets mine. "They appear to be humans, Rory."

"HE IS CORRECT, MY QUEEN. A LARGE

GROUP OF HUMANS IS APPROACHING THE CASTLE FROM THE EAST." Ashgrave's voice booms, shaking the piles of coins and jewels that surround us.

I shake my head as I wonder about the people approaching the castle. Why would humans come to Castle Ashgrave?

I'm in a state of shock. Humans traveling to the castle of a dragon is unheard of.

"Ashgrave, tap into your connection with the bees and confirm that the people approaching aren't hostile, please?"

"AT ONCE, MY QUEEN."

"Do you see them?"

"I DO, MY QUEEN. THE HUMANS APPROACHING OUR BORDERS ARE NOT CARRYING WEAPONS AND DO NOT APPEAR TO BE HOSTILE, MISTRESS."

"Thank you, Ashgrave. Please open a safe pathway for our visitors."

"RIGHT AWAY, MY QUEEN."

Tucker puts his small screwdriver on the table next to the clear plastic cage of the last orb. "Are you going to meet them in the throne room?" His lips pull into a dazzling smile.

I nod my head and wink at him. "Do you want to meet our visitors with me?"

"Hell yeah! This is exciting." He approaches me as his gorgeous green eyes twinkle and he plants a kiss on my forehead. "We have human visitors."

My gaze goes to the clear plastic box. "Brett, have you ever seen this kind of nonexistent lock before?"

"I have." Brett nods his head.

"Will you try to get it open, while Tucker and I go and meet our guests?"

The feeling of pride coming from Jade has a smile crawling up my face.

"Ashgrave, please take me and Tucker to the throne room," I tell my murderous castle.

"RIGHT AWAY, MISTRESS." My castle's voice booms as the wall to our right slides open and a tunnel appears.

Tucker grabs my hand and flashes me one of his trade mark goofy grins. "Let's go meet our new friends, babe."

His excitement is contagious, and I feel my face returning his grin as he pulls me into the magical tunnel.

Tucker and I walk up the stairway that appears. "Good idea, babe."

I pull my weapons expert to a stop. "I love you,

but I have no idea what you're talking about, Tucker."

He places his calloused hand on my cheek. "If the case is booby-trapped, it's better that Brett takes the hit rather than me." He gives me a gentle kiss on the lips. "Thanks for choosing me over Brett, babe." His body shakes with laughter as the wall ahead of us slides open.

My adorable weapons master grabs my hand and pulls me through the open wall, and we approach the ornate double doors of the throne room.

"Ashgrave, have my men meet me in the throne room, please. I'd like them to be seated by my side to greet our visitors."

"RIGHT AWAY, MY QUEEN."

Drew, Jace, and Levi race down the stone staircase toward us with worried expressions on their faces.

"Are we being invaded again?" Jace asks as Levi and Drew gaze at my face.

"No. We have human visitors." My gaze drops to the beautiful marble floor. "I figured we should all be together when we greet them."

"Good idea, Rory." Drew's black eyes glimmer with pride.

"BOW BEFORE THE ONE TRUE QUEEN OF

ASHGRAVE AND RULER OF DRAGON MAGIC,"
Ashgrave announces as the doors swing open and I
spot over one hundred people on their knees with
their heads dipping to the floor.

My men and I approach the dais that holds our
thrones, and we look out over the people bowing to
us. I notice that there are several different smaller
groups of people. The smaller groups are dressed
similarly, making me think these people are from
different countries and joined this procession as a
type of pilgrimage.

As my men and I take our seats, I'm in shock that
this many people would come to see me. To see us.

"You may rise," I announce.

The large group of humans rise to stand. A
woman who appears to be around sixty years-old
with grey hair curled on top of her head and wrin-
kled laugh lines around her mouth and crow's feet,
approaches the raised platform where our thrones
sit. "Good day, my queen." She lowers her bright
green eyes toward the marble floor at her feet. "I am
sure you are wondering why we have traveled to
visit you this fine day," she says with a Polish accent.

I give the woman a nod and make sure my face is
an emotionless mask.

"We have come from many different countries

for many different reasons." She points to the corner of the large room near the door to those who are dressed in fine silks. "The people from France have come to visit the infamous Castle Ashgrave." She then points to the group of people dressed in furs near the stage and to the group in the far corner dressed in wool coats. "Our brothers and sisters from Siberia and the United Kingdom have come to pay homage to the queen who freed them from the dragons who ruled them with an iron fist."

My fists involuntarily clench at the thought of dragonkind ruling over humans. It seems as though a few dragon families believe humans are their slaves and not their equals. I figure it's up to me and my family to set them straight.

The grey-haired woman points to the group behind her. "The group from Poland has come to thank you for saving us and our loved ones from the Vaer dragons, who have been attacking and punishing humans who are actively supporting you and your family." The woman's green eyes twinkle as she points to the group dressed in rags. "These groups of stragglers from different countries are all seeking protection and safety." She makes a circle with her arm in the air, indicating everyone in the room. "But we all, my queen, have come to give you gifts from our regions of the world."

Drew draws my attention as he clears his throat. He gives me a knowing look. The woman keeps calling me her queen. My fire dragon knows that I have to be the queen I'm meant to be. And, I have to say, I believe it.

My eyes travel to Levi's ice blue ones, and his gaze is strong and silent but also reveals his pride. Jace is fidgeting next to me, and I can tell he's eager to get back to training my army. My mate does look pleased though, as a sexy smile graces his full lips.

"Ashgrave should start giving tours," Tucker whispers as he sits next to Jace. My weapons expert swings his left arm out to his side and mimics my castle's booming voice. "AND HERE IS WHERE WE TORTURE THE POOR FOOLS WHO DARE DEFY THE ONE TRUE QUEEN."

"Oh my gods, Tucker will you please shut up, you adorable goof?" I place my head in my hands and stifle a chuckle.

I compose myself and raise my head, making sure my face shows no emotion. I can't allow them to see any type of weakness.

"You are all welcome to our home," I announce in a loud yet kind voice. "Feel free to explore the main floors of the castle. However, I ask that you stay away from the lower floor, the west wing, and the area around my private rooms." I take a deep breath and slowly allow it to escape through my lips. "Please know that you are free here, no matter where you came from. We choose to treat each other with kindness and respect. I promise to do everything in my power to ensure your safety while you're here. Feel free to introduce yourself to me and my lords—we're here for you." I smirk as my eyes meet Jace's, and a frown pulls his lips downward. I stand and raise my arms out wide to my sides. "Welcome to Castle Ashgrave."

The crowd erupts with applause, and a few wolf whistles pierce the air as my men stand from their thrones and approach my side.

My men and I walk down into the smiling throng of humans, and some split off to grab their bags from outside the throne room doors while others approach Jace, Drew, and Levi with their phones out, asking to take pictures with them.

A grin pulls my lips upward as I think that if my men want me to be queen so badly, they're going to have to get used to being my lords.

CHAPTER TEN

I walk through the crowd, taking time to shake outstretched hands and hugging those who embrace me. I catch Tucker's gaze. He looks toward the doors and wiggles his eyebrows up and down. My weapons expert knows that I still don't do well surrounded by people, and I love that he knows that. My eyes roam over the crowd, and I spot Levi posing for a selfie with a young man that appears to be about sixteen or seventeen years-old, and I point to the door, letting him know that I'm heading out of the room. My ice dragon gives me a small nod, and I head for the exit.

The doors to the throne room are sitting open, and I exit the room and walk around the corner to allow the beating of my heart to slow. I doubt I'll ever enjoy being in a crowd of people, especially a group of over a hundred strangers who are offering me gifts for doing the right thing. But I guess that's part of being a queen. It's part of stepping into my new role as a ruler and protector.

As I stand in the hall with my eyes closed and my head leaning against the wall, the clacking of boots hitting the marble floor has my muscles tensing. My eyes spring open, searching for an attack. A sigh rushes from my lips as I spot the culprit—Tucker.

"Are you okay?" He grabs my hand and pulls me up the stone staircase.

I allow him to lead me away from the commotion in the throne room. My weapons expert gently tugs on my hand, pulling me toward my private rooms so we can be alone.

As we walk toward my bedroom, Tucker pulls me to a stop. "I know something's bothering you by the way the corner of your eyes turn up when you're concerned about something, babe." He gently kisses the upper corner of each of my offending organs of sight. "Kind of like how I knew something was getting to you when your vein turned blue the other day when we were in the surveillance room."

"You do have a strange knack of seeing through

the emotionless mask I wear." My head bows toward my chest.

My weapons expert tugs on the tips of my fingers. "Rory, you and I are alike in a lot of ways. One of which is that we have both been taught to hide the emotions we have inside for our whole lives. We were raised to wear emotionless masks. So, it makes sense that I can see through your mask now." Tucker plants a gentle kiss on my lips as his gorgeous green eyes stare right into my soul. "Tell me what's on your mind, beautiful. I won't laugh or tell you that you're worried over nothing. I promise."

As I look into his eyes, I feel my emotional wall crumble. "I had a couple visions of the dragon gods."

His eyes widen. "When? You had another one?"

"It happened a little while ago. I was in the treasury and I touched Morgana's dragon armor." I slightly tremble. "It felt like I was in their presence, Tucker. Like all I had to do was reach out my hand, and I'd be able to touch all three of them. Morgana's voice felt like it was going to burrow its way into my body. It was horrible, and it felt so real." I place my head on Tucker's chest, and he wraps his arms around me as if his strong shoulders alone will protect me from the dragon gods. "I worry that I won't be ready when they come for my magic, Tucker."

"That's why we need to get the last orb out of that box and fix it," he whispers into my hair. "So we can have Ashgrave at his full strength and back you up."

I tilt my chin upward to search his face, and I find his adorable goofy grin on his lips. "It's not only the dragon gods," I confess. "I tense up every time I think about my eventual showdown with Kinsley."

Tucker kisses my forehead. "We will follow you to hell and back, babe. You know that, right?"

I nod my head against his muscled chest. "If I fail, a lot of people will suffer and die, Tucker. Especially those closest to me."

My weapons expert grabs my arm and spins me out of our embrace. He turns me so my back is against his chest and he pushes me into the wall of our secluded hallway as his strong calloused hand encircles my waist, pinning me in place.

"Abandon the thought of failing, babe." He whispers into my ear from behind me. "You won't. You're the strongest person I know."

"If this is your way of convincing me," I tease, "I'd like you to prove how persuasive you can be."

"Is that a challenge?" Tucker growls in my ear then bites my earlobe.

I nod my head as a moan escapes my lips.

Tucker's hands move from my waist to my breasts. He pulls on my growing nipples with his fingers and thumbs through my shirt and bra as he plants heated kisses up and down my neck. My dragon coos in preparation of having our weapons expert control us, and I let out a groan of need and want.

My weapons expert keeps teasing my nipples with one hand as he unbuttons my jeans and pulls them down, exposing my ass to the air. His long thick fingers then start to explore my sensitive folds as he continues to kiss and nibble on my neck. His other hand continues to tweak and pull at my over-sensitive nipples. My need to be filled by him pools between my legs as Tucker's fingers stroke my clit, making me arch into his hand.

He slides a finger into me and I grind against his hand, wanting him to fill me completely as the throb of a blossoming orgasm starts to build in my core. He pumps his finger in and out of me in a rhythm that brings takes me to the edge of an orgasm.

He removes his finger. "Am I starting to persuade you, babe?" he growls in my ear. He continues to nibble and kiss my neck as I feel his freed enlarged cock against my ass.

I arch into him as he leans my chest and face over into the wall and spreads my legs wider to give him room to enter me from behind. As the tip of his member enters me, I gasp. Tucker teases my entrance by entering a little of himself at a time, making me push my ass against him, forcing him to give me more.

He follows my lead and pumps every inch of himself inside me, making my muscles clench around him. My orgasm has me biting the inside of my cheek so I don't scream out in pleasure.

Tucker waits for my muscles to loosen up and starts a pumping with a rhythm that has another throbbing orgasm starting to build. He nibbles and kisses my neck while continuing to tease both of my nipples with one hand and holding me close to him with the other. My head rolls back onto my shoulder as my orgasm rips through me, and I feel Tucker's release inside me.

My weapons expert kisses my neck and slaps my naked ass. "Consider yourself persuaded, my love." He turns me around and gives me a heated kiss. "You, Rory Quinn, will never fail. Failing isn't in you. It never was and it never will be. You, babe, only succeed. It's what you do." Tucker pulls up my pants and buttons them for me. He plants a gentle kiss on my lips as he pulls up and buttons his own. "Your fire is one of the many reasons I fell in love with you. You got this, babe. And no matter what happens, you will always be my queen."

CHAPTER ELEVEN

As the sun sets over Ashgrave and the surrounding area, I search the surveillance room, war room, and dining room for my sister. I need to let her know that Brett opened the clear plastic box and that we are one step closer to our goal of taking down Kinsley. I want to share the good news with her, but I can't find her in any of her usual spots, so I climb the stairs of the west tower, hoping she's gone back to our dojo days and she's at one of the highest points of the castle. The only tower higher than this one is the central tower that's directly above my private rooms.

I climb the stairs to the tower and remind myself that we've only had the orb for a little over thirty hours, and we now have the box opened and are ready to start putting the final orb back together. Ashgrave will finally be at his full power. *Very* soon.

As I round the last turn of the stairway, I find the door to the tower open. I walk through the door and find Irena sitting on the ledge of the tower, with her legs dangling over the side of what could be more than a hundred foot drop if she's not careful. But she's unbothered—stoic. She breathes in the fresh night air and watches Jace lead hundreds of dragons and about ten of Ashgrave's massive mechanical dragons in a mid-air drill.

"There you are," I say. "I've been looking for you."

"Oh yeah, why?" Irena's bright green eyes turn to meet mine.

"Brett opened the box. We can start putting the orb together." My lips curve into a smile as I approach my sister.

"That's good." Her gaze goes to the dragons as they dance around each other in the air, and she shrugs her shoulders.

"What happened at the Washington facility? Why did you hesitate to kill the Vaer soldier who was attacking you?" I place my hands on the ledge next to her and turn my head to observe Irena's face as I narrow my eyes.

My sister takes a deep breath and lets it out

slowly through her pursed lips. "Is it possible to have a connection to someone to the point that they're almost literally in your head?"

"I experienced something close to it." I nod. "Isaac Palarne telepathically invaded my thoughts once." My eyes meet my sister's, and I shrug to hide my internal cringe at remembering the feeling. "But on the other side of that unpleasant coin," I say as I let out a strained chuckle, "Levi and I share thoughts when we touch each other. I can feel what he's feeling, and the same goes for him. We also communicate telepathically when we have skin-to-skin contact, so there's that bonus. It's something special that only Levi and I share."

Irena's eyes start to glow again, and I take an unconscious step backward. My sister's eyes are so much like Kinsley's when they glow that it's offsetting.

She closes her glowing eyes and shakes her head. "I saw myself in the mirror in my bathroom and slammed my fist into it, shattering it. I don't want to look at myself anymore, Rory," my sister confesses. "I feel like Kinsley is a part of me, and I can't stand it."

I approach Irena and place my hand on her

shoulder and look out at the surrounding hills. My mind searches for the right words to soothe her.

As I observe the beauty of the rolling hills and valleys, I spot a tall chocolate skinned man walking toward the main road of the castle. I narrow my eyes to see which of the Palarne brothers are approaching. By the way he slumps his shoulders and drags his feet, it has to be Payton. Isaac always walks with his back ramrod straight and with a confident purpose.

"PAY—" Ashgrave starts to announce.

"I know. Payton Palarne is approaching," I interrupt. "Thank you anyway, Ashgrave."

Irena takes my hand off her shoulder and swings her legs to the inside of the tower, placing her feet on the floor of the tower. "Do you want me to come down to the throne room with you?"

"Nah, I've got this." I turn and spy Flynn walking toward us. His hazel eyes light up at the sight of Irena, but my sister doesn't acknowledge it.

Flynn approaches us with his gaze locked on Irena's, and my big sister doesn't turn away or lower her gaze.

Could it be that Irena has a thing for Flynn? Maybe. I'll just have to keep my eyes open and hope my sister keeps her heart open to the possibility of happiness with the rebel leader.

I slip away and trek toward the throne room to see what brings Payton all the way to the castle.

As I walk down the hallway to the stone staircase that leads to the throne room, I take in the beauty that is Castle Ashgrave. The rich marble floors, the ornate woven carpets, the beautifully framed art pieces and sculptures that line the hallways. The fact that even though the sun has gone down, my castle isn't dark. The hallways are all brightly lit with elegant crystal sconces on the walls and small chandeliers that hang from the beautifully sculpted ceilings.

I approach the double doors of the throne room and they swing open automatically. As I enter the room, I notice that Payton is standing in the center of the large room with his head bowed toward the ornate carpet at his feet. The muscles in his neck and shoulders strain with tension.

"Hello, Payton." I walk across the large room and take a seat on my throne.

The Palarne heir tilts his head to look at me as he chews on the inside of his cheek and clenches his hands into fists. I wonder if the Palarne found the bug we planted at their capital and traced it back to us.

"Kinsley Vaer launched an attack on a Palarne stronghold this morning," he says, barely able to control his anger.

"Oh no! I'm sorry to hear that." I search his round black eyes with my own. "Is everyone okay? Do you need us to do anything?"

Payton shakes his head. "Isaac sent me directly to you because of the nature of the attack."

I lift a questioning brow at him. What is that supposed to mean? Kinsley has always orchestrated attacks without provocation and without mercy.

"Kinsley herself was present during the attack. She was wreaking havoc." He lowers his gaze. "Her powers were oddly enhanced. Kinsley did things that defied explanation." Payton observes me, perhaps to gauge my reaction. "Rory, her abilities this morning were far beyond her normal capabilities."

"What does that mean?" I ask.

Payton shakes his head and paces in a wide circle while clenching and unclenching his hands for a while as he decides how to answer my question.

I slam my hands onto the arms of my uncomfortable chair, letting Payton know that I need an answer.

"Before my brother gave you Esmeralda's diary, he studied it at length himself." Payton places his hands on the top of his head and leans his head back to look at the ceiling. "I used to mock him for it, but now, after witnessing what Kinsley did, I have to say that the gods must be stirring, and in some strange way they're within Kinsley Vaer."

CHAPTER TWELVE

The bright yellow glow of the morning sun shines through the large arched windows of my bedroom. I roll toward Drew's large body and accidentally get a face full of his long beard. I poke him in the ribs, and his top lip curls up into a smirk as he wraps his strong arms around me and pulls me into his hard-muscled bare chest.

As the images of our lovemaking run through my mind, heat pools between my legs. I'd love to spend the day in bed with my sexy fire dragon, reliving him having every inch of me, but we can't.

We have a lot of work to do.

Now, more than ever, I need to piece that broken orb back together. I need it whole in order to work. The orb will not only change my men into my lords by allowing them to have access to my magic, but it will also give them a piece of my soul. Placing this orb will give me and my men an unbreakable bond that we will have for the rest of our very long lives.

But its magic isn't limited to turning my men into lords. It will also return Ashgrave to his full power. I'll need my vengeful, murderous castle at full strength when the sleeping gods awaken all the way. I only hope that my evil butler remains loyal to me when Morgana returns.

I jut out my chin and rub it against the strong muscles in Drew's chest, and he releases me, turning his back to me and covering his chest with his hands, laughing.

"Hey, no fair. You chin tickled me," he grunts out through his laughter.

"Serves you right. We have a lot to do today, and you were trying to trap me in bed." I chuckle.

My fire dragon is a huge mountain of a man who demands attention wherever he goes. But it just so happens that this natural born leader is also extremely ticklish, but only I know that fact.

"Fine. Have it your way, slave driver." Drew shakes his head, chuckling. "Guess I should trim my beard this morning, so you don't choke on it."

I playfully slap his shoulder. "Yes, please. I love

your sexy beard, but it's in desperate need of losing a few inches of its length."

"Ashgrave, can you please get the team together for a meeting in the war room?"

"RIGHT AWAY, MY QUEEN. WOULD YOU LIKE BREAKFAST SET IN THE WAR ROOM AS WELL, MISTRESS?"

"Yes, please." I push myself up and sit in my fluffy cloud like bed and push the plush comforter off my body.

Drew sits up and throws his long legs over the side of the bed next to me as I plant my feet on the floor.

"You do know there's another side of the bed, right?" My gaze meets his dark eyes.

He nods his head. "I do. But I can't do this from the other side of the bed." He grabs my face in his large hands and gives me a heated kiss that has me wishing we could spend the day in this bed.

Drew pushes himself off the bed as I watch his naked body walk out the door, with my fingers touching my warm, wet lips. *Tease.* I'll punish him for that later.

I pull myself to my feet, raise my arms into the air, and stretch out my back muscles. I approach my large walk-in closet and pull out a pair of dark stone washed jeans and a black braided cord sweater. I make my way to my extravagant bathroom to brush my teeth and quickly throw my hair up in a low ponytail that hangs at the back of my neck.

As I look at myself in the mirror, my heart pangs with the ache of knowing that my sister doesn't feel like her strong confident self anymore. Every time Irena looks in a mirror, she sees Kinsley's glowing green eyes staring back at her, and she hates it. I rush to my sitting area and throw on a pair of dark socks and my favorite black combat boots as I make a mental note to remind my sister this morning that she is not Kinsley. Her name is Irena Quinn, and she is stronger, smarter, more loving, and more resilient than Kinsley Vaer will ever be.

"WOULD YOU LIKE ME TO MAKE A PASSAGEWAY TO THE WAR ROOM, MY QUEEN?" My castle's voice thunders through the room, making me jump to my feet.

"Yes, please," I reply as the wall to my left opens up and I enter the magical tunnel that my castle provides.

As I follow the dimly lit hallway to the stairs that lead downward, I think of soothing words to help my sister come to grips with her new identity. The wall at the bottom of the stairwell opens, and I step out into the hallway across from the door that leads to the war room and I straighten my back, drawing in a deep breath. Time to get this done.

I pull the door open and walk into my noisy war room. I find the center of the large wooden table covered with a small red velvet blanket with the broken orb pieces nestled safely on it. The fragments of the orb are all splayed out with the larger pieces surrounded by the smaller ones.

Jace and a freshly trimmed Drew sit facing the door and looking at a tablet my fire dragon is holding in his hand. Brett and Jade stand near the table of breakfast food, placing fresh fruits and yogurt on small plates as they whisper quietly into each other's ears with huge toothy grins plastered on their faces. Tucker and Flynn are talking loudly in the left corner of the room while Levi stands between them with his hand on his forehead. My ice dragon's eyes light up when he spots me. His sensual full lips pull upward at their corners, and he walks away from the rowdy discussion going on.

I search the room for my sister, but she's not here. "Ashgrave, where is Irena?"

"SHE LEFT THE CASTLE GROUNDS WITH A DOZEN OF HER FIGHTERS BEFORE DAWN, MY

QUEEN." My castle's voice booms, shaking the orb fragments that lie on the table.

Damn it! She's out on another sabotage mission, no doubt. Irena feels she needs to destroy Kinsley to prove to the world that she's nothing like the Vaer Boss my sister's eyes and magic resemble. My heartbeat quickens as I remember how my sister barely escaped with her life the last time she went on one of her sabotage missions. Irena had better make it back here safely so I can maim her myself.

I roll my shoulders and shake out my arms to loosen the muscles that tightened when I realized my sister left the castle and put herself in harm's way, yet again, just to prove that she's nothing like Kinsley Vaer.

My eyes roll involuntarily as I clear my throat to gather the attention of my team. My family.

"After studying Clara's diary and watching Ashgrave's memories in the mural room for a majority of the afternoon yesterday," I say as I meet each set of eyes in the room with my own, "I've figured out that in order to fix the orb, certain foundational pieces will have to be melded back together first." My eyes dart toward the large pieces of the broken orb, and I rise from my seat to stand ramrod straight. "This is going to be like putting together a jigsaw puzzle. Who's up for some fun?" I rub my hands together and move to sit near one of the larger pieces of crystal orb.

"I'm down for working on the puzzle, but I do have one question for you." Jade comes to sit across the table from me, and I'm flooded with the feeling of excitement.

"Shoot." I flash her a genuine smile.

"How are we supposed to fuse the pieces together?" Jade lifts an eyebrow at me, and I fight the chuckle that wants to fly from my lips at how much she resembles me when she raises a questioning brow.

My gaze drops to my lap. "I'll fuse them together with my magic."

I leave out the fact that I'll have to infuse a bit of each of the gods' magic into the orb while repairing it, though, as I struggle with the fact that their magic is dark and I want nothing to do with any of it.

Brett takes a seat next to Jade and starts trying to put the smaller shards of the orb together. Tucker grabs the chair to my left and Levi takes the seat to my right.

Drew playfully ruffles Tucker's chin-length, dark brown hair. "Looks like someone else needs a trim too." He winks at me and strokes his now neatly trimmed beard before my fire dragon takes the seat across the table from Levi.

Jace stalks silently across the room to take the empty chair across from Tucker and joins in on trying to piece together the fragmented shards of crystal.

A rush of happiness comes from Jade as she holds up two of the larger pieces of the broken orb. "I found two pieces that go together."

I take the broken pieces and hold them together as I concentrate all of the magic at my disposal into the two pieces of crystal in my hand. My palms exude the brilliant sapphire blue light of my magic into the fragments of the orb as I follow the directions from the diary. I shiver from the chill that invades my entire body as the crystal pieces fuse into one.

I place the now fused piece of orb on the red velvet blanket on the table and rub my hands together. My fingers tingle as the freezing cold slowly fades, and I turn my hands over in my lap as I search them, noticing that the ends of my fingers are stained an abalone grey color.

"I have three pieces here that go together." Tucker hands me the fragments, and as his hand brushes mine, he turns my hand over. His eyes narrow at the grey tinge of my fingertips, and his eyes search mine for an answer to his unasked question.

I gently pull my fingers from my weapons expert's vice like grip and concentrate my magic on combining the pieces of orb that lie in my hand. I watch as the blue light glows from my fingertips, fusing the small three fragments into a larger one as my body once again becomes ice cold. My muscles tense like I'm freezing into a solid block of ice.

The last time I had a vision of the dragon gods, the death god, Caelan, had an ash grey tinge to his skin. I figure the coldness and my grey fingertips have to be a byproduct of using Caelan's death magic.

Fan-freaking-tastic.

The only way to fuse the remaining orb is by funneling the gods' magic into it, and by doing that, I'm apparently at risk of becoming a grey popsicle.

No! I won't allow that to happen.

This is *my* magic, damn it. This power will listen to me—it's mine. It no longer belongs to the dragon gods.

A boot scrapes across the floor, and Tucker pushes his chair back from the table and rubs his calf. "What the hell was that for?" He glares at Jace.

"For putting that frown on her face." My mate nods his head toward me.

"Whatever! You're just jealous that I'm the favorite." My weapons expert wiggles his eyebrows up and down at Jace.

"Really? You think so?" My mate lifts his arms and flexes his biceps at Tucker. "You might have guns, but these guns are part of me." He gives me a wink, and I know he's trying to get a rise out of his brother.

"Just wait until we get this orb fixed." Tucker slaps his hand against the table. "You three might be dragons, but I'll be her lord."

"We will all be," Levi adds with his lips turning down. Drew hides his chuckle with the pieces of orb he's trying to put together.

The whole room erupts in uncontrollable laughter. Not one of us can keep it at bay any longer.

Leave it to my strong silent protector to put our resident jokester in his place.

My eyes roam over the faces of the members of this ridiculous family of mine, and I spy Brett and Jade with their heads so close together that they're almost touching. They carry on a whispered conver-sation while trying to put a few pieces of orb together, and a feeling of love washes over me from Jade.

My eyes take in the way Levi is sitting with his back and shoulders tense, and I lean into him as he turns two of the larger shards around in his long fingers. I place my hand on top of his and open our connection. I pour my love and concern for him into it.

How have you been sleeping? I ask my ice dragon through our special connection.

Better. He puts the shards he's working on down, turns his hand around and places his palm against mine, and laces fingers with me. *I haven't had any more nightmares. Not since seeing the Vaer elite warrior team at the facility in Washington. I was once a member of Kinsley's select team, and seeing all new members made me realize that I'm not the same person I once was.*

I'm happy you've finally come to grips with what I've known since I found you. I force more love and support through the connection. *You will never be anyone's pawn again, Levi.*

The more time I spend with you, the more I realize my purpose and my future with you. Our family is laid out for me to see. He gently kisses the back of my hand. *The old fear of falling back into being feral fades away.*

I'm happy to hear that. I gaze into his ice blue eyes

and raise a questioning brow. *But, what aren't you telling me?*

I wonder what it'll mean to activate the orb and receive part of your magic. Levi places his free hand over the back of the hand he's holding. *We're going to receive part of your very soul, Rory.* He shakes his head and drops his intoxicating eyes to our combined hands. *Won't that weaken you on some level? You need all of your strength. What, with Kinsley, and now with the dragon gods stirring. I just think we should wait.* An exasperated sigh escapes his sumptuous lips.

I need this, Levi. I put my free hand over his, making a double decker hand sandwich. *By making you guys my lords, it'll give you added protection and strength. It won't weaken me. I promise. It'll give me peace of mind and bond us all together, forever.* My eyes try to search his, but he won't look at me.

I can tell he doesn't believe me. I can feel it through our bond. I take my hand off his and gently untangle my fingers from his to stop the feeling of disbelief from flowing into me from the one man that makes me *feel.* I shake my head to remove Levi's feelings from my own.

I look at my tingling fingers and notice the grey coloring is gone. Good. Whatever Caelan's death magic is doing to me must be temporary.

Brett holds up four smaller pieces of the orb in his palm while Jade holds a larger fragment out to me.

"These pieces all fit together, Rory." Jade's feeling of happiness floods my mind as she speaks.

"Great." I allow my lips to drift upward into a smile. "Let's get them fused together." I put my hand out and Brett and Jade place the pieces in my hand.

As I place the pieces together, I focus my magic into the five pieces and they start to glow sapphire blue as they fuse together. Once again, a deathly chill floods my body. I place the newly fused section of orb on the red velvet blanket.

"Drew, can you hand me the other pieces I've fused together? I'd like to combine them all."

"Sure, love." He hands me the other two pieces that have been fused and doesn't notice the grey color of my fingertips.

Thank the gods that Drew was busy looking into my brown eyes. I know that if he realized this magic was doing something to me he would have questions, and I can't stop him from getting answers if he really wanted them.

I carefully arrange the three large pieces together and focus the flow of my magic into them. My hands glow as I force more of my power into fusing the orb together. A shiver runs down my arms as over half of the orb refracts sapphire blue light around the war room, and it becomes one large piece. My fingers ache as I set half of the fused orb on the red blanket, rise from my chair, and I clasp my hands behind my back and pace the large room.

"I need a break," I announce with my chin to my chest.

"Do you want me to go with you?" Jade asks with her concern for me coming through our strange connection.

"No." I flash her a smile. "I just need to rest for a little while."

I walk out of the war room. "Ashgrave, can you please open a passageway to the treasury?"

The wall in front of me opens and I'm thankful that my evil butler didn't say a word.

I travel through the magically lit tunnel and down the stairway. The wall in front of me slides open as the doors to the treasury open as I approach them.

As I enter the room of treasures, I search my still cold fingertips. From the second knuckle up, my fingertips are now a darker grey—almost a smoke grey, and the coloring is embedded deeper into my skin.

I reach down and pick up a handful of rubies, emeralds, sapphires, and diamonds and hold them in my hands. The jewels turn black and dissolve in my hand. As the last of the precious jewels falls from my hand like ash, I know that it has to be Caelan's death magic that's affecting me.

Bile rises in my throat, and I force myself not to give in to the sickening feeling. Wielding Morgana's chaos magic is one thing, but this death magic—it's an entirely different monster.

My mind wanders over that fact for a moment. If I make my men my lords, will they inherit some of this awful power as well? And if they do, what will it do to them?

I have to make sure I can control this deadly magic before I share it with my men. I don't know exactly how to tame it, but I won't allow this power to affect my men. Not ever.

CHAPTER THIRTEEN

As I exit the tunnel into the hallway across from the closed door to the war room, I stop, lean my head back into the now solid wall, and listen to the sounds of the bustling castle. There are people talking, pots boiling on the stove in the kitchen, and even someone's bout of laughter trickles down the stairway toward me.

I let out a soft sigh and push off the wall. As I silently open the door to the war room, I instantly wish I could change my stealthy ways. I find Brett and Jade with their bodies entangled, and my ears are assaulted with the sounds of their shared wet kisses. My mind is flooded with love and happiness from Jade, and my lips fight against turning up into a grateful smile. I clear my throat, making the lovers jump apart, and their faces turn a bright shade of pink.

"I don't mean to interrupt." I lift my eyebrows at them. "But we still need to get this puzzle pieced together. Where did the guys go?"

Brett is all too eager to change the subject from his and Jade's activities. "Drew got an important phone call and left for the surveillance room. Flynn said he was going to try and check in with Irena to make sure she's okay. Levi looked upset about something, so he was going on patrol," he blurts out the list of who's-doing-what as he ticks them off on his fingers without meeting my eyes. "And Tucker and Jace went to see Payton Palarne off and to ensure he didn't snoop around the war room. They basically thought it would be best to make sure the Palarnes stayed in the dark about us having the final orb of power."

"We can match up the final pieces of the orb and let you know when they're ready to be fused, if you want." Jade smiles sheepishly.

"That sounds like a good idea. I have a few thing to do." I return her smile. "Thanks."

I turn on my heel and walk out of the war room, making sure to close the door behind me. I might have to think about making some "Do Not Disturb" signs if Jade and Brett can't keep their hands off each other. I don't want our visitors scared in case body parts start getting bared, as the thought of Tucker and my sexual escapades in the hallway run through my mind and my dragon coos.

My feet move down the hallway toward the surveillance room as I go in search of Drew. I need to tell him about these bursts of what must be death magic. I also want to know how he feels about the Lords orb. I wonder if my fire dragon feels the same way as Levi does.

Drew's deep tenor voice comes from the open surveillance room door as I approach. When I enter the room full of computers and surveillance equipment, I spot my fire dragon sitting in his favorite plush computer chair with a smile on his face. As I get closer to him, Milo's voice comes from the phone my fire dragon is holding to his ear.

"Thanks for the information on the secret research facility, Milo," Drew tells his brother. "It really saved us a lot of time."

As my fire dragon continues his conversation, my phone vibrates in my back pocket, and I take it out.

It's a text from Irena.

Need to check on mom.

Shit! That can't be good. The coded message means I need to call my sister ASAP.

I step out into the hallway and dial Irena's number.

"Are you out getting into trouble again?" I ask when my sister answers her phone.

"Have you been keeping up on the bug that I planted on Kinsley's general?" she asks, and I shake my head as a smile creeps up and tugs on my lips.

I love the way Irena cuts to the chase. She's always been that way. It's one of the constants in my ever changing life.

"No, we've been fixing the orb all day," I admit. "Why? What is it, Irena?"

"I've traced some chatter that says Kinsley has arranged a meeting with Jett for tonight."

"I'm already aware that Kinsley is trying to get him on her side." I roll out the tense muscles in my shoulders. "I know Jett won't join the Vaer. He's been allowing Milo to help us. It wouldn't make sense for him to join the Vaer."

"Exactly," my sister says over the phone line. "Kinsley found out. The meeting's a trap. She's going to ambush Jett Darrington."

My mouth drops open as I listen to the last sentence my sister said, and my mind runs over

Payton's words last night. He didn't come out and say that her power was like mine, but he did insinuate that her newfound powers were tied to the gods awaking. Images of Kinsley turning dragons to ash flood my mind.

"I gotta let Drew and Milo know." I shake my head to rid my mind of this even more deadly version of Kinsley. "Don't die, sis."

"Stay safe, Rory." Irena clicks her phone off.

I rush back into the surveillance room to give Drew the information of a planned ambush on his father, so that he can tell Milo. I hope against hope that he's still on the phone with his older brother.

As I enter the surveillance room, I notice Drew is putting his phone on the desk next to him and my stomach drops to my toes.

Shit! I'm too late.

"Drew, can you call your brother back?"

"I just hung up with him. Why would I want to call him back?"

"Because Jett has a meeting with Kinsley tonight." A chest rumbling sigh escapes my open mouth. "And it's going to be an ambush."

"Shit!" Drew picks up his phone and dials what I assume is Milo's private secured phone number.

I listen to my fire dragon tell his brother about

Kinsley's ambush as my mind swims with what-ifs. What if we can't reach Jett? What if Kinsley is using this to trap me? What if the Vaer Boss is planning to use the Darrington Boss as her excuse to start the dragon war?

Drew's deep voice cuts through my invading thoughts. "Well try again."

I raise a questioning brow at my fire dragon, and he puts his hand over his phone.

"Milo can't reach our father." Drew's shoulders draw up toward his ears. "Jett's already left the capital."

"Do they know where the meeting is supposed to take place?" I whisper.

Drew nods. "Milo's getting me the coordinates for where Jett is meeting Kinsley."

"We'll both go, big brother," my fire dragon says into the phone and hangs up.

My jaw drops and I wait for Drew to answer my unasked question.

My fire dragon puts his phone on the desk then places his hands on top of his head. He gazes into my eyes and sits back into the computer chair.

I approach Drew and place a hand on his shoulder.

I understand. He needs to save his father, and I'm going with him.

"I'll tell Tucker to get the chopper ready," I say quietly as I fight the emotions that struggle to break free.

CHAPTER FOURTEEN

As the horizon turns bright pink and purple with the setting sun, Flynn and his group of rebel dragons surround the chopper as it starts its descent to the beautiful island of Santorini, just southeast of Greece.

Levi, Jace, and Drew growl as we spot a group of fire dragons who are led by a large red fire dragon, fighting with an army of orange and black dragons among the whitewashed buildings of the city.

Gunfire thunders through the air, making my metallic castle hover to look out the window of Tucker's second favorite toy as Tucker lands about fifty feet away from the brewing battle.

I unbuckle quickly and join Levi, Jace, Drew, and Ashgrave at the open door of the chopper.

As I peer out the door, I spot humans yelling and screaming as they run for cover from the battling dragons and the gunfire.

A roar of pain slices through the air as an orange fire dragon crashes into the dome of a nearby building, and glass rains down on the people below.

A large jagged shard falls from the broken dome, heading for a couple who're frozen in each other's embrace. I don't think—I exit the chopper and shift. I gently push the couple back against the building as glass rains down, to protect them from being impaled.

"Save my little boy," the woman I just saved screams at me. "Please, Miss Quinn."

My eyes scan the near empty street and I spot a little dark-haired boy in the middle of the road with wide eyes staring at another extremely large shard that is plummeting straight for his head.

I search my dragon claws and remember the feeling of the cold death magic and the way the precious jewels dissolved in my hands.

My sapphire blue magic brightens the sky around me as I send a freezing cold blast toward the offending shard. The large piece of glass instantly disintegrates as the death magic engulfs it and the frightened boy runs into the arms of his parents.

Ashgrave rushes toward me as Levi, Jace, and Drew step out of the way of whirring chopper blades and shift into their dragon forms.

An angry roar pierces the air as golden Andusk dragons approach the area in a tight formation around a group of Nabal ice dragons.

Tucker's chopper takes off and hovers near me, and I wink my golden dragon eye at him. I know my weapons expert will be able to help us better in the sky. His ability to maneuver his flying toys rivals the flying capabilities of most dragons I know. My metallic steampunk castle races off to assist Tucker in taking out the new threat that's approaching.

An earsplitting roar erupts from my mouth. Flynn and his rebels rush to help Milo's massive red dragon form as the Darrington heir fights against the Vaer who are trying to hold him to the outer most part of the island.

Drew presses his massive red forehead into mine as his large golden eyes search mine, and he opens up the dragon telepathic connection. *I'm going to find my father.*

A blast of ice strikes the ground next to me as I notice that more Nabal and Andusk dragons are closing in. I need to help Tucker. He's an excellent pilot, but he's still human.

I'll catch up when I'm finished taking out some of the Nabal and Andusk. I remove my forehead from Drew's and flap my dazzling white wings to take to the sky.

My massive fire dragon blasts the Vaer dragons who are trying to force Milo back toward a cliff with raging waters below it, making the ice dragons roar in pain and take to the sky as he and his brother fly toward the middle of the island to search for Kinsley and their father.

"I'm glad you came to help," Tucker's voice booms from the loud speaker attached to the outside of the helicopter. "You know your castle hates me."

I let out a snort of blue smoke. Leave it to Tucker to crack a joke in the middle of a battle.

A blast of fire hits me in the leg and I let out an angry roar. I'm glad it was me who was hit and not Tucker, but it still hurts. I search the sky for the Andusk who fired at me while I was distracted. I spot a golden dragon with a black stripe from the top of her head to the tip of her tail. She hovers in the air about ten feet away from me, staring at me with eyes that sparkle like jewels in the setting sun. Elizabeth Andusk.

A blast of Jace's blue thunderbird magic hits her in the side, and she lets out a whimper of pain and roars an order to retreat into the sky. All of the golden Andusk dragons turn from the battle and fly off toward the setting sun.

Figures, Elizabeth has always been up to fight in a battle she can win, but if the going gets tough, the Andusk Boss gets going. Now that the Andusk's numbers have been decreased by Flynn and his rebels leaving and joining me, I'm sure that Elizabeth will only do the minimum to keep her alliance with Kinsley.

I turn my big white head, searching for my mate. And I find him battling with some Vaer and Nabal alongside Levi and Flynn below me. My ice dragon sends a blast of ice magic into a familiar orange Vaer dragon, freezing him instantly. Flynn slams his huge black tail with a silver stripe into the dragon we encountered at the secret government facility in Washington, shattering him into hundreds of little ice shards.

Out of the corner of my eye, I spy a Vaer soldier dressed in all black with a familiar green "V" embroidered on his shoulder, pulling a rocket launcher up onto the "V" and aiming it at me. The loud pitched whistle of the rocket being fired screams through the air. The loud whir of Ashgrave's metallic wings has me turning my head to watch his little steampunk body crash into the rocket that was aimed at my head. My evil butler crashes into the ground in a plume of smoke.

My worry and anger battle inside me. I know my murderous castle isn't dead. He can make another mechanical body—he's told us as much. But I hate the idea of him getting hurt. I know firsthand that being hit by a rocket hurts. It *hurts* like hell.

I tuck my wings into my side and dive to find my evil butler's body as Tucker lands the chopper nearby. My body shifts to my human form, and I roll to my feet and approach the area where he landed to check and see if Ashgrave is okay.

The thick black smoke floats in the air, concealing the debris that covers the ground, and I put my hands out in front of me and drag my feet to make sure I don't trip over anything.

The scream of a rocket launcher slices the air as a slight wind starts to clear away the heavy smoke. I'm tackled to the ground by the strong arms of my weapons expert as a rocket explodes into the ground about five feet away, making more dirt and smoke fly into the air. My stomach suddenly churns as the ground gives way and we fall into the earth beneath us.

Tucker and I lie on our backs and shift positions

in response to the rocky dirt beneath our backs. We catch our breaths as we scan the area around us, trying to gauge how far we've fallen, and where.

I pull myself up into a sitting position and observe what appears to be an underground tunnel system. There are hollowed out walkways of rock and dirt that are big enough for me to walk through, and it looks like the tunnels go on for miles.

Screams and cries echo down to me as gunshots ring out. I spot the shimmer of Flynn's silver stream as he sends his thunderbird magic into something or someone to the left of our hole in the ground.

"Ashgrave," I call out. "Where are you? Damn it, answer me you smiteful castle."

"Hey, babe." Tucker places a comforting hand on my shoulder and sits up. "You know your evil butler will be okay, right?"

"Tucker, we're in a hole." I shake my head. "There's no room for me to shift in here." I drop my chin to my chest. "Not safely, anyway. And if I try to set off a blast of magic to tell everyone where we are," I let out a deep sigh as a pang of dread strangles my heart, "I could bring everything down on top of us. We're trapped."

I lie back on the rocky dirt and close my eyes. This is not how it ends for me. My team needs me.

Drew needs me, and I'm stuck in a tunnel unable to help.

Tucker lies back next to me and grabs my hand in his. "You've got this, babe. You're the most intelligent person I know. You've got what it takes to lead our team, our army, and the world." He rolls on his side to look at me and uses his free arm to gently stroke my forearm. "You never give up, and seeing you like this makes me want to fight harder, not quit. I've seen you take the dark magic of the dragon gods and use it to help others, make their lives better. A cave-in is just a minor setback. Considering what we've been through, this is nothing."

Tucker's words cause my dragon to stir. I reach inside myself and connect with her and the power that's swirling within me. Caelan's cold death magic wraps itself around me, and I push it away, knowing it's not going to help me and Tucker out of the cave.

My soul listens to the chaotic clash of swords and armor of Morgana's magic. I push that away too. It's not right either.

Razorus's magic rushes forward, enveloping me an illusion of Tucker pumping into me while I lie on a field of wildflowers. There we go. The magic of altering reality. This could work.

I focus the illusory magic into the earth and

debris surrounding us, and I force them to turn into light, dead leaves. Then I pull on a bit of chaotic magic and form a wild wind to blow the leaves away, creating an opening.

The wind whips at my hair, and I open my eyes to find the area around us clear of the tunnels. It's now just a huge rocky hole in the ground.

I roll onto my side. "You ready to get out of here, babe?"

Tucker's eyes are as big as saucers, but he flashes me one of his trademark goofy grins and nods. He pulls me up to stand on my dirt covered feet.

"Okay, stand back." I straighten my arms and turn in a circle. "I'm going to shift and get us out of here."

My dragon presses against me, and I allow her to take control.

My hands turn into claws, and I roar into the sky before I carefully grab Tucker in my talons and carry him to the surface.

I gently place my weapons expert ten feet away from the hole we were trapped in and observe our surroundings. The clickity-clack of metal hitting against itself has me peering through the smoke to find Ashgrave's cat-sized steampunk body limping as one of his wings hangs lifeless with the huge rocket launcher in his mouth. He releases the mangled weapon from his spiked metallic teeth, dropping it at my clawed feet.

Ashgrave steps back and an earthshaking roar escapes his little metallic body. I respond with my own earsplitting roar.

I set my large dragon head on top of Tucker's to open the telepathic link. *Will you be okay if I leave you here to care for our damaged castle?*

We will be fine, babe. Go kick Kinsley's ass. He steps back, grinning, and he breaks our connection.

I spread my wings and take to the sky to find Drew and his family and to destroy Kinsley once and for all.

CHAPTER FIFTEEN

I search the raging battle below me for Drew, Milo, or Jett. An earsplitting roar cuts through the cool night air and it pulls at my soul. I tuck my wings and dive, aiming my body for the dark tenuous pull.

The pull leads me to a large black volcanic crater with sharp dark rocks jutting up from its surface. As I get closer, I spot Drew, Milo, and Jett on one side of the massive black hole in the ground. A large dragon with a black cloud floating over its body stands across from them, and three familiar-looking orange fire dragons are at its back.

My claws send black volcanic rock flying into the air as I land and make the ground quake beneath me. As Drew and Milo approach me, I roar a threat of violence into the cloudless black sky. I don't recognize this new dragon, but I'm not going to allow it to hurt my fire dragon or his family.

I brush the tip of my wing against Drew's to open our telepathic connection. *Who the hell is that dragon who's covered in a black floating oily film?* I ask. *I don't recognize it.*

I don't see a film over Kinsley. He shakes his head. *I do know she has power that mimics yours though. She shot me from the sky, and it felt just like when you shot me in the tunnels under the dojo.* Drew runs the tip of his wing up mine. *I don't know what happened to her, Rory. But she's lost her ice magic and gained—*

Kinsley unleashes her dark soul-pulling roar into the air. She gathers a royal blue shade of magic into her throat, meets my gaze with her dull forest green one, and blasts the center of Jett's back with her enhanced magic. The Darrington Boss crumbles into a motionless heap. Milo lets out a dangerous growl and narrows his eyes at the dragon who dared blast his father. He returns the favor, unleashing an intense blast of fire, and Kinsley takes to the sky, evading the Darrington heir's deadly blast.

I take a moment to examine Kinsley Vaer. Her white skin that would normally shimmer in the moonlight has a black smoke that swirls like oil floating over her entire body. The dark film dulls her glowing emerald green eyes to a lackluster, deep forest green.

What did Kinsley do to herself?

Out of the corner of my eye I spot an orange fire dragon blast Drew's older brother in his damaged wing. Milo roars out in pain, and I rush over to help him defend his father who's lying on the hard black rock in his dragon form. Drew flies straight up into the air and lands silently behind one of the warriors he's facing off against and blasts him with a blue-green flame, turning the orange dragon's head to ash, and the Vaer warrior falls dead at Drew's huge red claws.

As I approach Milo, I send a blast of my icy death magic into the orange dragon trying to seize Drew's big brother in his snapping jaws. Milo's lifeless left wing hangs by his side, and he shuffles forward, snapping his jaws, trying to force the Vaer warrior away from his fallen father. As I send more power into the concentrated blast of Caelan's death magic, the Vaer warrior turns charcoal and starts to disintegrate and blow away into the moonlit night.

A blast of dark, cold magic slams into my back and robs the air from my lungs as I fall to all fours in the volcanic hole.

I shake my head and force my lungs to fill with cool night air as I wonder what the hell I was just hit with. I've never felt power like that before.

Drew's words come rushing back to me, and I realize Kinsley just blasted me with magic like my own.

Damn it!

How did Kinsley mimic my magic? She's the Vaer Boss and one of the most powerful ice dragons to ever walk the earth, not a dragon vessel. Payton Palarne was right—she's conspiring with the gods somehow, and they're using her as a means to take me down because I'm the one possessing their full power.

So, what did they promise Kinsley?

She has definitely done something to enhance her powers.

And it's up to me to take her out before she can hurt anyone else.

I roll over onto my back as I pull on the death magic inside me and aim for the Vaer Boss. But she's already flying away. Kinsley roars an order to retreat into the sky, and all of her elite warriors, soldiers, and allies take to the air and scatter in different directions.

I flip over onto all fours and push myself up—like

hell I'm going to allow her to leave. A deafening and deadly roar escapes my mouth and erupts into the sky. I want that bitch to face me here and now.

Out of the corner of my eye, I spot Drew struggling with two of Kinsley's orange dragons who ignored her order of retreat. I silently stalk up behind one and hit him in the middle of his back with my large, golden-striped white tail, causing him to fall face first into the sharp volcanic rock. I circle around to his head as smoke and blood trickles from the cuts on his nostrils, and he gives me a venomous glare. A snort escapes from my nose. If I can't take out Kinsley, I'll take out one of her lackeys—her elite warriors. I send a freezing blast of death magic into him as screams of pain escape from the dragon that Drew's battling. I turn my back on the disintegrating dragon at my feet and spy the orange fire dragon lying at Drew's large red feet in a pool of blood.

A deep rumble with a heavy intermittent wheezing has me searching the area for Milo and Jett. They're about twenty feet away, and Milo has shifted to his human form and is kneeling next to Jett's broken dragon form, running his palm over his father's snout. My gaze meets Drew's, and we shift to our human forms and rush toward them.

Jett is barely breathing. He's bleeding profusely

from over a dozen large cuts on his huge red chest. One of his wings appears to be torn from its socket, and the huge Darrington Boss's left side is soaked with blood. A cut over his right golden eye has his majestic face covered in tar-like blood. I don't know if it's part of Caelan's death magic, but I can *feel* the life slipping away from Jett. Even if we were to call for medical assistance, it would be too late.

Both Milo and Drew touch the top of their dying father's head, and I step back to allow the Darrington men time to say their good-byes. Jett turns his massive red head toward Milo first, telepathically talking with his firstborn son. Milo gives Jett a nod with watery eyes and his nose flares, but he doesn't shed a single tear as he steps away from his dying father, allowing Drew his own final farewell.

Jett turns his one good golden eye toward Drew, and my fire dragon lays his open palm on the top of his father's head as they communicate. My fire dragon bends over his dying father and places his head against Jett's.

"I know. Me too," Drew whispers to Jett, and he pulls himself up to stand as my fire dragon's head hangs like he can't find the strength to look at anyone or anything.

Jett's eye takes me in, though I'm not touching him or linked with him. His eye seems to be pleading with me to stick by his youngest son and to take care of him. I give the Darrington Boss a subtle nod, and Jett Darrington shifts to his human form as he exhales the remaining air from his chest.

I'm speechless. I've seen people die before. Hell, I've killed a lot of dragons while I lived under Zurie's control as a Spectre. But I've never felt like my world was knocked askew like it has been with the death of Jett Darrington. Despite the underhanded and selfish things Jett did, he was and always will be Drew's father. I hope whatever he told Drew in his last moments gave them both the closure they needed.

I wrap my fingers around Drew's wrist and pull him into my chest and embrace him. He squeezes me in his arms so hard that I struggle for breath.

"I'm sorry, Drew," I whisper into his muscled chest. He plants a kiss on the top of my head.

The slam of a fist thumping into a chest has Drew releasing me and turning toward his brother, who is standing with his right fist raised into the air above his head as he stares into the crescent mooned sky.

Milo's face screws up in pain, and he struggles to

replace the expression with a composed mask that lacks emotion. "I should have come with him. I thought this was just another routine meeting where Kinsley would flex her power, try to bribe him to her side, and he'd give her another 'Maybe.' They've done this dance several times before."

Drew approaches his older brother and places a hand on his shoulder. "This isn't your fault, Milo. I promise we will get Kinsley."

Milo nods and turns his head to meet Drew's gaze. "I'll take care of father's body and make the funeral arrangements."

Drew nods at his older brother. "Okay, Milo."

I figure it's good that Milo is taking the initiative and making plans for what needs to be done, but the obvious question hangs in the air—which one of the sons is the heir and will lead the Darrington family?

The whirring blades of choppers and the scream of jet engines rush to my ears from the Greece mainland. Help is on the way for the citizens of Santorini. We have to leave. Now.

"Go! None of you can be seen here. I'll take care of the fallout." Milo puts his hands on his waist and gives us a sad smile that doesn't reach his eyes. "I've been good at cleaning up messes. Hell, I've made a few of my own that needed to be cleaned up."

Drew's eyes go to his dead father's body as he envelopes my hand in his large one. "Are you sure, big brother?"

"I'm positive. Now, go." Milo points to Jace and Levi who are standing on the edge of the crater. "Get your family to safety, Drew. I'll let you know when the funeral will be so you can return to the capital. We will have a lot to talk about."

Drew nods at his brother. Her turns and spots Jace and Levi as they stand like silent sentinels, tall and rigid. He pulls me along with him as we approach them.

"Tucker has Ashgrave in the chopper," Jace says, looking to the sky as the whir of helicopter blades becomes too loud to hear whatever else he was going to say.

Tucker sets the chopper down close to us and we rush toward the open door and get in. Flynn roars an order for our soldiers to surround the chopper and retreat.

As I'm buckling up in my seat, Drew sits next to me and grabs my hand, holding it in an iron grip, like he's afraid that I'll be taken from him. I put my free hand over his to reassure him that I'm not going anywhere, not without him or all of my men, anyway.

I search the inside of the chopper for my metallic castle and find him in the front seat next to Tucker. Jace sits across from me, holding a blood-stained rag against a cut to his forehead. Levi sits next to him, rubbing his scarred chest that's already healing. I figure one of the elite warriors must have tried to open the scar Kinsley gave him years ago.

As we fly away from the small island of Santorini and head for our castle, I'm thankful for these men at my side. I turn and watch the choppers and planes coming from Greece as they become visible through the windows of Tucker's second favorite toy.

A sigh escapes my lips as I realize the humans are safe, but I don't know if Drew will ever heal from his loss. I put my head on my fire dragon's shoulder and feel it quiver beneath my cheek. Losing a parent hurts, and I hope that Drew will allow me to take care of him.

CHAPTER SIXTEEN

As we set the chopper down on the helipad at Castle Ashgrave, the crescent moon starts its descent in the sky through the helicopter's windows. Tucker turns the whirring blades off, and for several minutes we sit in silence.

My weapons expert finally turns around in his seat to look at a frowning Drew. "I'm sorry about your dad, bro."

Tucker stands and puts his hand out toward the large fire dragon at my side. Drew reaches up and grasps it.

"I'm here if you want to talk," Tucker leans in and whispers.

"Thanks, Tucker," Drew responds in a low voice while holding onto my hand.

Jace and Levi unbuckle and approach us as Drew frees my hand and unbuckles his own five point harness. I unbuckle and squirm in my seat.

I've never been comfortable with these types of emotions, and with the sense of loss hanging like a heavy cloud inside the chopper, the old me wants to run—but I know Drew needs me to be strong for him. I stand and reach out my hand toward him to do the same.

Drew places his hand in mine and stands up from his seat as Jace extends his hand toward my fire dragon. "I'm sorry for your loss, Drew. You know that Jett and I rarely had kind words for each other, but he was your father, and he needs to be acknowledged for that fact alone. Without Jett, there would've never been you, and I'm thankful for you, my brother." Drew releases my hand and pulls Jace into a bear hug.

Levi places his hand on my fire dragon's shoulder while Drew and Jace hug, and Drew drops his arm from around Jace and pulls Levi into a brotherly embrace.

My men. Brothers by choice. Family forged in war and love.

The door to the chopper flies open as Flynn sticks his head inside.

My men pull out of their group hug, becoming the deadly warriors that they are by spreading their legs shoulder width apart and clenching their fists at the sudden intrusion. They quickly realize it's just Flynn, and they step back and put their hands on their hips while they glare at the thunderbird who interrupted their brotherly moment.

Flynn clears his throat, and he lowers his head. "Do you guys need anything, Rory?"

I straighten my back. "Alert Brett to what happened on Santorini and tell him to keep an eye on the news, dragon channel chatter, and among the different networks we have access to as to how Kinsley is going to spin this against us, please?"

My eyes involuntarily roll into my head at the thought of what the Vaer Boss will do with Jett's death. Knowing her, she will blame it on me and Drew. Kinsley has always been mean, but with her enhanced power, she's become savage.

"Right away." Flynn rushes toward the castle. Part of me wonders if he's moving quickly due to the heartache that is clear on all of our faces. No one likes to see their friends in pain, and I figure that's what has Flynn running into the castle now.

The clicking of metal scraping against itself has

me searching for Ashgrave. I find him dropping to the floor in the front of the chopper.

His brass eyes meet mine. "I AM SORRY FOR THE DEATH OF YOUR FATHER, MR. DREW." His voice booms inside the small cabin of the chopper. "NOW I WILL REQUIRE MR. TUCKER'S ASSISTANCE IN REASSEMBLING MY BODY, MY QUEEN."

I catch Tucker's gorgeous green eyes and mouth a "thank you" to him.

My weapons expert gently lifts Ashgrave by his dented wing and half-carries, half-drags him out of the chopper toward the castle. Under the bright lights of the air strip, I notice that the wing opposite Tucker's hand is bent up at a ninety degree angle while his left leg is hanging on by only wires and is spewing what must be hydraulic fluid as my castle tries to put weight on it. I spy the cat-sized metallic dragon also has a fist-sized dent in his chest as Tucker turns around to blow me a kiss.

"Don't you worry, Ashgrave, I'm good with machines and will have your body fixed up in no time." Tucker turns around and heads toward the castle again.

"THANK YOU, MR. TUCKER," Ashgrave's voice booms.

Tucker's laugh cuts through the cool night air. "It's going to be a long night if you keep calling me mister. How about just Tucker, okay little friend?"

"FRIEND? I AM NOT YOUR FRIEND, JUST TUCKER," my castle booms.

Tucker stops dead in his tracks and his eyes take in the damage to the metallic dragon in his grasp. "We will be friends by the end of the night. I promise."

I shake my head at Tucker and my castle. But Ashgrave did thank Tucker, so that's a first. And if anyone can become friends with my murderous castle, it'll be my goofy weapons expert. Hell, he can pry a smile from the always serious Levi. That's saying a lot.

Jace approaches the open door. "I need to go and prepare our army for the new Kinsley."

"It's the middle of the night, Jace," I say.

"Rory, the more we practice with the magically infused weapons the better." He walks back and kisses me on the head. "Plus, we have an army of soldiers and they're used to training at all hours. It helps them prepare for battle."

My mind wanders back to when I was younger and Zurie would wake me up in the middle of the night to perfect a fighting technique.

"You never know when the enemy will invade, Rory," she would always tell me. *"Practicing while you're tired will help you in a real battle."*

I allow my head to drop toward my chest. Jace is right. He's the general of my army, and he is protecting his soldiers by equipping them with new knowledge. They need to practice so that when we meet the Vaer Boss in battle, we will be victorious.

I give Jace a nod, and Levi moves up beside him. They both exit the chopper and head toward the west wing of the castle, leaving Drew and me alone in the helicopter. My fire dragon wraps his arms around me.

"Let's go and have some alone time," I tell him.

He kisses the top of my head. "Sounds perfect."

I wiggle out of his arms and grab his hand, and we leave the chopper's cabin. Once outside, Drew closes up the door of Tucker's second favorite toy and gives me a smile with sorrowful eyes. He grabs my hand and we walk silently toward the castle and the privacy of my rooms.

We make our way inside and up to my bedroom door. I turn the knob and open the door and silently tug my fire dragon in behind me, leading him past my sitting room to the room with my king sized comfy bed with the fluffy white comforter.

I pull him to a stop beside my bed. "Do you want anything? Something to eat or drink, maybe?"

Drew shakes his head. He sits down on my bed and heaves a heavy long sigh with his face pulled down and his eyes out of focus.

I know that look on his handsome face—regret.

I was too young to pay attention to the way Irena took care of me when our mother died, but I know I need to help Drew heal. After all, he just lost his father, even if Jett was a real prick, he was still Drew's dad.

I wrap my arms around his drooping, muscled shoulders. "Drew, I'm here for you. Whatever, whenever, I'm here. Okay?" I whisper into the side of his head and place a tender kiss on his forehead.

He turns his head up toward mine and gives me a fierce kiss full of need.

I run my fingers through his ear length black hair. "I love you, Drew."

"I love you, Rory," He whispers against my lips. His hands frame my face, and he turns my body so that I can sit on the bed next to him. He wraps an arm around me, and I sit next to him.

Drew opens his black eyes and I shift on the bed to turn toward him. "Are you going to allow Milo to take his place as the Darrington Boss, or do you want the title and duty?"

Drew shakes his head as his piercing black eyes watch me. "My place is here, with you. Always, my queen."

Drew places his hands on either side of my head and gives me a toe curling kiss that has my dragon cooing with desire for our fire dragon. He leans me back onto the bed and rolls me on top of him.

CHAPTER SEVENTEEN

I pull the pillow over my head to shield my eyes from the bright sunlight that's pouring in through my large arched windows. Once my vision is clear of the glimmers that were dancing in them from the rush of white light, I roll over and gaze at the large sleeping man next to me. Drew had an impossibly painful night. I figure I'll let him sleep in, and I silently leave my comfy bed and rush to my closet to throw on a pair of acid washed jeans and a sapphire blue corded sweater. I run into my private bathroom that resembles some fancy spa and silently close the door before quickly brushing my teeth and running a brush through my tangled hair. I kick on a pair of new black combat boots and step lightly as I head out of my bedroom in search of caffeinated goodness.

As I round the corner to the kitchen, I stop in my tracks to take in my silent castle. Castle Ashgrave hasn't been completely silent since before Flynn and his rebels and the dojo soldiers joined us. I revel in the quiet kitchen and reach to get a coffee mug from the cabinet above the constantly full coffee pot. I figure the pot is always full because Ashgrave knows that coffee is a need for me, not just a want, and I smile to myself.

The thought of Kinsley covered in an oily black smoke has me leaning against the granite counter top sipping my coffee and wondering what she did to enhance her magic. How did she obtain access to the gods' magic without being a dragon vessel? What sort of ritual or bargain did she engage in?

I refill my coffee cup and head to the treasury to go through the Astor Diaries. I know whatever Kinsley has done to herself, there has to be an explanation for it in at least one of the diaries. If I can find the answer, then I can stop her.

As I head to the treasury, I wonder how Ashgrave and Tucker are getting along, and my lips turn up into a smile. I push the double doors of my treasury open and I'm greeted by a sparkling rainbow. The brightness of the sun lights up the precious jewels in the room from the inside, and they shimmer and cast the vivid colors of the gem stones onto the walls and ceiling, washing everything inside the room the colors of a glowing technicolored rainbow.

I approach the pedestal that holds Clara's diary, and I pick up the ancient book and carefully thumb through it to find out if I forgot something when I memorized it before. No, I didn't. There's nothing in the book relating to Kinsley's new power or how she could've gotten it. And if I'm remembering correctly, there's nothing about obtaining new powers written in Esmeralda's diary either.

"Ashgrave," I call out to my castle.

"YES, MY QUEEN?" Ashgrave's voice booms, shaking the piles of coins and jewels and making the glowing rainbow dance on the floors, walls, and ceiling.

"How is your body doing this morning?"

"MUCH BETTER, MISTRESS. TUCKER TAPPED OUT THE DENTS IN BOTH OF MY WINGS ALONG WITH THE DENT IN MY CHEST. I BELIEVE I CAN BLAST OUR ENEMIES WITH MY MAGIC ONCE AGAIN," He informs me in his thunderous voice.

It's hard to believe that his loud voice is

becoming normal to me. In the beginning, his volume had me—and everyone else who calls the castle home—jumping. But now, it's just how Ashgrave talks.

I shake my head. "What about your leg?"

"THANK YOU FOR NOTICING, YOUR HIGH-NESS. TUCKER HAD TO REMOVE THEN RE-WIRE AND RUN THE HYDRAULICS AGAIN FOR MY LEFT LEG. MY BODY IS FUNTIONING AT ONE HUNDRED PERCENT NOW THAT TUCKER HAS REPAIRED IT."

I'll have to thank Tucker personally for how he helped my evil butler. At the thought of a naked Tucker writhing underneath me, my dragon coils in desire. The hussy. We made love to Drew just hours ago.

I push the thought of a naked Tucker from my mind and return my thoughts to Kinsley and what she could have done to obtain the appearance of god-like power.

"Ashgrave, do you recall what Brigid taught or revealed in her diary?"

"I AM NOT PRIVY TO THAT INFORMATION, MY QUEEN. BUT FROM WHAT I REMEMBER ABOUT HER AS A PERSON, BRIGID IS THE ONE

WHO BETRAYED THE GODS BY USING THE ASTOR CRYSTALS TO WEAKEN THEM WITH THE HELP OF THE KNIGHTS."

"Do you remember if the crystals had any other applications?"

"SOME OF THE CRYSTALS WERE USED BY THE PRIESTESSES TO COMMUNE WITH THE GODS, EVEN TO RECEIVE SPECIAL MAGICAL FAVORS FROM THEM. FOR EXAMPLE, THE ICE DRAGONS WERE CREATED BY MORGANA TO CAUSE CHAOS FOR THE FIRE DRAGONS. SINCE FIRE AND ICE ARE OPPOSITE SIDES OF THE SAME COIN, MORGANA MADE THE ICE DRAGONS AT THE BEHEST OF ESMERALDA WHO THOUGHT THERE SHOULD BE CHAL-LENGERS TO THE FIRE DRAGONS. BUT MORGANA MADE THE ICE DRAGONS FEWER IN NUMBER, SO THE GODDESS WOULD ALWAYS HAVE THE FINAL SAY.

"That explains some of why ice and fire dragons react to each other the way they do." I nod my head. "What about the thunderbirds? Did Morgana make them too?"

"MOST DEFINETLY, MY QUEEN. THE THUNDERBIRDS WERE MADE TO BE THE

RARE GEMS OF DRAGONKIND. SECOND IN RARITY AND POWER TO THE DIAMOND DRAGONS OF THE GODS THEMSELVES. THUNDERBIRDS HAVE THE ABILITY TO NOT ONLY BREATHE FIRE BUT ALSO ELECTRICITY. AND, THUNDERBIRDS AS YOU KNOW, MY QUEEN, ARE THE ONLY KNOWN BREED OF DRAGON TO HAVE THE MATE-BOND."

I reach over and take the coin off the diary page that lies on the pedestal meant for Brigid's diary and pick it up to examine it. The script on the page is different from the other two Astor Diaries. Jade gave it to me after she confessed to using it to make her power-stealing crystal.

Kinsley must have part or the rest of Brigid's diary. That must be how she received some of their power.

I shake my head and lift it as though the top of my head is being lifted by a magical tether anchored in the ceiling, lifting me to stand taller than I can imagine. So, the gods really are stirring, and they're lowering themselves to using Kinsley to get to me— the one and only dragon vessel. Let them try their best shot. I'll take Kinsley and the gods themselves down for hurting my family.

"HARPER FAIRFAX IS AWAITING YOUR

ARRIVAL IN THE THRONE ROOM, MY QUEEN." My murderous castle's voice rattles the piles of coins near me.

I place the single page of Brigid's diary back on its pedestal and put the single golden coin on top of it. I promise myself that the rest of the diary will be added to the pedestal soon.

"Ashgrave, will you please take me to the throne room?"

"AT ONCE, MY QUEEN." The double doors swing open and the wall across from them slides open.

I approach the hole in the wall and follow the stone stairway up to the opening in the wall that empties into the hall opposite the ornate doors to my throne room. As I approach the double doors, they swing open.

"ALL HAIL THE ONE TRUE QUEEN OF ASHGRAVE AND ALL MAGIC," Ashgrave announces, drawing a girlish giggle from the Fairfax Boss.

I rush to Harper and give her a hug that she returns. Her expression grows serious. "How's Drew doing?"

"He's doing as well as can be expected." I pull out

of our hug but keep my hands on her shoulders. "But in a way, he's still processing it all."

Her girlish face pulls down in a deep frown, forming a "V" in the center of her forehead, and her eyes are trained on the ornate rug at her feet. "After what happened in Santorini, a lot of people are turning against the Vaer. There is actually video footage that some of the survivors took. They all show you and your men defending and saving humans from Kinsley's forces, Rory." She lifts her gaze and her eyes meet mine.

"I suppose that's the one good thing that's come out of all of this," I say. "Another is the fact that I'm actually tapping into, using, and controlling more of the gods' powers."

The buzzing of a phone interrupts our conversation. Harper takes her phone out of her back pocket and looks at the screen.

"Your sister is one hell of a troublemaker. You know that, right?" She steps away to read her text in private.

I hold back the groan that wants to erupt from my lips. Where is Irena? And what the hell is she up to, now?

Harper walks back toward me and tries to hide the smile that's climbing up her face. "A Vaer stronghold has just gone up in flames, and Irena just texted me some intel based on a bug she planted. I have to go—the Fairfax can make some devastating blows in Kinsley's resources if I act now."

Hmph. So, Irena thinks she's slick by texting Harper and not me. It's probably because my sister knows I wouldn't approve of yet another dangerous sabotage mission and would tell her off. But, what's done is done, and it seems she has some pretty important information for Harper.

Harper wraps her arms around me. "Stay safe, Rory. I'll keep you updated on anything else that I come across."

"See you soon." I step out of my friend's embrace.

I watch as Harper walks through the double doors and out of the throne room. I grab my phone out of my back pocket and push the numbers of my sister's private cell phone number.

"THERE IS A DARRINGTON DRAGON REQUESTING AN AUDIANCE, MY QUEEN," Ashgrave announces, and I put my phone back into my pocket.

I walk the steps up to my throne and take a seat in the uncomfortable wooden high back chair. "Usher the person in, Ashgrave."

"Good morning," the dragon shifter says as he

enters the throne room. His eyes are lowered to the floor beneath his feet as he approaches the middle of the room. "My name is Darius Flack, and Milo Darrington has instructed me to deliver a letter to Andrew Darrington."

That's odd. Why didn't Milo just call Drew if he wanted to talk to him?

I approach the tall forty-something man with flame red hair and a matching beard whose chest is as wide as Drew's.

I extend my hand and accept the red envelope he's holding. "I'll give it to Drew when he awakes." I turn my back on him and walk back to my throne.

The man—Darius Flack—stands where I left him, in the middle of the floor with his chin tucked to his chest.

"Is there a problem?" I ask.

"No, Your Highness." He lifts his head and his eyes meet mine. "I was ordered to watch Andrew Darrington read the letter himself."

I roll my eyes. "Ashgrave, is Drew awake?"

"YES, MY QUEEN."

Darius covers his ears and searches the room for the thundering voice, and I let out a cough to hide my chuckle. I don't think I'll ever get over how people react to my beautiful castle and his loud voice.

"Will you please tell him to join me in the throne room, please?"

"RIGHT AWAY, MISTRESS."

I observe the Darrington dragon in front of me. He doesn't move from the center of the room until the double doors fly open and Drew walks in. To my surprise, they rush to give each other a manly version of a hug and pat each other on the back.

"Rory," Drew says, "Darius was one of my mentors growing up. He taught me to control my flame after my first shift and he's been the one I'd go to for advice for most of my life." Drew steps away from his mentor and places a firm hand on the older man's shoulder.

"He brought you a letter from Milo and said he can't leave until he watches you read it." I approach the men and hand the red envelope to my fire dragon.

Drew breaks the wax seal on the back of the envelope and takes out the white paper to read it. As my fire dragon's eyes float over the words that are written on the pages, his eyes narrow and his luscious lips screw up into a scowl.

His eyes meet mine and they soften. "It's a

summons from Milo." His gaze swings to his mentor and then back to me. "My brother is asking me to meet with him to settle the question of who will be the Darrington Boss. He wants me to meet him in the capital in two days to bury our father and come to a final decision."

Drew turns his attention to his mentor. "Tell my brother that I'll be there, Darius."

Darius places a hand on Drew's shoulder. "I told him to wait, Andrew. But he is your father's son and is just as stubborn."

"I understand, Darius." Drew looks his mentor in the eyes.

Darius drops his hand from Drew's shoulder. He turns and walks out the double doors of the throne room, leaving the castle.

"Isn't it brash and insensitive to do this right now?" I wrap my arms around Drew's waist.

He turns in my arms and faces me so we can look at each other. "It's just how things are done." He plants a gentle kiss on the tip of my nose. "It's dangerous to not have a visible leader right now, especially when we're at war."

I lean my head against his muscled chest. "Not if we can stop the war."

He lifts my chin with a strong finger, and I plead

silently with his black eyes. "This is something I knew would come one day—and I have to face it."

I place my head back against his chest and listen to his steady heartbeat. "Fine. But I'm coming with you."

CHAPTER EIGHTEEN

The mid-morning sun shines through the chopper's windows as we fly over the white Nova Scotia landscape. Tucker's neck muscles remain rigid and tense as he flies Drew and me toward the Darrington capital. The clicking of metal against itself has my eyes searching for my cat-sized steampunk dragon as he shifts his weight to get more comfortable while he sits at my feet on the floor, pretending to sleep.

Ashgrave's body has no signs of the damage he endured in our battle on Santorini. His sleek metal exterior has no dents, and his left leg seems better than new. He glimmers in the bright sunlight.

Tucker really is a mechanical genius.

My thoughts go to Irena and the fact that I haven't been able to get in contact with her over the last two days. She hasn't returned a single message. And since Kinsley likes to retaliate in horribly vicious ways, I'm worried for my sister's safety.

I asked Jace, Levi, and the others to remain at the castle and for them to keep the army alert. I wouldn't put it past Kinsley to try another strike, considering the circumstances. Or, if Irena comes speeding toward the border again with Vaer soldiers on her heels, at least my army will be there to assist her.

Drew grabs my attention by placing his large hand on my thigh and giving it a squeeze as a dozen red dragons surround the chopper. My mind wanders to the first time I came to this capital with only Drew by my side. My heart skips a beat with a pang of loss as I'm reminded that this time is different—Jett is no longer in charge of the dragons flanking our helicopter. Milo is, at least for the time being, and he's our ally, of sorts.

The red dragons keep a safe distance away from the spinning blades as they escort the chopper toward the large red and yellow spires and golden walkway of the Darrington capital. As we get closer to the city where my fire dragon grew up, I spy more red and orange Darrington dragons lining the walls of the massive fortress, and once again they only leave a small circle for our chopper to land in.

Tucker sits the chopper down in the center of the Darrington dragons and flips the switch to stop the blades from turning. He turns in his seat and gazes at me. My weapons expert then quickly turns his attention to the large red banners with a black fancy script "D" that has two swords crossed over them. They flutter in the wind as they hang from the walls and arches in the courtyard while two red flags with the same coat of arms whip in the breeze as they fly at half-mast.

The dragons surrounding us have dark circles under their eyes, and their heads dip toward the ground. I figure the death of their Boss has affected them all.

My weapons expert unbuckles and rushes to open the helicopter's door for Milo who is approaching with an entourage of six dragon shifters in human form while Drew and I unbuckle and take off our headsets.

Who does Milo think he is, approaching us with an entourage? I raise a questioning brow to my fire dragon.

"My brother must show strength during this

fragile time. He has to appear as the one true Boss of the Darrington family," Drew whispers into my ear. "I have to as well."

My fire dragon stands, turns his back toward the door and his brother, and extends his hand toward me. I place my hand in Drew's and stand up.

"You, my love, are the most powerful threat here," Drew whispers into my hair and kisses me on top of my head.

"Go ahead, guys," Tucker says out loud. "But do me a favor and don't allow your faces to turn into the solemn masks the people and dragons around us are wearing. I'll stay here and keep Ashgrave company." He leans in to give me a kiss on the cheek. "I'll keep my comms on in case you need me."

Drew holds my hand as we exit the chopper and approaches Milo. "I wish we were visiting under different circumstances, brother." Drew extends his free hand to the eldest Darrington.

"Me too, little brother." Milo shakes Drew's hand. "Follow me, please." His face is pulled down in a frown, and circles the color of deep bruises are under his eyes.

Drew and I step up next to Milo and are quickly surrounded by the entourage as we follow the golden pathway through the capital. All of the dragons and shifters I spot have the same frowns, and the tension in the air is palpable. With their Boss gone and the question of his successor hanging in the balance—especially with a brewing dragon war —I don't blame them.

By the way everyone is walking around with an air of sadness and loss, I figure the Darrington family is definitely feeling the absence of their Boss. No matter how much of an ass Jett could be, he kept them all safe for many years.

Milo leads us through a large archway and into a beautiful garden with blue-green grass. In the center of the garden sits a raised platform surrounded by blooming red rose bushes that holds a massive casket that can easily hold the body of Jett's molten-lava red dragon. A red silk drape covers the large casket, and at its center is the same fancy script "D" with two swords crossed over the top.

As I take a moment and scan my surroundings, I notice that there are hundreds if not thousands of shifters present in the garden. Some of the women wipe their eyes with red silk handkerchiefs as they sit in folding chairs, and the men sit with their backs straight and gazing at the casket as their eyes go in and out of focus.

"It's time to start," Milo quietly tells us and points

at two of three empty chairs facing the crowd on the raised platform.

Drew drops my hand and ushers me up the short wooden stairway toward the empty chairs. My fire dragon places a reassuring hand on my back as I make my way to my seat. Milo, Drew, and I take our seats, and we face the crowd in a moment of silence. Drew's big brother clears his throat, stands up, and approaches a clear glass podium with a microphone built into it that stands next to the massive casket.

"We are gathered here today to pay homage to our Boss. Jett Darrington wasn't always an easy man to get along with, but he always had our best interests at heart…"

I allow Milo's words to dull to a low hum in my ears as I lean over to place my hand over Drew's. "Are you planning on saying anything?"

My fire dragon laces his fingers through mine and shakes his head. "Anything I wanted to say was said to my father in those last moments." He squeezes my fingers in his and leans closer to me to plant a kiss on my cheek.

"Today," Milo continues, "we will finish mourning the loss of my father. Today, my brothers and sisters in arms, we will start looking forward to the Darrington family's future." The shifters in the crowd jump to their feet as deafening applause erupts through the garden.

People are shouting Milo's name. The large television cameras near the outside wall of the garden pan the area, capturing the crowd's response. People with their phones out record the scene and continue chanting Milo's name.

This is all rubbing me the wrong way. I know Milo helped us out a couple of times, but why does there need to be all of this pomp and circumstance? And why are there cameras everywhere? It seems like Milo has something up his sleeve, and it's something Drew and I won't like.

I know that we wouldn't have escaped Chinatown without major damage if it weren't for Milo and his soldiers. Hell, we might not have even beat the Vaer to the last orb if weren't for Milo's intel. But with Jett's death and the Darrington Boss title up for grabs, this could take a really bad turn really fast. Shit, some people become irrational and selfish in the aftermath of the death of a loved one, and a power grab would definitely tempt Drew's brother.

Milo places both of his hands on the clear podium and turns his head toward Drew and me, and his lips pull up into a grin while his black eyes gleam.

Damn it! I can't tell if his grin is sincere or if Milo's planning something—and that bothers the hell out of me.

CHAPTER NINETEEN

T he stained glass windows of the massive
dining room paint the walls with fiery images
of fire dragons in different battle scenes as the mid-
morning sun shines through them. There are large
images of two red and an orange fire dragon facing
off against two cobalt-blue ice dragons who make a
large pool of water beneath their feet as they blast
their magic at each other. Ten golden fire dragons
are depicted in a fight as they gather in tight forma-
tions against a massive red fire dragon and three
orange fire dragons.

The fire dragons in the image blast fire in the
shades of blue, green, yellow, red, and orange as they
circle each other in the air. Two black thunderbirds
are also part of the stained glass scene. The thunder-

birds appear to have been captured in a net by a group of seven red and orange fire dragons who are attempting to drag them from the sky. But the thunderbirds blast their silver and gold electric magic at them, and the brilliant colors wash over three of the four walls of the large room.

One of the windows stands over the fireplace that's big enough for me to walk into in my dragon form. It bears the image of a massive red dragon dressed in black armor. His right eye is bloody and mangled, and he faces off against a glistening green diamond dragon who's dressed in white and gold filigreed armor. I'm certain that the exact same white and gold dragon armor is sitting in my armory back at Castle Ashgrave, and my mind wanders back to the first vision of Morgana in her dragon armor. I wonder if this is an image of the same battle or from one of the many skirmishes she took part of.

My mind replays the vision of the dragon king, a fearsome red warrior covered from head to tail in a suit of black dragon armor. A long gouge covers his eye, a long silver line cuts through the matte black armor showing the route a talon had taken when it scarred him. I shake myself from replaying the vision of Morgana dealing the final death blow to the dragon king.

The squeak of ungreased tires has me turning my attention from the beautiful images to the carts full of racks of lamb, yams topped with marshmallows, carafes of red and white wine chilling in buckets of ice, cakes, donuts, eclairs, and cream puffs.

I turn to my left and catch Drew's eye and lift a questioning brow at him while the servants place huge amounts of food on the extra-large cherry dining table in front of us. I turn my head and search the room for the other people who will be joining us to consume this feast, but there's no one else. Just Drew, Milo, and me sit in the over-sized room full of food and wine. Drew and I sit on one side of the table and Milo sits directly across from us. Thank the gods I talked Milo out of us sitting at the long ends of the table. I'm not sure I would see him let alone hear him. This massive table could easily sit over fifty people.

The click of a door closing tells me the servants have left us to talk. Drew and I fill our plates with the savory and sweet foods in front of us as Milo sits forward in his chair. He pushes his white, gold-trimmed place setting back toward the middle of the table and pours himself a glass of blood red wine.

Drew and I finish filling our plates, and my mouth waters. Ashgrave does a great job of setting our table with delicious and nutritious foods for breakfast, lunch, and dinner, but I've never seen this much food set for a meal for three people. I can't allow it to go to waste.

My fire dragon takes a lamb chop and puts it near my mouth. I roll my lip up at it. Oh, I like lamb well enough, but Drew's chop is dripping with mint jelly.

The eldest Darrington brother takes a drink, sets his goblet down on the table, and studies Drew's face.

"What?" Drew pulls his white linen napkin from his lap and wipes at his face. "Do I have mint jelly on my face?"

I shake my head. "I have a question for you, Milo."

"Ask away, Rory," Milo and Drew say at the same time.

"It's the middle of January, and Jett's casket was surrounded by blooming red roses. How are—"

Drew turns his head so he can watch my reaction. "Our mother's favorite flower was the red rose. Jett hired gardeners to ensure the roses bloomed every day in remembrance of her. And since we're fire dragons, weather has never really been a problem for us. Unless, of course, it's the type of frozen tundra that Ashgrave sits in the middle of."

"You're right, little brother," Milo shakes his head. "That kind of cold is for ice dragons." He clears his throat. "With diamond dragons being the only exception."

The Darrington brothers chuckle under their breaths while their cheeks turn pink.

"Let's get down to business, shall we?" Milo takes another sip of his wine and watches his brother continue to eat his lamb chop. "Do you want to lay claim to my title, little brother?"

I swallow a bite of sweet yams covered in marshmallows, and I instantly regret eating the deliciously sweet food as my stomach churns and threatens to empty.

Drew finishes chewing the meat in his mouth as his eyes narrow at his older brother.

"NO! You idiot." Drew takes my left hand in his and rubs little circles on the back of it with his thumb. "I'm with Rory, and we live together at Castle Ashgrave. She is the only Boss I'll follow." Drew takes a drink of wine from the goblet near him and swishes the wine around in his mouth before he loudly swallows it. "And that's never going to change, big brother."

Milo nods his head. "I'm glad to hear that."

Drew places his free hand on the table and leans in toward Milo. "I've been observing you, Milo. I see how much you've changed and what you're made of. How you'll handle all of this." Drew waves his hand in the air in a wide circle.

Milo's chin touches his chest and he squirms in his high-back wooden chair. "I confess I feared the family would back you, Drew. That I'd be left out in the cold." Drew's brother lifts his head to gaze at his little brother as he swallows hard. "But, I figured after all we've been through lately, it was worth a shot to just sit down and talk with you about it."

My mind wanders to the brewing war. Jett never declared the Darringtons for one side or the other.

I take a drink of the sweet red wine in my goblet and place the golden rimmed glass on the table with a clink. "Milo, since Drew has no interest in being the Darrington Boss, will you consider officially declaring the Darringtons for our side and using your full forces against Kinsley?"

Drew's thumb stops making circles on my hand. His head snaps to meet my eyes with his, and he raises an eyebrow. I shrug my shoulders at him and raise my own brow as if to say, "What? It needed to be asked."

"Yes." Milo takes another drink of wine. "On one condition—that Drew forever disavows his claim to the title of Darrington Boss."

I search my handsome fire dragon's face for a sign that someday he might regret his decision to reject the Darrington Boss title. My heart pounds against my ribs as I wonder if the way he feels about me now could change in the future.

Drew's thumb starts making circles on the back of my hand again. "I don't have a problem with that." Drew nods at his brother, pulls my hand to his lips, and places a gentle kiss on the back of my hand before he starts rubbing circles on it again.

The door the servants left through swings open, and three men in pinstriped suits enter the room, carrying briefcases, manila file folders, and pens. The men push Drew's half empty plate away from him and place the open folders on the table in front of him.

What the hell? Milo couldn't wait until our lunch was over to bring in the lawyers. I struggle to control the curses I want to let fly. A blond haired man who appears to be in his thirties hands Drew his own copy of the legal paperwork that he needs to sign. The other lawyer, with dark hair and about the same age as Drew, lets out a sigh as my fire dragon reads the papers he was handed.

As Drew continues to read his copy of the paperwork, Milo rises from his chair and approaches me. "Do you really need the support of the Darringtons? I'm willing to give you everything you need and more." Drew's older brother places his hand on my shoulder and leans into me. "If you'll marry me?"

Without thinking, I backhand him, almost knocking him off his feet. "I'm not now, nor will I ever be a bargaining chip." I stand up and glare at Milo. "Is that understood?"

Drew tries to hide his chuckle with the pen he's signing the legal forms with. Milo lets out a loud belly laugh and rubs the quickly forming bruise on his cheek.

"Now I see why you like her so much, little brother. I'm sorry, but I had to try." Milo continues rubbing his bruised cheek. "She might be a diamond dragon, but her fire can match any fire dragon in our family."

CHAPTER TWENTY

As we fly back to the castle, I catch a glimpse of the crescent moon hanging in the starlit sky. Drew sits next to me with his hand on my thigh as Tucker whispers something to my little metallic castle who is buckled into the swiveling co-pilot chair.

I lean my head on my fire dragon's bicep, and I'm thankful that he chose to be with me. Drew gave up ever becoming the Darrington Boss so we could continue our lives together. He chose me over ruling his own family.

Well, he's not getting out of ruling that easily. Once my men become my lords, they're going to help *me* rule. Whether they like it or not.

The buzz of my cell phone cuts through the

steady hum of the whirring helicopter blades as we fly over the Northern Sea route.

I take my phone out of my pocket and look at the caller ID. It's Brett.

"Yeah, what's new?" I ask as Drew blinks the sleep from his eyes.

"The final pieces of the orb are all matched. All we need now is for you to use your magic glue, Boss."

A chuckle bubbles from my lips. "Good to know. Thanks for working on that while we were gone."

"Anytime, Boss," Brett replies.

"Good-bye, Brett. We will see you soon." I disconnect the call and put my phone back in my jacket pocket.

Drew sticks his arms up over his head and stretches them while he yawns loudly, making Ashgrave's wings flutter.

"Sorry for disturbing you, Ashgrave." Drew looks up toward the nose of the chopper at the steampunk dragon who rolls his brass eyes at my fire dragon before closing them again.

"Brett and Jade matched up all the orb pieces," I tell Tucker and Drew. "All I have to do is fuse them together and the orb will be complete."

"About damn time," Tucker says. "Then we can all

become lords. That'll be better than being a Boss, won't it Drew?"

My fire dragon lets out a deep chuckle. "I totally agree with you, Tucker. All of the fun and none of the responsibility." He takes my hand in his and kisses each of my fingertips.

"Hold on a minute." I turn in my seat and adjust my headset. "You guys are going to be bound to me forever, through my magic and soul."

Drew pulls one lip up in a smirk. "And... that's supposed to be a bad thing?"

"Don't think that you guys won't have more responsibilities once you become lords." I grin. "We will run our kingdom, not just me. We're all going to be responsible for the care and safety of our people. We're a team."

"A family." Drew grabs my hand and kisses it. "A chosen family."

"The best kind of family is the one you choose to be in," Tucker says over our headsets and reaches out to touch the little metal dragon next to him.

My heart beats in a happy rhythm at the thought of us becoming a real family. Me, my men, my castle, Irena, Flynn, Jade, and Brett. I put my head back against the wall of the chopper and drift off to sleep.

After a while, Tucker's voice blasts into my ear. "Wake up, sleepyheads. We're home."

It only felt like I was asleep for a minute or two, but the crescent moon is heading for the horizon as my weapons expert lands his second favorite toy in the middle of the "H" on the helipad at Ashgrave's private air strip.

"Time to fuse the orb pieces, Rory." Tucker flips off the whirring blades, turns his chair around to leave, and his face pulls up in his trademark goofy grin.

I quickly unbuckle my harness and take off my headset as Drew does the same. Ashgrave hops out of the co-pilot's seat and approaches the door, following Tucker.

Tucker opens the door and the stairs descend from the chopper. "I'll meet you in the war room once I get the chopper locked down."

"I'll just go with you, unless you want me to go get the others." Drew stretches his arms out and stands, making his hands flatten against the ceiling of the chopper.

"I'd love your company." I give him a wink and walk away, heading toward my castle with Ashgrave hovering closely behind me.

As I walk through the front doors of my castle, I

let out a sigh. The Darrington capital is beautiful, but nowhere and nothing compares to the beauty and riches that are held here in Castle Ashgrave.

Drew opens the door to the war room for me, and I spot the orb sitting on the red velvet blanket in the middle of the table. Half of the crystal orb has lines running through it while the other half is smooth and flawless, giving off a slight royal blue glow.

I pull out the chair closest to the orb and sit down while Drew stands behind me and places his large strong hands on my shoulders. My hand wraps around the orb, and I pull it toward me, cradling it gently in both of my palms. I call on the gods' magic. A freezing chill passes through me as I funnel the power into the crystal orb in my palms. My hands take on the sapphire blue glow of my magic as I force more energy into the ball in my hands, focusing all of my power into it. The orb takes on the blue glow of my magic as purple and pink bolts of lightning arc inside the orb, making the colors mix and dance together within their crystal home.

Gently, I place the newly fused orb back onto the velvet blanket and watch the electrical storm continue inside the crystal sphere. My hands are ice cold as I observe the tips of my fingers and watch them turn from abalone grey, to ash black, and then back to their normal peachy pink color. Drew's hands tighten on my shoulders, and I turn around to look at him. But his eyes are trained on the orb as the purple and pink lightning continue to dance through the swirling blue glow.

"I think it's time for us to gather the rest of our family." I turn around to wrap my arms around Drew's waist and put my face against his strong chest.

"I think you're right." Drew kisses the top of my head.

"Ashgrave, can you please have our team meet us in the main hallway, please?"

"RIGHT AWAY, MY QUEEN. WOULD YOU LIKE FOR ME TO MAKE A PATHWAY TO THE LORDS DOMAIN ONCE THEY HAVE ALL ARRIVED?"

"Yes. That'd be great. Thanks, Ashgrave."

"IT IS MY HONOR, MISTRESS."

As Drew and I make our way to the main hallway with the final orb, I hope I'm making the right choice by bringing Ashgrave back to his full power. If he decides to remain loyal to Morgana, it would be certain death for my family. I study the orb as it dances with beautiful light in my palms, and I mull over the possible answers to the nagging question in my mind. I'll have to be prepared for any scenario.

Brett's voice carries over to me. "I don't know why she wants Jade and me here too, Tucker. Why don't you ask Rory yourself?"

Drew pulls on my forearm. "Maybe we should let them fight it out?" He kisses my head and gives me a devilish grin. "I got fifty bucks on Tucker."

I stick my elbow into his ribs and he jerks away from me. I walk away from him and step around the corner into the main hall. "Because you're all members of this family, Tucker. That's why. But only Drew, Jace, Levi, and Tucker are going to become my lords."

Out of the corner of my eye, I watch Jade pull Brett to her side, and he slides his arm over her small shoulders. My lips curve upward into a genuine smile. Jade and Brett really do feel like they're family. Jade's my little sister and Brett is her boyfriend. I shake the image of them making out the other day from my head as Jace, Levi, and Flynn come around the corner from the west wing.

I give them a slow nod as my eyebrows wag. "Are we all ready for this?" I meet the gaze of each of my men.

When I get to Levi, his ice blue eyes make my

heart skip a beat. I need for him to want this too. Time seems like it's standing still as I gaze into the face of the one and only man who makes me feel grounded in a special way. My ice dragon's nostrils flare, but he nods his head.

The wall behind Jade slides open. She sticks her head into the magical tunnel and grabs Brett's hand to pull him through with her. Jace, Levi, and Flynn follow the lovebirds, and Tucker walks in front of me and Drew as the wall seals itself once we are all inside. The magical tunnel is lit by blue magic along the top of the wall and near the floor of the tunnel. Up ahead is a stairwell that goes downward. We silently descend the set of stairs and continue to move toward the Lords Domain at the end of the east wing of the castle. The shuffling of footsteps and our breathing are the only sounds inside the four-person-wide tunnel. The wall on the right slides open, and our procession steps out into the hallway across from the training room Irena and I practiced in when she was first able to tap into her powers.

"Ashgrave, this isn't the Lords Domain. It's the Hall of Heroes."

"THE LORDS DOMAIN IS LOCATED INSIDE THE HALL OF HEROES, MY QUEEN. IT IS

BEHIND THE BRONZE SUIT OF ARMOR. THE ORB WILL UNLOCK THE DOOR, MISTRESS."

The double doors of the Hall of Heroes swings open as we approach them. Jade and Brett step to the side, and Flynn joins them.

"You guys are coming too, right?" I search their gazes for an answer.

"Won't we mess up the magic?" Jade asks, and I'm flooded by her worry for our safety.

"ABSOLUTELY NOT, MISS JADE. THERE IS A MECHANICAL DEVICE THAT THE QUEEN AND HER LORDS WILL BE REQUIRED TO PLACE THEMSELVES IN. THERE IS NO WAY THAT YOU CAN INTERVENE IN THE TRANSFER OF POWER UNLESS YOU ARE WILLING TO RISK YOUR OWN LIFE."

A rush of relief comes to me from Jade as Brett and Tucker let out chuckles that are disguised as coughs.

"Let's get this over with." Drew pushes into the massive room that could easily hold three football stadiums.

We follow his lead and spread out to search for the bronze suit of armor. I search in the corner near the door, and the rest of my family spread out to search for the one bronze suit of armor in a room that is wall to wall armor. In front of me are two silver, one gold, and one copper suit of armor.

I shake my head as frustration rushes into me from Jade and move down the wall to search for the needle in the haystack. The crystal orb in my hands starts to vibrate. I hold the orb out to my left with both hands, and the vibration stops. I swing it out to my right and the orbs starts to vibrate again. I walk along the wall of armor to the right, and the vibration becomes faster. I scan the suits of armor ahead of me, and I spot a bronze battle axe with its handle leaning out toward a bronze glove, and my heart bangs against my chest.

"Over here, everyone!" I shout as I approach the only bronze set of armor in the Hall of Heroes.

Levi stands behind me and places his hand on my shoulder. "I'm ready when you are, Rory."

As I lift the glowing orb toward the shield of the suit of bronze armor, the marble stand the armor is perched on rotates toward the wall as a loud screech has everyone but me covering their ears. I hold the orb out in front of us to light the way as we walk into a small room with no ceiling.

Jade and Brett are the last to join Jace, Tucker, Levi, Drew, Flynn and me in a room that appears to hold a metallic spider with a blue glowing bowl in its center.

"Flynn, Jade, and Brett—stand against the wall. I don't want you hurt." I place the lively orb in the center of the glowing bowl, and the metallic spider sinks into the ground without any squealing from the metal or grumbling from the solid stone floor.

Four stone tables and a stone throne rise from the solid floor that parts like water to allow the new additions to the room.

"YOU FOUR MUST EACH LIE ON ONE OF THE STONE TABLES WHILE OUR QUEEN SITS ON HER THRONE," Ashgrave's voice booms, causing pebbles to rain down from the tall walls.

My eyes meet the steely grey gaze of my mate first. He blows me a kiss and takes the stone table near him. Next, I search the green eyes of my weapons expert, and he salutes me and jumps on the table next to Jace's. The black eyes of my fire dragon widen then he gives me a flirty wink before jumping up onto the table next to Tucker's. The fire in the ice blue gaze of my ice dragon sends heat pooling between my legs, Levi kisses my check and jumps up to lie down on the last table.

"All we need is you, babe." Tucker urges me to take my seat on the stone throne.

As I sit on the throne, the earth beneath my feet shakes, making my hands cling to the arms of the throne. Metal manacles snap closed around my wrists as a high pitched scream pierces the stagnant air. My body is drenched in fire. It burns through every single cell in my body as my heart races and pounds. The light of my soul is being sucked from me as if a powerful vacuum is attached to my very being and is pulling it from me. My brain screams for the burning and pulling sensations to stop. I pray to whoever will hear me to make it stop. Suddenly, it does. It all stops, and my throat is raw. I realize the high pitched scream I heard was from me.

As I open my eyes, I spot Jade wrapped in Brett's arms, sobbing loudly. Flynn is standing with his back to me as he rests his forehead on the stone wall of the small room.

A chest rattling cough comes from my right, and I jump up from the stone throne and rush toward the sound to find the sexy green eyes of Tucker staring at me as he bangs on his chest.

"Shit. That hurt like hell." My weapons expert pushes himself to sit up on the stone table.

"I've felt worse." Levi jumps from his table and lands on his feet noiselessly.

"Feels like I've been hit by a Mack truck, again."

Drew sits up and hangs his legs over the end of the table.

"Pffft… baby," Jace says to Drew as he slides from his table and his feet hit the floor.

Jade rushes toward me and wraps her arms around me. "That pain was horrible, Rory. I felt every bit of it." She looks over her shoulder toward Brett. "Brett wouldn't let me help you. He and Ashgrave kept telling me if I intervened that I would die."

"The pain was necessary, Jade. It's okay." I return her hug. "We're all okay."

"How okay?" She raises a questioning brow.

"Let's find out." I grab her hand in mine and leave the small room that houses the Lord Domain and head into the Hall of Heroes.

We all file into the massive room with its walls filled with suits of armor. As Flynn, being the last in line, leaves the domain room, the suit of armor rotates back around to face the Heroes room and melts seamlessly back in line with its fellow soldiers.

I grab Drew's hand and close my eyes. "Circle up, guys."

An icy coldness washes over me, and my heart skips a beat as the familiar massage of Levi's mind relaxes me.

Well, this is new, he says through our connection.

How is this happening? I ask my ice dragon.

Our magic is amplified. I guess there's no need for us to touch to communicate anymore. His hair ruffles around his ears. *This will make it easier to check in with each other, even when we're apart.*

I keep my eyes closed and try to sense my men in the huge room. The cool magic and the voice of my ice dragon is directly behind me. The pull of my dragon has me moving toward the left. I wrap my arms around my mate and give him a heated kiss.

"You found me." Jace places his hands on my hips. "Now, go find the others." He taps the tip of my nose with his fingertip. "No cheating, Rory. Use our magical signatures."

Magical signatures… the way each of my men affect me.

I concentrate on the free feeling I get when I'm with Tucker, and I'm pulled to the far corner of the room. Even with my eyes closed, I spy the goofy grin he gives me as I approach him. I stretch up on my tiptoes and plant a kiss on my weapons expert's cheek.

Tucker places his hands gently on my shoulders. "Find Drew so we can discover what other magical powers we have, babe."

With my eyes still closed, I concentrate on the fiery leader who insists I'm his queen. Heat pools between my legs as Drew's warm breath washes over me, and he materializes in front of me.

"How did you drag me from over two hundred feet away?" Drew wraps his large arm around my waist, chuckling.

My eyes fly open. "I did not."

Out of the corner of my eye, I spot Flynn trying to hide his laughter. Tucker is holding his stomach, laughing, while Levi and Jace's cheeks turn a bright pink. Jade is leaning her back against Brett's chest as they both try to hide their chuckles.

"Stand further away. Let's see if I can do it again?" I point to the other side of the room.

"I say we try our powers. Everyone but you watched me get pulled across the room like a damn fish caught on a pole being reeled in." Drew rubs the back of his neck as his cheeks turn pink.

"Fine," I breathe out.

Five practice dummies rise out of the stone floor.

"Thank you, Ashgrave."

I focus my magic into a small stream and shoot a hole the size of an ink pen through the dummy in front of me.

The sizzle of fire magic has me turning to watch

Drew burn a hole in his dummy with blue-red flames.

"That's new." Drew looks at his hands. "It's even hotter than before. Nice."

The crackle of electricity has both Drew and me turning toward Jace as he fires his now royal blue magic at the dummy, causing it to turn to ash and flake to the ground.

"Holy shit! Did you see that?" My mate shakes out his hands. "My magic feels more like yours now, Rory." He approaches me and Drew, offers his brother his knuckles, and then kisses my cheek.

Out of the corner of my eye, I spy a sapphire glowing orb and realize Tucker is holding magic the color of mine in his hands. My weapons expert's eyes narrow at the dummy opposite him as he winds up his arm like he's throwing a baseball. In one smooth motion, he releases the magical ball toward the dummy. The sapphire ball hits the dummy in the chest and sends pieces of burlap and rice scattering in the air.

"Yee-Haw!" Tucker looks at his hands and then at the hole in the dummy's chest.

"Your turn, ice man." Flynn leans against the wall.

Levi shakes his head. *I've never used my magic in my human form.*

Tucker's never had magic at all, I remind him through our bond.

Levi nods as he forms a cerulean ball of ice in his hands. He drops the ball of ice at his feet, and it shatters into millions of blue ice crystals. His gaze meets mine, and he focuses on the center of the dummy's chest and blasts a clean hole through it.

"THERE IS A BANQUET IN THE DINING ROOM, MY QUEEN," Ashgrave's voice echoes in the massive room.

"Great idea." I grab Tucker's hand and lead him to the dining room.

Tucker swings my arm as we walk through the hallways decorated with beautiful women being saved by knights and the rest of my family follows closely behind us.

My thoughts travel back to the magic that Tucker wielded. It was a bright sapphire blue like mine and Jade's. My weapons expert has magic.

My men and I are connected. This is a joyful occasion—a silver lining during a time of loss and death.

I am connected to my men.

And, they're connected to me, for the rest of our lives.

CHAPTER TWENTY-ONE

My eyes flutter, trying to adjust to the bright morning sun that shines in through the large arched windows of my bedroom. I roll over in bed and reach my arm out for Levi, but I find that my silent protector has already started his day. I sit up in bed and raise my arms up toward the ceiling to stretch out my muscles. As I pull the fluffy cloud-like comforter off my legs, I swing them over the side of the bed and stand up.

I curl my toes in the white fur rug underneath them as a chest rumbling sigh escapes my lips. A smile crosses my face as I remember the way my men are connected to me now.

My mind goes to my four strong lords, and I get a mental picture of Drew and Jace blasting the ground near each other's feet as they do front and back flips to evade the shots of magic they send at one another. Drew fires a blast of blue-red flame at Jace's feet and my mate does a back flip, missing the fiery blast by inches. Jace returns the favor by sending an arc of blue lightning into the dirt under my fire dragon's feet. Drew does a diving forward roll, jumping up, then putting his thumbs in his ears and wagging his fingers at my mate. A chuckle flies from my lips at their silliness.

I concentrate on Tucker and Levi and find them in the west wing training arena, not far from Jace and Drew. Tucker is forming a sapphire blue ball of magic in his palms. The ball grows larger as he spreads his hands further apart and moves them in a circular motion. My weapons expert's brows furrow as a hood appears over his gorgeous green eyes and sweat beads at his temples. Levi silently approaches Tucker from behind, pooling a ball of cerulean ice in his hands. Tucker suddenly turns around and sends his magical ball at my ice dragon. Levi pulls at the ice ball in his hands, forming an ice shield that glimmers in the morning light.

Through the mental window that I have to my men, I chuckle to myself at the way they talk to one another, as I stand in my room with my eyes closed, concentrating on the way they each call to my soul.

"No fair, Levi. I haven't learned that yet." Tucker's head drops and he kicks at the patch of grass with his toe.

Levi approaches my weapons expert and puts his arm around his shoulders. "We're learning together, brother."

My heart skips a beat as I realize my men really are brothers now. They all hold a piece of my magic and my soul which binds them tighter than brothers born from the same parents. We all share a soul.

Good morning, beautiful, Levi says through our connection as I rush to my closet and throw on a pair of black jeans, a black sweatshirt, and a pair of black sneakers. *I didn't wake you when I left, did I?*

Nope. I just woke up. I rush to my bathroom, brush my hair and teeth, and pull my long dark brown hair into a high ponytail. *Can you gather the others and meet me in the surveillance room, please?*

See you soon. Levi steers Tucker toward Jace and Drew, and I drop our mind-to-mind connection.

As I walk down the stairs, heading toward the surveillance room, the Polish woman I met in the throne room approaches as she makes her way up the steps.

She lowers her head when our eyes meet. "Good morning, my queen."

I lift her drooping chin with my fingertips. "Are you enjoying life at the castle?"

"Very much so." She nods her head. "Everyone is so kind. We're all planting a garden near the eastern wall of the castle's grounds." She hides a giggle with her hand, and I notice soil under her fingernails. "The castle told us it was safest to plant there."

A chuckle rushes from me as I nod my head. "You'll get used to his booming voice. I did."

"Thank you, my queen." Her gaze strays up the stairs.

"Do you need to do something?" I place a hand on her shoulder. "Please, don't let me keep you."

"A young woman from France is showing signs that she is ready to deliver." The Polish woman's chin meets her chest. "I believe it's time to deliver her baby."

My eyes widen. "I didn't notice a pregnant woman in the crowd."

"The woman hid it under her robes, mistress. She was afraid you wouldn't allow her to stay." The Polish woman shakes her head. "I told the young couple that you were different and would ensure the babe had what it needed, but these are proud people who've been taken advantage of for generations, my queen."

I massage circles on the shoulder my palm is on. "I'm guessing you're a midwife, right, uhh… I'm sorry. I don't believe you told me your name."

"My name is Lena." Her gaze meets mine as a beautiful smile pulls her lips upward. "And you're correct. I've been a midwife for many years."

"Well, Lena, I'm sure you'll be able to deliver the baby without any problems." I drop my hand from her shoulder and turn to finish my trek down the stairs. "But if you run into any problems, the castle has an infirmary with a staff of doctors and nurses."

"Thank you, my queen." She turns to continue up the stairs.

"Lena," I say, turning toward her. She twists on the balls of her feet to face me, and I give her a wink. "Please let me know when the baby arrives so that I can give the newest member of our household a proper welcome."

"Surely, your highness." Lena smiles and rushes up the stairs.

I shake my head as I rush toward the surveillance room.

A baby in the castle. Now that's something.

Drew's deep voice comes to me out of the open

door of the room that houses all of our fancy computer equipment. "How do you know Rory wants to meet us here, Levi?"

I rush through the open doorway and spy Levi sitting in a chair in front of one of the computer stations. Jace leans back in the chair across the room from him, rubbing his calf. I figure Drew must have caught him with one of his fiery blasts. Tucker spins in the over-stuffed computer chair next to Levi while Drew sits in his favorite computer chair near the door, giving my ice dragon a look that would thaw the North Pole.

"Because I told him." I pull out a chair and sit down. "All of our magic has changed," I say, winking at Levi.

"Did you see that Levi froze my arm, babe?" My weapons expert kicks my ice dragon's chair. "Before, I could have lost my arm." Tucker lets out a wolf whistle. "But now, just a little bruise." He pulls his shirt off to show me his bicep, but there's nothing there, just his tanned muscles.

"I don't see a bruise, babe." I stand and walk toward him, planting a kiss on his bare upper arm.

Tucker's lips pucker into fish lips and drop open into the shape of an "O" as he puts his long sleeved Henley back on. "Just a couple of minutes ago, when we all sat down, there was one. Honest, babe."

Jace rushes to back up Tucker. "There was a deep blue-black bruise that took up his whole bicep, Rory."

"You must have dragon healing now." I pull out one of the free comfy computer chairs and take a seat.

"He's healing faster than any dragon I've ever seen." Drew's eyes meet mine, and he rewards me with a wink of his large black eye.

I shake my head as my men tease each other, and my mind wanders to the full power of the last orb being in use. Ashgrave is now at his full power. My men have all received enhanced magical abilities. Abilities that match Kinsley's.

As my thoughts drift to Kinsley Vaer, I know we need to focus on either catching the Vaer Boss off guard in some way or even luring her out so we can deal with her once and for all.

Irena's bug has been eerily silent. There hasn't been any chatter from it since Santorini, so that won't help me catch her off guard.

The only way to accomplish this is to figure out what her endgame is—what does she want above all else? And how can I use that against her? I ponder

Kinsley's motivation. Some of the Bosses wanted to own me, like Elizabeth Andusk, who wants to stash me away like a precious gem. Others, like the Bane, want to sell me to the highest bidder. But Kinsley— she keeps referring to me as a goddess with an air of disdain.

The Vaer Boss is powerful in her own right. She didn't need to enhance her powers. Hell, if Irena wouldn't have intervened when Kinsley attacked my castle, I might be dead now.

It seems being a powerful Boss isn't enough for Kinsley. The Vaer Boss has hundreds if not thousands of ice and fire dragons who follow her every command, and she is one of the most powerful ice dragons to ever walk the Earth. Yet, she resents the fact that I'm the dragon vessel. My heartbeat speeds in rhythm as my thoughts drift to the fact that if Kinsley's already made and used an Astor Crystal to commune with the dragon gods to increase her strength, I wouldn't be shocked if Kinsley wants to drain my power. Especially if the Vaer Boss believes all of the gods' power should reside in her. It seems to me that Kinsley believes only she is worthy of controlling the gods' magic.

This is it. I can use Kinsley's jealousy of me and her unbridled ambition against her. The only question I have is should I lure her into a trap or force her to make a misstep. As blind and as desperate for power as she is, I can make that happen.

The thunder of footsteps on the stone floor in the hallway head toward me, and it rips the thoughts of Kinsley Vaer from my mind. Flynn rushes into the room, his face red from exertion. He bends over and puts his hands on his knees as he sucks in air to fill his lungs. He holds up a finger toward me.

Tucker shakes his head and smirks. "You gonna be okay, dude? Or should we get you to the infirmary and get you some oxygen?"

"This castle is massive." Flynn wheezes. "And I just ran its entirety and its surrounding grounds looking for Rory."

"What's so important that you had to run all that way?" Drew stands up from his chair and offers it to Flynn.

"Irena should've been back last night." Flynn takes the offered chair and places his head between his knees.

"How do you know?" I cross my arms over my chest.

"We made plans to spend time together." Flynn lifts his head to meet my gaze, and I raise a questioning brow at him, urging him to continue.

"This would've been our third date, Rory. I made plans to make it extra special." His hazel eyes pierce mine. "I put red rose petals on her bed and—"

"I don't want to know your special plans, Flynn." I shake the image of Flynn and my sister from my head. "Do you know where she went?"

Flynn shakes his head, places his hands on either side of his dark hair, and drops his eyes from mine. "She wouldn't tell me where she was going, or her plans. I know she went on another sabotage mission, and this time she may have gotten too cocky. Irena may not admit it out loud, but she still hates the fact that she is a dragon with Kinsley's magic. She will die proving that she's nothing like the Vaer Boss."

Black dots appear on the surveillance screen behind Flynn. They're approaching the southern border. I count the dots—about a dozen people are walking toward the castle. Irena left with that amount.

"Ashgrave, escort the people approaching to the throne room, please?" I ask.

"RIGHT AWAY, MY QUEEN."

I head out the door and rush down the hall toward the throne room with Flynn on my heels, followed closely by my men. As I throw open the doors to the throne room, I spot a group of twelve men and women who are all bleeding from various injuries. Two men are holding up a man between them whose leg is mangled and dripping blood on the stone floor near the raised platform where my uncomfortable throne sits. A woman cradles her twisted arm against her chest.

"What the hell happened?" Jace shouts.

"We are the Spectre rebels that accompanied Irena," the man being held up says. "We burned down the Vaer stronghold, but Kinsley surprised us. Her magic…" He shakes his head as his eyes gloss over.

"Where's my sister, and why didn't she come back with you?" I demand.

"We would've stayed. We wanted to stay. But Irena ordered us to leave and come back here while she held off Kinsley," a woman who's holding her coat to her head says, shaking her bleeding head softly. "She said she was responsible for our safety."

I swallow down the curses fighting to escape my lips. This is my fault. I wanted my sister to be a considerate leader, but not like this.

Flynn's eyes widen to the size of saucers as his gaze meets mine. "Do you think Kinsley…"

"No. If my sister was dead, we'd know." My heart

pangs with dread as I wonder what the Vaer Boss is up to.

My phone buzzes and interrupts my thoughts. I pull it out and look at the caller ID.

Unknown.

I hit the green button, place my finger to my lips, put it on speaker mode, and say nothing.

Kinsley's voice comes over the line. "Some dragon vessel you are. You can't even protect your own sister." A laugh that makes my bones ache comes through the speaker. "Even with all of your power, you failed to save Jett Darrington, and you'll fail to save your sister too—unless you meet me in a formal duel."

Levi's thoughts and feelings of anger, certainty, and love, rush to me. *It's a trap, Rory.*

I know, but I need to end this. I show him mental images of my plans for Kinsley's death, and his love and hope fill me.

"When and where?" I say into the phone as Levi nods his head and my men's faces all pull up into devilish grins. They know I have a plan.

"In two days' time at the Chained Monument on Mason Greene's property."

My heart pounds hard against my ribs at the mention of the place that started my new life with my new family.

"I'll be there." I end the call.

My mind wanders back to the night Mason threw me into the Chained Monument of the dragon gods, hoping to end my life. But instead, the gods chose me to be the dragon vessel, changing not only me but also my future. The old me died in the pit, and the real Rory Quinn was born.

If I hadn't become the dragon vessel, I wouldn't have found the loves of my life—my men. I never would have found Castle Ashgrave, Jade, Brett, or Flynn. I never would have found or been able to heal Irena without the help of my men.

Hell yeah, I'll meet you at the Chained Monument, Kinsley.

The Vaer Boss may think that she holds all the cards, but I'm resolved to win this game and end her, once and for all.

CHAPTER TWENTY-TWO

F lynn, his five hundred rebels, and Ashgrave in his cat-sized steampunk form with fifty of his giant metal dragons land near where I freed Levi at the back of Mason Greene's property. It has now become a Vaer stronghold. My mind travels back to my castle where I left Jade, Brett, the dojo soldiers, and the remaining metallic dragons of Castle Ashgrave, and I hope they keep their eyes and ears open while they guard the castle and Ash Town.

A series of loud squeaks has my eyes spying the massive metallic dragons as they form a circle beneath the chopper as Tucker hovers above them. Once my weapons expert believes he has enough room, he lowers the chopper and lands us in the open field.

Drew takes off his headset and unbuckles his harness, while Jace, Levi, and Tucker do the same. None of them are joking or talking. Their faces are all emotionless masks as we ready ourselves for battle.

I place my headset next to me and unbuckle my harness, as Levi's mind brushes against mine. *We're here if you need us. Just reach out to me, and we will all jump in.*

I know. Thank you. But I'm sure Kinsley will set some rules for this duel of hers. I shake my head at how the Vaer Boss will make sure to take advantage of the situation. *Don't step in unless I tell you to.*

Okay. Levi's unwillingness to see me hurt leaks through the bond.

I stand from my seat and place my hands on either side of his face. *Promise me.*

His gaze drops to the chopper's floor. *I promise, Rory.*

My ice dragon wraps me in his arms and pushes his love and admiration through our new bond as he gently kisses my lips. He releases me and grabs a bag of guns from beneath my seat and walks toward the door. Tucker steps up next to me, taking his brother's place, and gives me a kiss on the cheek, then rushes to open the door of the chopper and the stairs descend. Drew places a kiss on the top of my head as Jace follows him and gives me a heated kiss that curls my toes and has heat pooling between my thighs.

Drew and Jace exit the helicopter first. They stand outside my weapons expert's second favorite toy with their arms crossed over their chests as their heads pan back and forth, searching the area surrounding the chopper.

Flynn and his rebels surround the massive metal dragons that encircle the helicopter, and they send plumes of smoke up into the air from their nostrils. Jace gives a silent nod, and my cat-sized steampunk dragon flies toward the chopper.

"THE MAJORITY OF THE VAER FORCES ARE ON THE NORTH SIDE OF THE CHAINED MONUMENT, MY QUEEN," Ashgrave's voice thunders, shaking the branches of the evergreen trees over one hundred feet away from us.

"Thank you, Ashgrave." I step out of the chopper and let out a deep breath. "Are there others in the area?"

"NO, MISTRESS. THE REMAINING MEMBERS OF THE VAER FAMILY ARE NOT IN THE SURROUNDING AREA. THEY MUST BE ELSEWHERE, YOUR HIGHNESS."

I knew Kinsley wouldn't be here alone. But hell, if she has most of her army here, the Vaer Boss is planning to pull something. And knowing her, it's something *big*.

Tucker steps up behind me. "Babe, I think we should leave a couple of the big copper tanks here to guard the chopper."

I nod. "So do I, babe."

Levi approaches my weapons expert's side as Jace taps two of the metallic dragons that tower over the rebels, and they take two steps toward the helicopter. Tucker lets out a deep breath through his teeth, and his shoulders drop as he steps up next to me, giving me a wink. Tucker will be able to concentrate on the mission ahead, knowing his chopper is safe.

My men and I walk through an opening in the circle of metallic giants, and Flynn leans his giant black head toward me, the silver stripe that starts between his eyes glimmers in the light of the half moon.

I touch his head. *Rory, I'll keep my eyes open for Irena. If I get the chance to save her, I'll get her out of here during your duel.*

My heart pangs with dread at the thought of what my sister has suffered at the hands of Kinsley

Vaer. The Vaer Boss is notorious for her cruel, torturous punishments.

I remove my hand and give Flynn a knowing nod.

My men, Ashgrave, and I approach the south side of the Chained Monument surrounded by Flynn and his rebels and the metallic giant dragons. Ashgrave's metallic dragons separate at the marble dragon chained to a marble platform, who's grabbing at the chains that bind him, howling at the sky. Half walk in one direction around the edge of the pit, and the rest walk in the other one, putting their giant metal bodies between our side and the Vaer. Flynn's rebels split in half. About two hundred and fifty golden fire dragons take five huge dragon steps backward and turn around, in case Kinsley orders a sweep attack and we're surrounded. Jace wants us to be protected. The remaining rebels spread out along the rim of the pit, leaving enough room for Flynn, Jace, Levi, Drew, Tucker, Ashgrave's little metallic body, and me.

As my eyes search the area of the familiar pit across from me, I spy a raised platform with another chained dragon with his shoulders squared and his arms crossed as he howls into the night air with Kinsley, three of her elite warriors, and someone who is being shielded from my view by the tall men dressed in black with green script "V's" embroidered on their shoulders.

My eyes search the surrounding area, and I spy the third chained marble dragon, howling into the cool night air. The way the statues' eyes all glowed red the night I became the dragon vessel is burned in my memory. I scan the area for any sign of Irena, but I don't spot my sister anywhere. More than likely, the concealed and guarded person is her.

"The rules of the duel are simple," Kinsley's voice echoes into the night air. "We both can have our supporters who will serve as witnesses present. But, under no circumstances are they to intervene until this duel to the death has ended. Is that understood?"

My eyes search Kinsley's. "Understood. Where is my sister?"

Kinsley waves her arm in the air, and the three men next to her step aside. Irena has dark circles under her glowing green eyes, and a thin metallic headband device is on her head. The device glimmers in the moonlight as it sits unassuming over her long black locks of hair.

I nod and descend into the pit. My eyes take in the cracks of the once smooth marble walls. The last time I was in this pit, it lit up with red light, but tonight the only light is the silver-blue illumination of the moon. My mind goes to the conversation I had with the dragon gods the last time I was here as I step up to the image of a dragon worm eating itself in the center of the pit.

Morgana's bone burrowing voice echoes through my mind.

"Trust no one but us," the goddess of chaos told me.

A smirk pulls at my top lip as Kinsley approaches me.

Cheers, boos, and roars ring out into the freezing January night from both sides. And the Vaer Boss turns her back on me, raising her arms into the air, like she's already won. I crouch down and sweep her legs with my right leg, knocking her flat on her back.

Kinsley jumps to her feet and leans in toward me. "Do you like Irena's new accessory?"

"What the fuck is that on my sister's head? A bomb?"

"Oh, come now, Rory. Why would I harm my own blood?"

I punch the Vaer Boss in her nose, filling the air with a sickening crunch of bone and knocking her to the ground at my feet. "She's not your blood, you evil bitch. She's nothing like you."

Kinsley pulls herself to her feet and faces me again, spitting blood onto the grey marble at my feet.

The blood from her nose washes the ground at her feet red. "Well, she certainly obeys me." Kinsley raises a single finger over her head and Irena gives Kinsley a blinding smile. To my shock and disgust, my sister actually cheers for the Vaer Boss.

What the hell?

Why is my sister rooting for this murderous bitch?

"That beautiful headband your sister's wearing enhances the mind-link we share. It allows me to control her," Kinsley confesses as she wipes the blood from her nose with the back of her hand.

Rage boils through me as my dragon snarls and snaps her jaws at the Vaer Boss. Me and my dragon are on the same page—we both want to rip Kinsley's throat out and spit down her neck.

I allow my dragon to take control and shift. Kinsley waves her arms in the air and shifts too. She snaps her jaws at me, and the duel begins.

CHAPTER TWENTY-THREE

I step back and pace around the once brilliant white ice dragon, whose scales now have an oily smoke covering her entire body. She narrows her dull forest green gaze at me as she blasts me with her Astor Crystal enhanced powers, knocking me flat on my back. I twist on my side to get away from the large dragon claw aimed for my face.

I roll to all fours and flap my wings to rise into the air. Kinsley roars her soul tugging roar into the sky and rises to meet me. I send a blast of Caelan's death magic at her. It hits the tip of her wing as she rolls out of the way, and Kinsley lands with a loud thud in the center of the pit. Her left wing hangs limp at her side, turning an ash grey color. She blasts her magic at me from below. A blast of her enhanced magic hits me in the leg, making it feel like it's a lead weight. I fall through the air, and my body crashes into the hard marble of the pit.

Kinsley stalks toward me with the ash grey magic moving up toward the first joint of her wing. She sends another blast of magic at my head, and I jump up from the ground. The blast of magic hits the ground where my head was just moments before, sending bits of marble into the sky and hitting the Vaer soldiers that are lining the pit.

The Vaer soldiers boo loudly. They can go screw themselves. I send a blast of sapphire blue magic into Kinsley's injured wing, making the ash grey magic crawl further up her wing. Kinsley's forest green eyes stare me down as the death magic turns the tip of her wing black. Her eyes go in and out of focus, and Irena jumps down from the platform, aims an anti-dragon gun at my head, and fires.

My wings flap hard, and I take to the sky as the dragons on my side roar into the sky in shock. Kinsley's fighting dirty. I expected she would… but I didn't anticipate she'd use Irena to do it. She knows I'd never harm my sister.

"No fair!" Tucker shouts.

"What the hell, Kinsley?" Drew asks.

"There are duel rules for a reason," Jace interjects. "How is this not breaking them?"

"Stop your belly-aching," a dark haired Vaer elite warriors shouts. "*We* can't intervene on Kinsley's behalf, but if someone on Rory's side does it—it's fair game."

Irena runs down into the pit, throws a bag at Kinsley's feet, and aims the large gun that's propped against her shoulder at me again. I tuck my wings and dive, shifting in the air and somersaulting to my feet in front of my sister. I knock the aim of the gun on her shoulder to the side and elbow her in the face. I'm done with this shit. It's time to beat some sense into my big sister.

Irena turns in a circle, using the butt of the gun like a bat, and hits me in the side of the head. As I shake the white spots from my vision, she grabs my head and places it under her arm, grabbing me in a head lock.

Out of the corner of my eye, I spot Kinsley in her human form, placing her remaining Astor Crystals and a book in a circle on top of the symbol in the center of the pit. Her blood drips on them, but she moves steadily and with purpose. Whatever she's up to is not good, and here I am struggling to get loose from Irena's death grip on my head without killing her.

"SHE IS AWAKENING THE GODS, MY QUEEN!" My castle's voice booms across the pit.

My heart picks up its pace at the news that the dreaded dragon gods are waking up from their millennia long slumber. We all need to leave this place. *Now.*

I stomp on my sister's instep and she releases her hold on my head. My lungs sting as I suck in air, and the white spots fade from my vision. Irena wraps her long fingers around my throat, strangling me. I lean into my sister and head-butt her. Irena stumbles backward, dropping her hands from my neck. My arm snakes out, and I grab my sister's forearm, pulling her toward me. Irena's muscled back hits me hard in the chest, knocking the air from my lungs, making the white spots return with a vengeance. I reach up with my free arm, pluck the silver ring from Irena's head, and my sister turns around to see who has a hold of her. The vacant look in her eye turns into one of recognition, and she throws her arms around me in one of her bone crushing hugs.

My heart jumps against my ribs at the fact that my sister is free from Kinsley's mind control device. Irena's eyes tear up as she realizes Kinsley used her against me, and I return her hug, letting her know she is forgiven.

Tension hangs in the air like a heavy blanket—it's thick enough to cut with a knife. Both sides realize the tides have turned.

Kinsley stands in the middle of the crystals she had placed on the symbol that's now glowing like it's on fire, and tosses the book to the north side of the pit. She looks to her elite soldiers, gives them a subtle nod, and the Vaer elite warriors shift. Orange fire dragons blast fire at my massive metallic dragons. The giant metal dragons retaliate as blue magic erupts from their throats. They aim for the Vaer side of the pit, and those still in human form turn to ash.

The elite warriors take to the sky. Some of Flynn's rebels rise up to meet them, and an orange dragon blasts two rebels, scorching their golden wings. They scream out in pain as they crash into the evergreen trees of the forest surrounding the ancient pit.

Out of the corner of my eye, I spot my men with their backs turned toward each other with my cat-sized castle hovering over my men's heads. They take on ten of Kinsley's elite soldiers. Tucker throws a sapphire blue blast of magic, hitting one of the orange dragons in the chest as it circles over their heads. Ashgrave adds his blue magic to my weapons expert's, and the Vaer soldier crashes next to Kinsley in the center of the pit, making the marble shake from the impact as he draws his last breath. Jace and Drew take turns shooting their improved magic at any dragon who dares come close to them. Levi sends streams of his deadly ice magic through the wings of the orange fire dragons who fly too close to Irena and me.

Levi's mind caresses mine, and his excitement and worry flood into me. *This is fun, but can you end this before Flynn has a heart attack from worrying about Irena?*

My head turns like it's on a swivel toward the black thunderbird, who's sending his silver magic into an orange dragon attempting to stalk my sister. The dragon silently grabs his chest as it erupts with Flynn's silver electrical flames that paint the surrounding sky an eerie silver and white. The orange dragon falls over dead. My lips pull up in a toothy grin as my gaze meets his. I can't get mad at him for wanting to protect my sister, but she might.

A black ice dragon with missing wings screams out in pain as he plummets from the sky, and the giant metallic dragons, roars in victory. The body of the black dragon barrels into the pit, spewing marble into the air and forcing me and Irena to rush toward the glowing red symbol in the center of the pit. We barely evade being crushed by the large dead body of the Vaer ice dragon.

As I face Kinsley, I notice her eyes are black.

Fan-freaking-tastic!

This has to end. Now.

My mind goes to the trickster magic inside me. I focus on Razorus's power and form a special illusion for Kinsley.

The Vaer Boss attacks me with a blast of her enhanced magic, forcing all of the air from my lungs. I fall down on my hands and knees, and Kinsley approaches my sister, hitting Irena so hard in the face that my sister's bones crunch from the blow. It knocks her onto her back as blood spills from her broken face. I watch helplessly as I struggle to suck air into my damaged lungs.

Kinsley approaches me with a silver dagger in her hand. "Now all of the gods' power will be mine."

She slices the blade across my throat, spilling my blood onto the glowing symbol and the Astor Crystals in the center of the pit. The Vaer Boss yells out her victory into the cold night air.

As Kinsley is yelling, still caught up in the illusion I placed her mind under, I grab her forearm and give her a deadly smile. I force Caelan's death magic through my hand and Kinsley's body turns abalone grey, then a deep ash grey, and finally charcoal as her body begins to flake away and floats off into the sky.

The Vaer Boss screams an echoing, "NOOOOOO!" into the cold dark air.

All of the fighting stops as Kinsley's golden ring with a glowing green stone falls from her right hand as the last of her remains float away, making a loud tinkling sound as it rolls across the marble.

The Vaer soldiers' mouths drop open as the dragons land and shift. The men all bow their heads, hesitant to make a move after my display of power. Now they see it for themselves—there is only one dragon vessel who commands the gods' power, and only a fool would challenge me. My men's muscles tense, but they keep the tentative peace as they swivel their heads searching the inside of the pit for any signs of the Vaer Boss, as they stay on the edge of the pit.

I won the duel.

But, that may not be enough.

The symbol near my feet burns hot as the marble quakes and the figure of a short, majestic woman with black hair and no eyes materializes in my mind's eye. Then, the image of an extremely tall white man with white hair and red glowing eyes emerges, as well as a man with white hair and gold eyes standing a little taller than my ice dragon. More than ever, I feel their presence. They are no longer shadows haunting this world—they are in it. And they want my power. The dragon gods are awake.

Shit!

We gotta get out of here.

My heart beats a staccato rhythm against my aching ribs. I look into my sister's glowing green eyes and nod. Irena and I shift, and we flap our wings hard as we lift ourselves to our side of the pit and land near my men. The eyes of the three chained dragons glow red, and the marble suddenly turns to ash. The glowing symbol that holds Kinsley's Astor Crystals collapses and falls about ten feet into the ground. The marble around it cracks and falls into the new hole in the pit as a high-pitched roar of a dragon cuts through the air—and my soul. My dragon urges me to attack the new threat. Morgana.

But instead of attacking or confronting me, the green diamond dragon and the two black diamond dragons slither out of the hole and take to the sky as if they can sense something no one else can. They halt mid-air and turn their heads in different directions as if they're looking for something, then fly off,

with their soul shaking roars into the silvery
moonlight.

I know in my gut that they're off to devour any
remaining Astor Crystals left in the world. They're
too weak to challenge me now. The fact I'm still
standing here confirms it. However, I know they'll
be back. And I will be ready for them when they
return.

I will remove the dragon gods' darkness from the
world, even if it kills me.

CHAPTER TWENTY-FOUR

The cold January night is silent, except for the grinding stone as the image of a dragon worm eating itself rises in the center of the forty-foot deep pit. The wind groans as it blows the dancing pebbles from the huge marble hole in the ground.

A beam of silver-blue moonlight catches my sister's bronze wing, making it glimmer as she roars into the sky. Irena's eyes glow brighter, casting emerald green shadows on the naked men in front of her as she rushes the Vaer side of the pit.

A tall blond man, who I recognize as the leader of the elite warriors we met in Washington, steps forward from the crowd of Vaer and shifts into his orange dragon form, roaring into the sky. The Vaer all shift into their dragon forms as they stand behind the commander of the Vaer elite warriors. He's challenging my sister even though she has Kinsley's blood in her veins.

I shake my head at his audacity and roar into the sky. I'm not allowing this craziness. My sister isn't facing off against Kinsley's cruel warriors.

Drew places his hand on my leg. *Rory, remember the chaos that can happen when a Boss's seat is left vacant?* I turn my large white head toward him, and the moonlight shimmers over my golden stripe, sending small beams of golden rainbows into the dark sky. *If Irena can win this, the war will be over. She'll be the undisputed Boss. She's your sister, Rory, so trust me—she's got this.*

My golden eyes search my sister's green ones as she stands on the other side of the pit. By the look she gives me, I can tell she not only wants to do this, but she *needs* to do this.

I give her a small nod. Drew's right. Irena can do this and end the war.

Irena jumps down into the pit as her glowing green eyes stare at the dragon daring to challenge her. The orange dragon launches into the air and flies over her head, and she blasts him with her green ice magic. His wings freeze mid-air, and he plummets like a rock into the huge marble hole in the ground, landing ten feet away from Irena's bronze dragon. My sister rushes him. She knows she doesn't have time for a drawn out fight. She steps on his head with a sickening crunch, and the challenger shifts from his dragon form to his human one. His body lies still as an exhale of air escapes the hole in his crushed skull, and Irena stands over his dead body, victorious.

Before my sister can celebrate her victory, another orange fire dragon steps around out of her line of sight. He blasts my sister in the middle of her back, making her roar in pain. I snarl in response as blue magic crackles from my nostrils. I watch the other Vaer dragons to ensure no one else tries to step in or cheat, and I remind myself that my sister's got this. Irena flaps her wings hard and takes to the sky, and the sucker punching dragon follows her. The orange dragon blasts magic at my sister, and she barrel rolls away from the orange-red flames that were aimed for her head. Irena tucks her wings and dives toward the line of Vaer dragons, making them scatter as she pulls up at the last minute, flying inches above the heads of the dragons who refused to move. She extends her leg, knocking the stubborn soldiers in the head. The large bronze dragon pulls her neck upward toward the half-moon that is descending in the west, doing a loop-de-loop in the sky, and coming up behind the orange dragon challenging her. She blasts her green ice magic into his back. A green glow fills the challenger's chest as his body turns into a green chunk of ice that shatters as it hits the marble platform that Morgana's dragon was chained to.

Irena lands in the center of the pit and roars her victory into the sky. A black ice dragon steps forward and blasts the ground at her feet before taking to the sky.

My sister stands and watches as the black dragon does several loop-de-loops in the sky over her head. The black dragon continues to try and challenge my sister to take to the sky and battle him. He flies toward her at full speed and pulls up at the last second, but Irena stands perfectly still and doesn't take the bait. She's new to her dragon and knows better than to give up any edge in a fight. The challenger continues to charge at Irena and do loop-de-loops as a form of celebration when my sister refuses to fly for about twenty minutes. Soon, his wings start to slow, and puffs of mist shoot from his nostrils. Irena is fighting smart. She's keeping her eyes on him and allowing him to wear himself out.

The challenger starts to slow down, and my sister's glowing green eyes meet mine. Irena gives me a wink and launches her bronze body straight up into the sky. The challenger doesn't have time to react when my sister blasts his wings, freezing them instantly. The large black ice dragon drops from the sky, landing on his feet at the edge of the pit with an earth shaking crash. He shifts into his human form with his arms still chunks of green ice.

The muscles in his neck and back are rigid as he faces my sister. "Give me an honorable death, bitch. I'll never follow you."

Irena lands on the ground in front of him, snapping her jaws at him. The challenger falls to his knees, bowing his head, and Irena roars her victory into the sky. The Vaer shift to their human forms.

I shift back to my human form, now that I know I won't have to rip anyone to shreds with my teeth and claws.

Levi's mind caresses mine, and his joy seeps through. *She did it. She defeated all of her challengers.*

I never doubted her, I send back to my ice dragon. I knew they would all fail. Irena's too good at what she does. Even during our brutal childhood training with Zurie, she's always been a little faster and stronger than me. Witnessing her battle today brings back the memory of a particularly savage training session that she no doubt had in mind as she fought today.

My small, skinny ten-year-old self stands across from my sister. My short brown hair is pulled back into a pony-tail, and I'm dressed in a red and blue striped tank top, blue shorts, and canvas shoes. Irena is twelve and stands almost two feet taller than me with well-defined muscles, wearing a red tank top, cut-off jean shorts, and the same kind of shoes as me.

My sister lashes out like lightning in the small room that's lit by a single bulb that dangles from the ceiling. She punches me in the stomach—I swear it feels like I was hit by a rock, and I double over as my belly aches. But that doesn't slow my sister's assault. She continues to land punch after punch to my legs, arms, and head, as I attempt to dance away from her.

"Hit her, Rory. Your opponents will always be bigger and stronger than you," Zurie shouts at me.

I growl and wrap my arms around my sister's waste, tackling her to the blue mat beneath our feet. My small fists pummel my sister's arms and legs as Irena tucks herself into a tight ball, not allowing me to hit her in the head or torso. My fists slow as I grow tired from the phys-

ical activity. Irena rolls onto her back and flips herself to her feet, head-butting me in the face and splitting open the skin above my right eyebrow with the impact. As blood runs down my face, blurring my vision, I cower in a corner of the training room Zurie set up for us in the tunnels beneath her home.

"Take her down, Irena," Zurie growls from the surrounding darkness. "The only way to make sure she's learning what to do is by making her hurt." The creak of stairs being stepped on floods my ears. "Do it, now. Or else I will, Irena. Make it quick, little girl, before I get angry and make you both suffer."

A heavy sigh comes from my big sister, who has always promised in the solitude of our room to protect me. She approaches me and lifts my chin. I peer into her brown eyes with my one good one, and she mouths, "I'm sorry," then punches me in the face and everything goes black.

A tall Vaer soldier with jet black hair approaches my sister and bows down in front of her. "I'm the new commander of your Vaer elite warriors," he says in a clear voice. He scans the crowd of Vaer spectators, daring anyone to say otherwise. He continues, "I declare you our new Boss. My queen."

My eyes roam over the remaining Vaer soldiers, and I spy a few pair of narrowed eyes. But the crowd contains even more soldiers who are tensing their jaws as they refuse to look at my sister.

Shit! This isn't going to be easy for Irena.

"Time to go congratulate the new Vaer Boss, babe." Tucker places his hand on the small of my back.

"Hell yeah!" Drew punches the air with his fist.

My mate nudges Tucker out of the way and wraps his arm around my shoulders. "I knew she could do this."

A flood of excitement comes from Levi. *She's almost as tough as you, Rory.*

Flynn roars into the air, and he and his rebels take off from the ledge of the pit, making the ground under my feet shake as they surround my sister.

My men and I make our way to Irena's side as my little metallic dragon hovers in front of us.

We approach my sister, and as soon as I reach her, I wrap my arms around her. "You did it."

She pulls from my arms. "You doubted me, little sister?"

"Not for a minute, Irena." I pull her close again.

The patter of footsteps against the marble of the pit we're standing in has me searching for the intruder as my men each take their turn in congratulating my sister. I spy the new commander of the

Vaer elite soldiers approaching us with something in his hand.

"My queen, please accept this as a pledge of our loyalty." He hands my sister Kinsley's golden ring with the glowing green stone. "This ring is only worn by the Vaer Boss."

CHAPTER TWENTY-FIVE

My gaze sweeps the area around the pit as my men and Ashgrave approach us. The wind picks up, lifting the branches of the evergreens that surround us as the half-moon settles on the western horizon. I take a deep breath, and the muscles in my back and shoulders loosen.

"BRIGID ASTOR'S DIARY IS CLOSE, MY QUEEN," my evil butler's voice echoes.

My mind goes to the book that Kinsley tossed to the north side of the pit, and I approach the area that I think the book landed in. Out of the corner of my eye, I spot the dark brown leather cover of an Astor Diary. I reach down and pick it up, flipping through the pages of writing and hand drawn images. The writing in this ancient book matches the page back in my treasury. I found it, the last Astor Diary is ours.

No one can ever use the power of the Astor Diaries against the world ever again.

"Ashgrave, can you please keep the book safe?' I ask my murderous castle.

My little steampunk dragon flutters over to me and his chest slides open, making the perfect sized storage compartment for Brigid's diary. I slide the final Astor Diary inside my evil butler and a deep breath escapes my lips.

I know I need to get back to the castle and prepare for the gods' next move. They can strike at any time, and I know Morgana will definitely want to take my evil butler from me as soon as she can. The goddess of chaos will want to control everything that Castle Ashgrave has to offer. From his weapons cache to his power, Morgana will want it all.

I take in a deep breath and clear my throat, making the eyes of my men, Irena, Flynn, Ashgrave, the rebels, and even the Vaer, turn to me.

"Flynn, can you and your dragons stay with Irena until Irena's guard has been selected?"

Flynn approaches me and lowers his head. I place my hand on the silver stripe between his eyes and open the telepathic link. *Rory, I'd love to stay with your sister and assist her in choosing her private guard. I've been pulled to her since I first saw her and will stay by Irena's side for the rest of my life... if she will have me?*

Do you think you and my sister share a mate-bond? I ask Flynn.

According to the discussions I've had with Jace, I believe we do. Irena has admitted to having a pull toward me as well. He breaks the bond, and his eyes search out my sister's.

A knowing smile graces my face, and I nod toward Drew and Jace. "We also need to get the word out that Irena is the new Vaer Boss and formalize her position."

"On it!" My mate and fire dragon yell out at the same time and reach for the phones in their pockets.

Flynn moves and stands in front of my sister and bows. Irena's eyes shine as she takes in the way Flynn's thunderbird lowers himself on one big knee to her, making me smile. Irena's face lights up as she runs her hand up and down Flynn's leg, and he stands up. It seems as though my sister has opened her heart to a worthy man. After the loss of Irena's first dragon lover and the hurt from a Spectre lover's betrayal, I didn't think I'd ever see her happy again. But watching the way her entire face glows as she looks at Flynn, my heart flutters happily in my chest.

"Huh-um… " Tucker's voice draws me from my thoughts. "We're not leaving her here with the Vaer, are we?"

"Irena is the new Vaer Boss, Tucker. Didn't you see them bow to her?" I roll my eyes.

"Yeah. But they're a bunch of cheats, smugglers, thieves, and gods know what else, babe." My weapons expert drops his gaze and shakes his head. "I don't trust them as far as I can throw them. And that's not far enough, for my liking."

Drew places a large hand on Tucker's shoulder. "Bro, she's the new Boss. They gave her the Vaer Boss's ring."

Tucker shrugs off Drew's hand. "I saw that, but I don't think she's safe with these—"

"Tucker, it'll be worse for her to just up and leave, since they've already declared Irena the new Boss." I grab his hand.

"I have to show that I have the leadership skills and the strength they need, Tucker. Have faith in me, brother. Please?" Irena approaches us with Flynn rising to his dragon's full height, glaring at my weapons expert.

"Besides," I say to Tucker, "Flynn and his rebels are staying behind with her. She's in good hands."

Irena nods at me then turns to face the Vaer shifters. "I've learned from Rory that a good leader stands with her people during the hard times. I know you weren't accustomed to it under your former leadership." A single boo rises from the Vaer, and Irena snaps her head toward it and raises her voice. "I've *also* learned from my sister to make examples of a few to strengthen the whole." She gives me a wink. "I'll rule with heart, strength, a clear conscious, with respect for those who respect me, and I'll treasure loyalty. Today is a new start for you, me—for all of us. But believe me when I say I will not allow anyone to live who attempts to hurt me or those I love."

I spy many of the shifters nodding in agreement, though some still wear doubtful expressions as if expecting a trap.

"Okay." Tucker shakes his head. "You got the Boss spiel down, Irena. I just don't want Rory to lose you again. It was hard to see her go through the emotional struggle she went through while you were in your coma and we couldn't find you."

"Babe, it's not like that anymore." I place my hand on his forearm and gently turn him toward me.

"Irena is a powerful ice dragon and the Vaer Boss. She's got this. My sister trained me to be the fighter I am."

He opens his mouth to argue with me, and I place a gentle kiss on his lips. "Plus, everyone here knows what I'm capable of." I turn to face the Vaer and raise my voice. "And they also know that if my sister needs my help in making examples of the few who remain unfaithful to her rule, I'll be more than happy to oblige."

"That sounds like it could be fun," Irena says.

"TUCKER AND I MUST READY THE HELI-COPTER TO DEPART FOR CASTLE ASHGRAVE, MY QUEEN," my castle's voice booms from not only my cat-sized steampunk dragon but from the giant metallic dragons that still surround the south side of the pit.

"Ashgrave's right, babe." My weapons expert gives me a wink, and I release the hold I have on him. "We need to go while the getting's good." He approaches Irena and wraps her in his arms. "Stay safe."

Levi's mind caresses mine, and his sadness rushes into me. *I'll go and help Tucker and Ashgrave.*

I nod and break our special bond, not wanting

his sadness at saying goodbye to my sister to magnify my own.

Drew and Jace rush toward us and envelope me and Irena in their muscled arms, forming a huge group hug.

"I should have the paperwork ready for you to sign soon," Drew whispers into the empty space of the circle of our bodies.

"Paperwork?" Irena's glowing green eyes meet my fire dragon's black ones.

"Transfer of properties, businesses, and that kind of stuff," Drew tells my sister.

"What are you talking about, Drew?" My sister asks.

"You will own everything that Kinsley owned— *everything,*" Jace informs my sister.

"But what if I don't want it?" Irena asks. "Kinsley owns some crazy shit."

"You're telling me," Drew interjects.

"Whatever you don't want to be tied to, sell it or destroy it," Jace recommends.

"Good idea." I peer into my mate's stormy grey eyes. "But to who?"

"No worries." Drew nods in Irena's direction. "I'll make a list of questionable businesses and facilities and compile a list of interested buyers for you, sis."

"I'm happy you guys are on my side," Irena chuckles.

"I think I say that ten times a day." I step backward and everyone drops their arms from around the person next to them.

The whir of chopper blades cuts through the dark, pre-dawn sky, and I pull my sister once more into my arms. "I really gotta go." My eyes meet Flynn's silver ones. "But you and Flynn need to stay in contact with me and let me know if you need anything."

Irena nods at me. "Don't die, little sister," she whispers into my hair.

"Stay safe, Irena." I drop my arms and step back toward Drew and Jace. With a rueful smile, I turn my back on my sister and her mate.

Drew, Jace, and I walk silently toward the chopper as the giant metallic dragons take off, shaking the ground.

The familiar caress of Levi's mind touches mine as I enter the chopper and pull on the sweats that are sitting on my seat, placing my phone that was lying on top into Drew's lap. *She's going to be okay.*

She's going to be better than fine, I tell him as I allow my happiness to flow to him. I buckle up and place my headset on. *I think she and Flynn might be mate-bonded.*

Really? He asks as his heartbeat increases with his joy. *Irena is the new Vaer Boss and is mate-bonded to a great friend and ally. This is a fantastic turn of events.*

The only downer of the night is the dragon gods are fully awake. I let a deep breath pass through my lips, slowly.

Yeah. But we got this. His faith in me, our bond, and our family, leaks through the bond. *You'll kill them with your light, Rory.*

I break mine and Levi's bond and put my open palm out toward Drew, who's sitting on my right side. "Can I have my phone back, please?"

"Anything for you, beautiful." My fire dragon hands me my phone and kisses the tip of my nose as the chopper takes off into the air surrounded by Ashgrave and his fifty giant metallic warriors.

I plug the accessory cord into my headset and dial Harper's number. I wait for her to answer as I spy my cat-sized steampunk dragon out the window of the chopper. My face draws down in a deep frown.

Now that Morgana's awake, the nagging question of who he will choose buzzes at the forefront of my mind. Will I lose my evil butler to Morgana? Or will he remain the faithful friend I've come to rely on?

"Rory, why are you calling me before the sun rises?" Harper lets out a loud yawn over the phone.

"Because I have news that I know you'll want." I stifle my own yawn with the back of my hand.

"News that needs to be shared at zero dark thirty?" The rustle of sheets comes through the line.

"Kinsley is dead," I say, and a rush of breath escapes into the phone.

"Are you serious? Do the Vaer have a leader? It could be—"

"Irena is the new Vaer Boss," I respond, cutting her off.

"Woohoo!" Harper yells in my ear, and I quickly turn the phone volume down as the shouting continues. "The threat of war is over."

"But," I say into the now quiet phone line and turn the volume back up. "There's an even bigger threat looming over not only me, but also the rest of the world."

"What threat could be bigger than a war with the potential to kill millions, Rory?"

"The return of the dragon gods, Harper. They're back. I saw them with my own eyes."

CHAPTER TWENTY-SIX

The golden rays of the sun peeks through the clouds as I raise my hands above my head and quickly drop them to touch the ground between my feet. I pull myself upright and fill my lungs with the cool mountain air. Jace and I are taking a break from training in our favorite spot at the top of the eastern mountain furthest from Ash Town. I'm still dressed in the sweats I put on a few hours ago and so is my mate who's standing in front of me with his gorgeous grey eyes sparkling with admiration.

"Are you ready to continue training?" My mate raises his eyebrow at me.

I nod at him as my gaze roams over the seven practice dummies with holes the diameter of an ink pen in the middle of their red "X's" that are lined up behind his hot self.

My dragon coos knowing we are alone with our incredibly sexy mate. *We need to get ready for the dragon gods. Fun time has to wait,* I tell her, and she sticks out her bottom lip at me.

"Maybe we should shift—" Jace interrupts my question by shifting into his beautiful black thunderbird form and sends a blue arc of electricity into the grass near my feet.

I stifle the chuckle that wants to slip out and leap into the air, shifting into my white diamond dragon as I pursue my mate through puffy white clouds hanging low over the mountains.

A strike of blue lightning lights up the cloud in front of me, and I flap my wings harder to catch up to my mate, enjoying the wind that wraps itself around my large body and assists me in flying faster.

As I pierce the puffy royal blue, cotton ball looking cloud with the tip of my nose, my whole body tingles with an electrical shock, and I barrel roll away from the electrically charged cloud. Well, that's new. I wonder if I can electrify objects as well.

A loud huffing that resembles sandpaper rubbing against itself comes from my right, and I spear my mate with my golden dragon eyes. Jace lifts his shoulders as he hovers in the air near a large white cloud. I fly over to him and place my head against his as we hover in the sky.

Teach me how to do that? I ask through our telepathic link.

Just send a concentrated blast of your magic into the center of the water-filled cloud, he tells me. *It'll be like sending a current of electricity into a pool of water, and the cloud will hold it until it rains or something enters the cloud to disperse it. Pretty cool, huh?*

Where did you learn to do this? I ask.

I just tried it out. I figured if tap water conducts electricity, then so would a cloud. Jace lifts his head from mine, and his eyes focus on a puffy white cloud beneath us.

I concentrate on turning the floating white sponge into an electrical net and send a sapphire blue stream into it. The cloud takes on a sapphire glow and I fly into it, not wanting to shock my mate. The charge travels through my body, paralyzing my muscles, and I drop like a rock toward the valley below. Within moments, I have control of my body again, and I flap my wings hard to get away from the tall trees blowing in the breeze, mere inches below my large dragon claws. But my wings aren't flapping hard or fast enough. Without thinking, I send an unfocused blast of magic into the copse of trees, turning them a deathly grey. They darken and flake away into the cool breeze.

What the hell?

I need to control this magic.

I tuck my wings and dive toward the flaking trees and land, shaking the ground and sending more of the trees flying into the air, like a charcoal grey plume of dust.

I close my eyes and picture the beautiful copse of healthy cedar trees swaying in the wind and focus Caelan's cold death magic on the glorious trees. Instead of death and decay, I pour healing into the magic.

My neck aches and my hands warm, then grow hot, almost as if they were submerged in Drew's flames. The heat flows from my hands and into the soft soil. The rumble of trees crashing into one another floods the cool early morning mountain air.

My aching neck relaxes as the ground next to me shakes, and Jace places his large head at the top of my back where my wings sprout from behind my shoulder blades. *Open your eyes, Rory. You did it. You healed them.*

My eyes open and my jaw drops at the sight. The

tall cedar trees are waving their green branches at the brightening sky.

My knees grow weak, and I stumble forward into one of the newly grown cedar trees. I place a steadying claw on its freshly grown bark, careful not to mar it with my sharp talons, and suck air into my lungs.

Jace brushes the tip of my wing with his. *Are you okay?*

I nod. *Just had to catch my breath.*

Let's head back to the castle and get some rest. It's been a long and eventful night, and I'm sure the coming days will test all of us. He removes the tip of his wing from mine, steps back from the new trees, and flaps his wings as he takes to the sky.

I follow my mate into the air, and we head toward home.

Levi's mind caresses mine. *I felt you weaken. Are you okay?*

Yeah, I tell him, and I send him the image of the trees I destroyed then healed. *I'm learning some new tricks.* His love and admiration leak from the bond. *I'm on patrol. I'd love to have you join me,* he says as an image of my ice dragon in his sexy naked human form floods my brain. *I'll be on the north side of the castle when you and Jace are finished.* He closes our mind-to-mind link.

My thoughts drift to the fact that I became weak after healing the trees, because I forced the magic to go against its deadly nature. But I was able to change it.

Now I know my magic can be applied in different ways, and it doesn't have to be used for evil purposes. I used death magic to bring life. I know that Morgana's chaos magic can be used to make peace. And I figure instead of tricking or manipulating others, Razorus's magic can be used to inspire peaceful resolutions, noble actions, and truth.

I know that I can use the dragon gods' magic against them—and I'm more determined than ever to take them out. I will defeat the gods. I *have* to.

If the gods win? They'll subject the entire world to their dark tyranny. Images of humans who are beheaded, dragons having their wings torn off, and ripples of all of the food sources turning grey until they flake and blow away flood my mind. The gods will destroy the planet and all who reside here. They'd be even worse than Kinsley would have been.

Hell, all Kinsley could do is kill millions of people on the planet, though that is grim in and of itself.

But at least she wasn't powerful enough to kill off the entire earth.

I suck in a deep breath and shake myself from my thoughts as I approach my mate and brush the tip of his wing. My castle's courtyard comes into view. *I'm going to go on patrol with Levi. I'll see you later. Okay?*

Sounds good. He shakes his big black head. *Do—?*

He's to the north of the castle. I turn my head and give a big toothy dragon grin as the bright morning light washes his face with dancing golden beams of shimmering light.

You two being able to read each other's minds will really come in handy in a battle. He returns my grin. *I'll be training with the army in the west wing. See you later.* My mate drops his wing from mine and tucks his wings close to his body so he can land in the courtyard.

I flap my wings and head toward the north boundary of my castle, being sure to keep my eyes and ears open for my silent protector. As I search the snowcapped mountains beneath me, a blue bullet shoots through the air, making me stop mid-air so I don't run into him.

Hahaha! Levi laughs through our mind connection, and his happiness at surprising me leaks through.

You definitely have the gift of stealth. My eyes search the sky above me, and I spot my ice dragon hovering twenty feet above me. *Is there anything going on out here?*

Just the natural beauty of the mountains. He shakes his big blue head.

Well then, let's enjoy it shall we? I give my wings a hard flap and turn away from him, closing our link.

Levi and I fly side-by-side as our eyes scour the lush green valley below. The area surrounding my castle has been green for months, even during winter. I figure that has to be due to Ashgrave's magic. He's able to keep the land within his boundaries producing the food we need.

My gaze meets the ice blue eyes of Levi, and I'm flooded with happiness and freedom. My heart fills with undying joy as my ice dragon and I fly over the fields of blooming wildflowers.

Levi's pride and peace leak though are bond. *I'm ready to do whatever it takes to defend you, our home, and our family.*

My soul sings at his fierce need to protect not only me, but our home. *Our family.*

I concentrate on my men, the pieces of my soul, and the way they all connect not only to me but to each other. They're true brothers, and I'm grateful for each and every one of them.

The wind howls like it's angry as it picks up speed, and the sky in front of me is filled with white blowing snow that sucks Levi from my side and my vision.

What the hell?

Where did the bright sunlight go? And where in the fuck did this blizzard come from?

A loud grunt followed by a roar of surprise has me squinting to spot my ice dragon. I can't see anything through these white-out conditions, so I concentrate on the special bond that only Levi and I share.

I caress his mind with mine. *Are you okay?*

Levi's surprise and anger flood my brain. *I'm falling, Rory.*

I focus on the way my emotions flow freely with my silent protector, and a tug on my soul tells me that my ice dragon is twenty feet below and fifteen feet to my left.

I tuck my wings, close my eyes against the blowing snow, and dive, focusing on the piece of my soul that belongs to Levi. The snow and hail pummels my hard dragon skin like miniature ice bullets as the image of my ice dragon being pulled from the sky fills my mind. It seems like someone or *something* has a magical lasso around his torso, trapping his wings in the invisible rope as he struggles to free himself by snapping his powerful jaws.

As I get close to my ice dragon, I spot a small woman with black hair that isn't affected by the snow and hail that blow with a vengeance. The whipping wind lifts her into the sky.

Fan-freaking-tastic!

I'd know that short, black haired woman with no eyes anywhere. It's Morgana.

CHAPTER TWENTY-SEVEN

My heart pangs with dread as I spot Levi struggle against the invisible bonds Morgana has him in.

I'm fine, Levi tells me through our connection as he fights the unseen chaos magic pulling him toward the valley below. *Just knock her down a few notches, and I'll get free.*

I close my mind to my sexy ice dragon and focus on the goddess who is using the winds of the blizzard to propel her toward me.

Hail, snow, and wickedly blowing winds pummel my body as I flap my wings and force myself to hover in the air.

Zurie and Irena have both preached Rule 42 of the Spectres—assess all risks. Act Second. Morgana has my silent protector captive. If this goddess of chaos, with her missing eyes and black sockets wants to fight, she's going to have to come to me.

Morgana's bone chilling voice cuts through the howling wind as she moves closer to me. "It's time for you to give me back my magic, little human."

I shake my head and roar into the sky. "You're crazy if you think I'm going to just give up my dragon."

The goddess of chaos forms ten blades of ice that swallow any sunlight they encounter and turn a sickly grey color. In one smooth motion, she releases them all, aiming them at my wings.

I pull my wings in tight to my back and lean my huge head toward the valley below, dropping like a lead weight out of the sky. The blades hurtling toward my wings fly into the mountain that was behind me, causing the snow from its peak to thunder into the valley below. There are no towns in that area of the valley, and since the Palarne army has been called home, there won't be any lives lost from the avalanche Morgana caused.

I flap my wings and rise into the sky to face Morgana. When I get within fifty feet of her hovering human form, I focus my magic at the grey-ish-white funnel of winds that are holding her in mid-air and blast them, scattering the dancing funnel cloud and causing the goddess of chaos to plunge toward the ground.

Morgana quickly changes her focus from fighting me to controlling the winds beneath her feet. The snow and hail that had been beating against me slow their assault on my dragon hide. She re-forms her funnel clouds, and once again the goddess is rising toward me as I hover above her.

The goddess's hands glow a green-grey color and she blasts me with it. My wings and lungs instantly freeze—and they stop working. My body turns end over end as I beg my lungs to fight against the deathly cold ice and wind. They're colder than anything I've ever experienced, and if I don't fight off the frost taking root in my lungs, I'm as good as dead.

I focus my chaos magic into my frozen body, directing it with order and purpose. It fills the pattern of my lungs and wings. My magic warms me, getting so hot that I think I might just burn up here in the middle of an unnatural blizzard that is a manifestation of Morgana's chaos, and my lungs draw in a quick breath. I quickly beat my wings against the blowing wind and rise in the air again to meet the goddess of chaos face to face.

Her jaw drops open, and a blood curdling screech escapes from her mouth. The blizzard stops as abruptly as it started.

Morgana's black eye sockets narrow at me as she stays afloat the funnel winds. "You are a thief."

A snort of blue magic escapes from my nostrils, and the goddess of chaos's winds move her ten feet away from me.

I keep my dragon face an emotionless mask, but inside, my dragon and I are both pumping the air with our fists.

"You will submit to me and give me back my powers." Morgana's voice makes my skin crawl.

I realize that if Morgana is this dangerous with just a shadow of her powers, she could devastate entire regions of the world with her full chaos.

I raise a questioning dragon eyebrow at her.

There is a loud crash beneath me about fifty yards to my right as trees are downed by something big and heavy.

"You will give me back the power you hold, or I will kill everyone you care about," the goddess of chaos threatens.

My magic glows blue in my throat. No one threatens those I love and lives. I blast the greyish-white funnel cloud that's holding the goddess afloat, and she suddenly drops in altitude as she struggles to control the swirling wild nature beneath her.

"Have it your way, dragon vessel. But the next time we meet, it will be the last," her screechy echoing voice says as the funnel cloud she's manipulating disappears along with her.

I let out a deep breath, grateful that my lungs are no longer frozen solid. My mind goes to the crash I just heard before Morgana threatened those I love. *Levi!*

Levi, are you okay? I ask as his pain and confusion flood our bond.

I scan the area below for my ice dragon, and I catch a glimpse of a large blue tail in a long trench that's surrounded by downed and broken trees.

I... Uh. Rory? Levi's head is throbbing through our connection, and his vision is swimming.

Don't move. I'm on my way. I send my ice dragon my love and reassurance as I tuck my wings and dive toward him.

My landing shakes the ground and knocks a teetering tree top on top of Levi's underbelly. My ice dragon lets out a grunt as his big claw pushes the top of the evergreen off his belly, gouging a scratch into his already marred skin. *Thanks. I don't think my body's scarred enough. Wanna add another one?* He jokes through our connection as he continues to slowly move the fallen trees from his body.

I think you and Tucker are hanging around way too much. I make a scuffing dragon laugh as the sunlight shines brightly above us.

Don't tell my brother that. You'll break his heart. His physical pain leaks through our bond as he tries to lighten the mood with a joke.

My men are amazing. Their love for me brought them all together, and now that they all share a part of my soul, they're becoming closer too. They all rely on each other. Trust each other. And even genuinely care about each other. We're all a true family.

Let's get you out of here and back to the castle, I tell him as I lift some of the downed tree trunks off him.

I remove a large fallen tree, and Levi's ice blue eyes pierce mine. *Where's Morgana?*

The goddess of chaos and her wild storm disappeared. His admiration floods my heart.

You kicked her ass, huh? His dragon lips curl up into a toothy grin.

I wouldn't say that. She's still around and threatening all of us. I lift the last tree from his body, lean down, and extend my front claw to help him out of the hole.

Thanks. Levi uses my claw and he crawls out of

the deep trench.

Are you okay to fly? I put the front of my head to his bleeding one so I can study his eyes.

I'm banged up, but I'll be okay in a few hours. I can't feel any broken bones. He takes his head from mine and stands up straight, flapping his wings.

We need to get back to the castle and work on tracking the gods, I tell him as I take to the sky.

I'd be shocked if Drew isn't already working on that. Levi joins me and flies by my side.

Well, we know for sure that Morgana is near. I turn my head and watch as the cut above his eye gives off a sapphire blue spark and heals. *We need to account for Caelan and Razorus, as soon as possible. Gods! They could be out there killing and manipulating people right now.*

I shake my head to close our bond, and images of Caelan killing cities full of people with a single blast of his magic rushes through my mind. I let out a deep breath as we approach the castle. Images of Razorus casting an illusion over hundreds of Fairfax dragons, forcing them to kill each other flood my brain.

I let out an earsplitting roar.

The gods have to be stopped before they get their power back.

CHAPTER TWENTY-EIGHT

The oranges, reds, and peaches of the setting sun shine in through the windows, glimmering off the piles of jewels. The gold and silver bars that line the walls are stacked neatly while the coins are scattered in piles on the floor of my treasury, painting the walls and ceiling with a fire-like glow as I sit in the center of the Astor Diaries pedestals. My legs are crossed beneath me with Brigid's diary open in my palms.

All that Brigid wrote about were the ancient Oracles and the instructions to make Astor Crystals. Thank the gods this book is now locked in Castle Ashgrave, as thoughts of Kinsley and her glowing Astor Crystals flood my mind.

I rise to my feet and approach the pedestal that

holds Brigid's diary, removing the gold coin from the single page, drop the coin in a pile of coins on the floor nearby, and carefully place the page inside the ancient book. As I place the Astor Diary on its pedestal, my eyes roam to Esmeralda's diary. I take the book from its pedestal, approach the center of the pedestals, and sit cross legged on the floor.

Drew and Brett are paying attention to the chatter on the dragon channels in addition to the television and radio stations for any possible signs of Caelan, Razorus, or Morgana. Anything out of the ordinary could be linked to them and help us trace them. Levi, Tucker, and the bee drones patrol the area surrounding the castle and Ash Town for signs of the dragon gods' return.

Jace is busy training our army to work together and lean on each other, which will be a huge asset when the gods show their faces near our home. My mate is working with the massive metallic dragons and the dragon shifter soldiers. They're learning to work off each other's strengths and weaknesses. The extra-large steampunk dragons have unlimited magic and are able to incinerate a threat over two hundred yards away, but they move slowly and can't spot dangers that are within fifty feet of them due to their size. While the dojo soldiers are fast and powerful, they don't have unlimited magical stores, and their field of vision is about fifty yards. By teaming up and working together, our forces will become unstoppable.

We will need every advantage we can get against the dragon gods. That's why I'm here. To find out more about the gods and their power.

My eyes narrow and my brows become a "V" as I read and re-read everything Esmeralda has written in her diary, paying close attention to the gods' powers and abilities. I make sure to scan and note any weaknesses or mistakes that Esmeralda makes reference to.

I shake my head to rid my brain of the weariness that is taking root and stand and approach the pedestal that usually holds Esmeralda's diary. Gently, I place the ancient book back on top of it, and I turn to spy the gold and white dragon armor that appears as though it's on fire.

The fiery glow has me walking toward the beautiful filigreed suit of dragon armor that Morgana used to wear into battle. A thought of what-ifs floods my mind. I wonder what it would mean if I put that on. Would Morgana be at risk of a deadly blow if I wear it into our next battle? My mind flashes to the battle with the fearsome red dragon warrior who wore a black suit of dragon armor and faced off against Morgana. Even then she looked formidable in her shimmering green dragon form. An image of the dragon gods confronting me replaces it, and the blue and white rippling magic surrounds me as the gods threatened me. Or, would the goddess of chaos be able to use it as a conduit to control me and my magic?

A knock comes from the closed double doors, drawing my attention away from the dragon armor.

My ice dragon's love and hope flood to me as I open the door, and the warmth from his ice blue eyes makes heat pool between my thighs. His bruised and bloodied face and arms are healed as we bathe in our love for each other for a few moments through our bond.

"I thought you were on patrol with Tucker?" I wink and step aside so he can enter.

"The bees are still out there. I just wanted to check and see how Drew is doing." He gently takes my hand and gives a strong tug that has me tripping over a few stray coins on the floor and stumbling into his muscled chest.

I raise a questioning brow. "And how is Drew doing?"

"He's calling in every favor he's ever been given

and checking every network he knows of to see if anyone has seen anything unusual." Levi gives me a toe curling kiss. "Drew's checking to see if anyone has been approached by any of the three dragon gods. He's also keeping watch for any signs of an attack by them."

My eyes narrow and I pucker my lips. My chin touches my chest as I wonder what kind of sneak attack the dragon gods will pull. Will they wait until their power has had time to rebuild, or will they launch an attack where we least suspect it? Morgana's threat runs through my mind, and I wonder if the dragon gods are bold enough to try to hurt or kidnap one of my men, Ashgrave, Irena, or Harper?

My ice dragon places a finger beneath my chin and tenderly lifts my gaze to his as his worry for me floods my heart. "Hey, are you okay, Rory?"

My eyes shine with love as a smile crawls up my face. "I'm fine."

Levi drops his finger from my chin and pierces me with his ice blue eyes. "Are you sure? I mean, that was a brutal fight with Morgana."

I place my palms on his chest. "I'm all right. I'm just concerned that Morgana will try to lure me out by taking human hostages or by trying to kidnap someone close to me." I put my forehead against his strong chest. "And it really bothers me that the death god and trickster god are on the loose."

The thought of Razorus or Caelan sneaking up on us and setting an illusion so we won't be able to see him coming, or striking some of our army dead, has my mind churning. I wonder if we can view what the drones are actually seeing while they're on patrol.

I slowly lift my head and give Levi a wink. "Ashgrave, if we call a bee drone back to the castle, will we be able to watch images from the other bees?"

"YES, MY QUEEN," my murderous castle's voice thunders, making the coins and jewels jingle and tinkle as they vibrate.

The high-pitched buzzing of metallic wings lets me know the bee is heading toward me. I extend my hand out in front of me and step out of Levi's embrace. The tiny metallic bee lands on my palm, and its little body shakes and bounces as the bee's abdomen, thorax, and head stretch into the rectangular shape of a ten-inch tablet. Its wings, legs, and antenna mold around the screen, making a metal frame that surrounds the images that are coming through the viewing screen.

A sigh escapes my lips as the buzzing of

metallic wings fills the treasury. Levi places his hand on my waist and leans his head over my shoulder to watch the visuals of the green leaves sprouting from the growing vegetables in the garden, the faces of the villagers that call Ash Town home, the breathtaking view of the orange sun setting in the mountains to the west, and the big black gun and silver wings of Tucker's jet as he approaches the runway of Castle Ashgrave's private airstrip.

Now we can watch the images that the bees see at the same time, but if any of the dragon gods attack Ash Town, it will take us costly minutes to get to them. The little town and all of the people who live there could be destroyed.

"Ashgrave, can we please send a dozen of the large metallic battle dragons to guard Ash Town? But please make new ones. Jace is training with the ones we have now."

"RIGHT AWAY, MISTRESS."

Thoughts of frightened people running for cover as twelve massive metallic dragons land in the middle of their town, possibly crushing homes, carts, orchards, or fields of food under their huge bodies rush through my mind.

"Please make sure that they stay out of sight.

There's no need to alert the villagers, unless the town is attacked," I add.

"YES, MY QUEEN," Ashgrave booms.

I hold the metallic screen that's continually projecting the images of what the bee drones are seeing and turn toward my ice dragon's strong chest.

"Rory, you've battled the goddess of chaos and sent her packing today. Don't you think you've done enough for one day?" Levi whispers in my ear, and ripples of heat radiate through my core.

"We can see what the drones can see. I just want to watch for Razorus and Caelan." I plant a kiss on his cheek.

"He wags his eyebrows at me. "Or, we could have our smiteful castle watch what's going on outside." He places a heated kiss on my lips that has me leaning into him with need.

I clear the huskiness that I'm sure is stuck in my throat. "Ashgrave, will you please keep watch over the drones and alert me to anything unusual?"

"IT WOULD BE MY HONOR, MISTRESS."

"Thank you, Ashgrave."

"WOULD YOU LIKE A PATHWAY TO YOUR PRIVATE ROOM, MY QUEEN?"

My ice dragon's hand gently cups my ass. "No thank you, Ashgrave. Levi will escort me."

"PLEASANT DREAMS, MY QUEEN. AND TO YOU TOO, MR. LEVI."

"Thank you," we both blurt out as Levi gently takes my hand in his, opens the door, and leads me down the hallway toward the stone staircase that will take us up to my room.

CHAPTER TWENTY-NINE

The rising sun washes my room with shades of pinks, purples, and blues as I roll to my left side and extend my arm over the cool sheets and my eyes go to the empty bedside table. My ice dragon must have taken the tablet that shows the bee drone footage in real time with him.

My heart thunders against my ribs at the thought of one of the gods attacking and that I somehow slept through it.

Is everything okay? I send to Levi through our connection as I try to slow my racing heart.

Everything is fine, Rory. Breathe, please? His calming thoughts rush through me. *I just wanted you to rest.*

Any news or sightings of the dragon gods? My heart

slows as I fill my lungs with air and slowly exhale through my mouth.

Nothing yet, Levi tells me as his calming thoughts continue to soothe my frayed nerves. *But you might want to touch base with Drew to be sure, once you're dressed.* An image of me sleeping naked floods my mind and need rushes to me from Levi, making heat pool between my legs.

I close our bond and rush to my closet to throw on a pair of black jeans, a black cable sweater, and a pair of black combat boots. Then I step into my humongous white marble bathroom to brush my hair and teeth before quickly rushing to open my door and head out into the hallway.

As I make my way toward the staircase, I admire the way the rising sun glimmers off of the crystal chandeliers that hang from golden chains above my head, throwing miniature glowing iridescent rainbows over the walls, floor, and ceiling. A sigh escapes my lips at the way the beauty of my castle takes my breath away in awe.

I rush down the stone stairway and head toward the surveillance room and my sexy as hell fire dragon.

As I approach the open door of Drew's favorite room, the voice of a male newscaster announces that not only the Tensaw River in Mobile, Alabama and the Whitefish River in Rapid River, Michigan, but also the Cape Fear River that runs through Wilmington, North Carolina are flooding their banks and causing the people in those areas to evacuate. I place my back against the wall of the hallway near the open door and listen to the rest of the report. My heartbeat increases with my intuition—this is the action of the dragon gods.

The deep voice of the male newscaster continues. "… there are an estimated two hundred and fifty thousand people being displaced by the rising flood waters and over six hundred twenty-five residents still unaccounted for."

I groan, but my ears remain perked and listening.

"The United States government is working around the clock to build up levies around the affected areas to ensure that the water flow can be contained. However, this station has recently been notified by an unnamed source that the levy around the Whitefish River in Michigan has collapsed and the entire town of Rapid River is currently under five feet of water."

My head shakes in disbelief and anger as the newscaster continues in a somber voice. "The over three thousand residents of the small northern town are being airlifted to Marquette over fifty miles north where they will receive not only food and lodging, but also medical care. Over half of the residents are suffering from dehydration, frostbite, and heart arrhythmia due to being in the freezing water and left outside in the below-zero temperatures overnight."

I ball my fists. This has to be them. All they know how to do is bring misery.

"Almost four hundred people who call this town home have already succumbed to the elements and perished," the newscaster says. "The real question is how did the Whitefish River flood? It should have had a one to two inch frozen crust over it. To discuss this…"

I tune out his voice, not wanting to hear about more destruction, suffering, and death.

My intuition nags at me that this is Morgana. She created a white-out blizzard out of nowhere yesterday morning. I have no doubt in my mind that the goddess of chaos can flood all of these rivers at once.

A deep sigh escapes my lips and rumbles my chest as I push off of the wall and walk through the door of the surveillance room.

Strong arms encircle my waist as Drew pulls me

into his strong embrace. "Levi told me about the fight you had with Morgana yesterday." He lifts my chin with his long thick finger and gently kisses my lips. "He also told me you sent her packing."

I shrug my shoulders and try to hide my chuckle at my ice dragon's choice of words by placing my head against Drew's chest. "She left, but I didn't see her taking any luggage."

My fire dragon places his hands on my shoulders and pulls me away from his muscled chest. He pierces my eyes with his sexy black ones. "You're right, love. The important thing is that she left, and no one was seriously hurt."

My gaze wanders to the two large screens behind him with images of people paddling beds, couches, and tables away from their flooded homes. I close my eyes. All of the destruction by the floods and the lives unaccounted for rush through my mind. Over six hundred twenty-five, over six hundred twenty-five, over six hundred twenty-five...

I turn my eyes away from the screen to meet Drew's dark gaze. "Drew, are you sure these floods are natural and aren't Morgana, Razorus, or Caelan causing them?"

My fire dragon's shoulders slump forward, and his chin meets his chest as he removes his hands from my shoulders and rubs the back of his neck with one of them. "Rory, I've checked and double checked. They're natural disasters and not the dragon gods causing chaos."

I lift his bearded chin with two of my fingers. "Are you sure?" I look into the depths of his black eyes. "The river in Michigan was frozen yesterday. How did it flood its banks last night, trapping thousands of people and killing hundreds?"

Drew returns my prying gaze. "Rory, I promise you, this is normal. These disasters were not caused by Morgana, or any of—"

My phone rings, cutting my fire dragon off, and I step out into the hallway and take it out of my pocket. My eyes search the screen. It's Irena.

I click the talk button and wait for my sister to start the conversation.

"Rory, how are you?"

"I'm good. How are you, big sister? Or should I call you Boss now?"

"Ha ha ha! Very funny, Rory Quinn. Or should I call you Queen Lorelei?"

"*Now* look who's got a sense of humor?" I pull the phone away from my ear and narrow my eyes at it. Irena knows I hate being called Lorelei.

"I've always had a sense of humor." Irena chuckles. "You just never appreciate it."

"How's everything going in Vaer territory?"

"Good. Flynn's been a great help. Do you mind if I keep him and his dragons for a while?"

A smirk pulls at the left side of my mouth. It sounds like my sister is actually happy.

"It's up to him. We have things covered here if he wants to stay and help you do whatever it is that you're doing."

"Oh, little sister, I've been so busy. I didn't feel comfortable at the Vaer safehouse near the Chained Monument, so I'm setting up a temporary capital at one of Kinsley's properties just outside Anchorage, Alaska."

"Is it easily defendable?"

"Do you think I would've chosen a location that wasn't? Nothing is as defendable as Ashgrave, but I have a mansion that is surrounded by mountains on all sides. Flynn's rebels run regular patrols, and with my elite warriors, nothing can touch me."

"Irena, I'm glad to hear that you're stepping into the role of Vaer Boss with grace and dignity. You're going to be an amazing leader."

"Thanks, little sister. I had a great teacher. I learned from watching you."

"Thank you for saying that."

"I mean it, Rory. You're an awesome queen, and if I can be half the leader you are, I'll be a great one."

"I'm so proud of you, Irena. Keep up the great work."

My fight with Morgana and the images of the American floods fill my mind.

"Oh, Irena—one more thing." I suck in a deep breath. "The dragon gods are on the loose, so be careful."

"I'll never forget the way the dragon gods made me feel as they flew off. They give off some really bad vibes, lil sister. I'll keep my eyes open."

"Will you please let me know as soon as possible if any of the gods approach you or any of the Vaer?"

"I promise. Don't die, little sister."

"Stay safe, Irena. And tell Flynn and the rest of the rebels that we will miss them around here."

The phone goes dead. I slip my phone into my pocket and head back into the surveillance room. One of the screens is showing images of a huge five-alarm fire at the Willis Tower in Chicago.

"Drew, how did that massive skyscraper start fire?" I put my hands on my hips and look at the back of my fire dragon's head as he turns his over-stuffed computer chair around slowly to look at me.

"A lightning strike." His gaze meets mine. "Lightning happens in Chicago, Rory."

"I get that." I nod my head. "But I thought the historic building is equipped with multiple lightning rods to make sure it doesn't catch fire."

"Something must have gone wrong." He stands up and approaches me, placing his large hands over my shoulders. "There has to be a simple explanation, Rory."

I open my mouth to ask another question, but Drew's mouth crashes into mine, and he kisses me so passionately that my toes curl up in my boots and heat pools between my legs.

Drew breaks the kiss, and we're both panting loudly.

"Have you had your morning coffee yet, love?" He drops his hands.

I shake my head. "I do need my caffeinated goodness. You promise to let me know if anything else happens." I pierce him with my gold-tinted chocolate brown eyes.

"I promise." His sensual mouth pulls up into a sexy grin. "I've got this, woman."

I turn and head for the open door. Drew is right —I do need my coffee.

But my intuition nags at me that these aren't true

natural disasters. The dragon gods are behind this. I'm sure of it.

With thoughts of attacking ancient dragon gods on my mind, I decide to wait for my coffee and head downstairs to check on Jace. My mate is training the metallic dragon army and the dojo soldiers to work together in battle scenarios.

Someone's soft humming pulls me from my thoughts, and I feel the tug that is uniquely Tucker as my weapons expert jogs around the bend in the large stone staircase with his head down. I clear my throat and narrow my eyes as he grabs onto the banister, stopping himself from tripping on the stairs.

"Shit! You almost gave me a heart attack, babe." He steadies himself on his feet and puts a hand over his heart like he's trying to slow its rhythm from the outside. "Why are you sneaking around your own castle?"

"I'm not sneaking." I hide my chuckle with my hand. "You just weren't paying attention, babe."

"I'm going to put bells on you and Levi so I can hear you two coming from a distance." Tucker's lips pull up into his goofy grin.

"That wouldn't be any fun." I smile and give him a flirty wink.

Tucker rushes toward me. He wraps his strong

arms around me, pinning my body to the wall and giving me a heat-filled kiss that has my dragon cooing with need.

"Would you like a repeat performance of the last time we were alone in the hallways?" His lips collide with mine again. A moan of passion escapes from me and is muffled by my weapons expert's mouth.

"THERE IS A HUMAN WOMAN AT THE FRONT DOOR, MY QUEEN. WOULD YOU LIKE ME TO ESCORT HER TO THE THRONE ROOM, MISTRESS?" My evil butler's voice booms through the castle, making the crystals on the chandeliers and sconces tinkle as they bounce off each other.

"That's okay, Ashgrave. Tucker and I will greet our visitor." I wiggle my eyebrows at Tucker.

I figure the woman is one of the villagers from Ash Town who's come to visit one of the residents of the castle.

Tucker drops his arms and steps back from me, freeing me from our romantic embrace.

My eyes meet his and he grabs my hand as we walk down the stairs toward the large wooden double entry doors.

"THIS IS THE WAY TO THE WHIPPING AND TARRING ROOM," Tucker says in a loud voice with a Russian accent as we approach the door. He pulls it open.

The newcomer is dressed in a black hooded robe and is looking at the stones beneath her feet.

"Welcome to Castle Ashgrave," I say in greeting to the woman.

She takes her hands from her pockets, and a grey foul-smelling ash falls from her fingers. I breathe through my mouth to avoid the decay from entering my nose.

The first thing I notice is the ash falls off her each time she moves. Second, is the sickly grey tinge to her skin. It's a deep grey, almost the color of slate. Her black hair hangs lifeless, almost as if it's just black string stuck to her head that hangs to her elbows.

The woman doesn't say a word as she slowly lifts the hood from her head and brings her gaze up to meet mine. Her eyes are black, but I know that face. I've seen that face every day of my life, until I was changed into the dragon vessel.

It's Zurie.

My heart pounds painfully against my ribs as I stand motionless, searching the face of my dead mentor.

Tucker turns his head toward me, and my eyes

narrow as I fight for air to fill my lungs. He places a hand on my bicep as his eyes search for answers in mine.

Like a lightning flash, Zurie buries a dagger hilt deep into Tucker's chest, leaving a trail of ashes in her wake.

CHAPTER THIRTY

I shake myself internally. I have to get over the shock of seeing Zurie alive. I have to help Tucker.

He puts his hand on the hilt of the knife sticking out of his chest and falls to the floor on his knees with a loud thud.

Zurie pulls another dagger from the pocket of her robe and lashes out at me with it. I quickly side-step her attack and grab Tucker's shoulders to pull him out of danger. He grunts in pain, probably unable to shout out or even take in a deep breath.

As I pull my weapons expert toward the base of the stairs, Zurie grunts and slashes at me with her dagger, cutting my bicep. My upper arm stings, but once Tucker is safe, I turn to face Zurie.

My ex-mentor circles me, looking for her chance to attack. She lunges forward, trying to stab me in the stomach, but I lift my leg and place a kick to her hand, spraying me and the stone floor of the ornate foyer with stench-filled ash as the blade falls from Zurie's hand. She roars at me, like a tiger, and gnashes her blackened teeth.

"How are you even here, Zurie?" I circle the ex-Ghost. "I killed you."

She doesn't answer me. She just narrows her dead black eyes at me and growls.

I wonder if she *can* answer. All I hear from Zurie are animalistic grunts, growls, and roars. But my ex-mentor can still fight. Her flexibility and fighting skills are all still intact.

My ex-mentor's skin is a dull slate grey, spreading ash every time she moves. The substance reeks of decay and death. Most noticeably, her once ice blue eyes are now black with no signs of life.

This has to be Caelan—the god of death's work. It appears that he not only brings about death, but can also control the dead.

Fan-freaking-tastic!

Zurie rushes me and tackles me to the floor, covering my face with ash and filling my nostrils with decay as she straddles my chest. She bangs the back of my head against the hard stone floor, making black spots dot my vision.

I relax my muscles and allow my eyes to slowly drift closed, the way Irena taught me to in order to break a hold like this. After a few moments, Zurie grunts and stops using my head as a hammer. She gets off my chest, stands, and roars into the large open room.

I lie on the stone floor and wait for my chance to pounce. My eyes open enough to spot Zurie moving away from me and toward a motionless Tucker.

I spring from the floor like my body is tied to a bungie cord and attack Zurie with my magical dagger, stabbing her in the back. As she turns to face me, she lets out an earsplitting screech and grabs at her chest. A blue light the size of a quarter glows in the center of her chest as she backs away to slowly circle me with her eyes narrowed.

My ex-mentor rushes toward me with a dagger in each hand, and the magical dagger in my palm starts to morph. The handle of my mace forms, and I swing the spiked ball over my head.

"YOUR LORDS HAVE BEEN MADE AWARE OF THE TRESSPASER, MY QUEEN." Ashgrave's voice booms, shaking the tapestries.

The clinking of metal hitting stone has me

searching Zurie's deathly grey face. I approach her, spinning the ball at the end of the chain faster above my head. Zurie's black eyes go wide as the spiked ball crashes against her skull, making it cave in, and she falls into a motionless heap at my feet in the center of the foyer.

I drop my magical mace from my hand, and it disappears into blue sparks of magic before colliding. with the beautiful marble floor.

I put my hands on my knees and suck in a huge breath of air.

The clatter of a knife bouncing off the floor has my eyes searching for a new threat. I jump to stand with my feet shoulder width apart and pool my sapphire blue magic in my hands, ready to blast anyone willing to attempt to sneak up on me. Especially now, since I just killed Zurie—again.

My eyes roam over the foyer, and I spot Tucker pulling himself up to stand against the wooden bannister of the large staircase with his hand pressed against his wound. Zurie's dagger lies by his left foot.

I rush toward my weapons expert. "Oh my gods! Tucker, are you okay?"

He takes a slow and steady breath. "I'm okay." He opens his shirt, and the wound sparks with blue magic and closes before our eyes. "I'm lucky I'm one of your lords—apparently one of the perks is not only dragon healing, it's miracle speed-healing.

The thundering of footsteps from down the stairs and the hallway lets me know the rest of my team is on its way.

Jade, Brett, and Drew rush down the stairs and come to a stop on the last step. Jace and Levi approach from the west wing hallway.

Is that Zurie? Levi asks through our bond.

"Yes, that's Zurie," I answer out loud.

Jade turns green and leans into Brett, as her dread and shock funnel into me. My public relations expert wraps his arm around Jade's small waist, comforting her.

"How is that even possible?" Drew asks.

"You turned her to ash when the Spectres, Knights, and Vaer attacked and destroyed the dojo," Jace adds.

"I understand all that, but she didn't seem like herself," I tell my family.

"You can say that again," Tucker adds, rubbing his chest. "We should've slammed the door in her face when she flaked off that nasty ass smelling ash from her hands."

"Do you want to tell this story, babe?" I roll my eyes at my weapons expert.

"Nah! You go ahead, babe. I was unconscious for most of it anyway." Tucker gives me a thumbs up.

"Tucker and I answered the door to what we thought would be a human woman coming to visit one of our human residents," I tell my family.

"I APOLOGIZE, MY QUEEN. SHE DID NOT APPEAR TO BE A THREAT," my castle thunders.

"It's okay, Ashgrave. You couldn't have known that she would be a zombie of my ex-mentor." My lips purse at the memory of Ashgrave's booming voice distracting Zurie. "Plus, if you hadn't warned me that my lords were coming, I wouldn't have been able to deal the death blow. So, thank you."

"IT IS MY HONOR TO SERVE YOU, MISTRESS."

"You think Zurie was raised from the dead to attack you?" Brett asks as he holds Jade close to him.

"I don't think. I know she was," I answer. "She stabbed Tucker in the chest with a dagger."

All eyes go to my weapons expert and a goofy grin crawls up his face as he lifts his shirt to reveal a pink scratch on his chest. "Zurie buried the dagger hilt deep into my chest. Hence the unconscious comment," he says, nodding his head.

"But…" Jade's eyes widen to the size of saucers as her confusion leaks to me through our bond.

"Better than dragon healing, Rory's lords have extra-fast speed healing." Tucker answers Jade's unasked question.

Jade, Drew, Jace, Levi, and Brett's jaws drop open.

"If I wasn't one of Rory's lords, I'd be dead right now." Tucker grabs my hand, turns it over, and plants a gentle kiss on my open palm.

"So how did you kill Zurie this time?" my mate asks with a sexy smirk on his face.

"I crushed her reconstructed ash head with my magical mace." I mirror his smirk. "But, from the time we opened the door, I knew something was off. She flaked off this foul smelling ash every time she moved." I shake my head to get rid of the memory. "She was also a slate grey color, and her hair hung straight like string or yarn, and what used to be her blue eyes were black and dead."

"Did you ask her why she was here?" Drew asks.

"I did." I nod my head. "But she couldn't talk. All she could do was growl and roar like an animal."

Levi's mind massages mine, and my memories flood into him. He sends me his disgust at the way Zurie was resurrected and refashioned in such an unnatural way. *I'm sorry you had to deal with that, Rory.*

My gaze meets my ice dragon's. *I'm just happy it's*

over.

"Are you thinking this is Caelan's doing?" Jace asks.

"I'm one hundred percent positive that this was the death god's work." I nod my head.

Drew clears his throat. "The only question we need to ask now, is how do we get rid of the body?"

"I say we give her the vampire treatment—just in case." Tucker draws his thumb across his throat. "Let's remove her head and burn her."

I extend my hands out in front of me, and the curve of my magical axe forms. I move toward Zurie's body and raise the large battle axe above my head and sever her crushed head from the rest of her body.

"Ashgrave, please put the body outside and burn it," I ask.

"AT ONCE, MY QUEEN." Metallic hands grab Zurie's grey head and body and drag them across the stone floor of the castle and out the entry way doors into the front courtyard. Blue flames erupt from the stone pavers, engulfing Zurie Bronwen's resurrected body.

"IT IS DONE, MISTRESS," Ashgrave announces as Zurie's ashes disappear from the castle, and the entryway door slams shut.

CHAPTER THIRTY-ONE

My blood boils as I pace the ornate foyer of Castle Ashgrave, stomping my feet to remove the thought of Zurie being brought back to life by Caelan. The way these gods destroy everyone and everything around them is ridiculous. No one attacks my men or my home and lives. That goes triple for the dragon gods who are hell-bent on taking my power from me. I suck in a deep breath and shake out my hands as I walk back and forth to remove the tension from my back, shoulders, and arms.

I need to take out Caelan before he brings an army of dead down on us and destroys my castle and all who live in it.

I stop pacing, and my eyes roam over the silent

faces surrounding me. Jade's eyes are watery, like a tear may streak down her face at any moment as her shock of seeing Zurie on the floor rushes through our magical bond. Brett rests his chin on top of her long black hair. His nostrils flare as he sucks air in through his nose.

Drew, Jace, and Levi surround Tucker, examining his now unmarked tanned chest. My fire dragon and ice dragon are taking turns poking my weapons expert in the center of his brown haired chest.

"Does this hurt?" Drew digs the tip of his finger into Tucker's chest.

"How about this?" Levi slaps my weapons expert, making the skin between his nipples turn a bright pink.

"Ouch! Damn it, Levi! That's not even where I was stuck." Laughter erupts from all of my men.

"He was just checking to make sure your funny bone was still intact, brother." Jace's eyes meet mine and his back stiffens.

"Rory, killing your lifelong mentor couldn't have been easier for you the second time around." My mate approaches me, and his brothers follow him. "Are you okay?"

"I'm fine." I shake the image of Zurie's dark grey skull caving in beneath the pressure of my magical mace and my blood boils again. "Have the army on standby."

"Aww, you have a plan brewing behind those sexy brown eyes, babe." Tucker clasps my shoulder with his strong hand.

"What are you planning, my beautiful mate?" Jace asks as the left side of his mouth quirks up in a smirk.

"I'm planning to pull all of the strings. Now that I have a better understanding of what they can do, I know what I'm fully capable of." A deadly smile crosses my lips. "I'm going to make the ancient dragon gods dance like puppets at the ends of my strings."

Jade's anger fills me, and my gaze meets hers. "Ready to help?"

"You know I am." Jade rapidly blinks the tears from her eyes. "What do you need me to do?"

"I'd like for you and Levi to go with Jace and help him train with the army. You're a fierce fighter, and our army can learn a lot from you." I give her a wink, and a charming smile washes across her face, making her eyes glimmer with pride.

Yes! Training with an army will be amazing after all of the time I've spent alone. Levi sends me his love and gratitude through our special bond.

I knew you'd enjoy that, I send to my ice dragon. *You're not alone anymore, Levi, and you never will be again.*

I know, Rory. Thank you for reminding me, he tells me before closing our special link and rushing after Jade. They follow Jace down the hallway that leads to the training area in the west wing.

My weapons expert clears his throat, and I search his face. "Yes, babe? Can I help you?"

"What do you want me to do?" A goofy grin crawls up his face, and he pats his cheek with his hand. "Continue to look pretty for you, babe?"

"You know it. Keep your pretty head on those sexy shoulders." I shake my head to keep the laughter in my throat from bubbling out. "I also need you to get your favorite toy ready for combat."

"Really?" My weapons expert's eyebrows rise up his forehead, and he bounces on his toes like an excited kid. "I have a few modifications to do to the anti-dragon gun and a couple of heat seekers to add to her." He pulls me toward him, and his mouth collides into mine, giving me a heated kiss. He pulls away and walks toward the front door. "This is going to kick ass, babe. Seriously, give me a few hours and those asshat gods aren't going to know what hit them." Tucker opens the wooden door, walks out, gives me a salute, and lets it slam closed behind him.

"Drew, you'll go with me to the treasury." My eyes meet my fire dragon's large almond shaped black ones.

"What do you need me to do?" Brett's voice draws my attention to him.

"Brett, you contact Irena, Harper, Milo, and Isaac. Let them all know to come to Ashgrave as soon as they can assemble their armies." A sigh rushes from my lips. "The dragon gods aren't going to go down without a battle. We're going to need every ally we have."

"Right away, Boss." Brett gives me a salute, mimicking Tucker as he turns around and runs up the stairs, heading for the surveillance room to make his calls.

Drew wraps his strong arms around me and plants a kiss on the top of my head. "What's going on in that incredibly enrapturing head of yours, love?"

I lift my head, look into his dark eyes, and give him a playful wink. "You'll see."

A chuckle erupts from his lips and he drops his arms, spreading an open hand out in front of him, signaling for me to lead the way to the treasury.

"Ashgrave, will you please make a pathway for

me and Drew to the treasury?" I ask my castle as the wall behind the third tapestry slides open.

I lead the way into the magically blue-lit tunnel with my fire dragon stalking closely behind me. His hot breath rushes down the back of my neck, making goosebumps erupt with need all over my body. I silently follow the stairway leading downward, and Drew walks next to me and places our palms together, interlinking our fingers. The wall at the bottom of the stairs slides open and sunlight floods the exit of the magical tunnel. Drew and I walk out of the pathway and into the hallway across from the huge wooden doors of my treasury.

Drew opens the door for me, and I walk into the huge room full of piles of gold and silver bars that are neatly stacked. The mountains of gold and silver coins littering the marble floor sit next to piles of rubies, emeralds, sapphires, and other precious jewels. They send glimmering rainbows of light across the walls and ceiling as the rays of sunlight dance over them. But my eyes are focused on the suits of dragon armor that sit on the left side of the room.

Drew pulls me to a stop. "Are you going to tell me what we're doing here, love?"

The memories of my visions of the dragon gods

rush into my head. The way the fierce red dragon warrior fought against Morgana's green diamond dragon while she wore the intricately carved gold and white suit of armor. My vision ripples with white and blue waves as the memory of the gods threatening to take my power from me floods my mind, and I shake my head to stop the images.

"Touching Morgana's dragon armor has sparked visions in the past, so I figure I can use it to act almost like a conduit to contact the gods and send them a message."

"How are you going to do that?" Drew raises his brow at me.

"By putting it on." I give him a mischievous smile.

"It's a suit of dragon armor." He points to the gold and white filigreed armor in front of us. "And you, my love, are in your human form."

"I can put on the helmet." I point to the beautiful golden piece of armor that Morgana used to cover her dragon's head. "If you're willing to take it down for me and help place it over my head?"

Drew approaches Morgana's dragon armor, and his muscles bulge beneath his sweatshirt under the weight of the massive dragon helmet as he takes it off the top of the golden and white well-cared-for suit of armor. He approaches me, aiming the part of the helmet that covers a dragon's nose at me.

"This is going to be heavy. Make sure you get into a fighting stance and get ready to balance this monster on your head."

I place my feet shoulder width apart, raising my arms into the air, and nod for Drew to lower the dragon sized helmet onto my head.

He gently places it over my head, and I support the sides with my hands as I drop the tip of the long nose down toward the floor. I spot Drew's muscled thighs through the eye holes and concentrate on the dragon gods. Drew's breath and the creaks of the floor above our heads cease to exist as my mind focuses on the images of the faces of Morgana, Razorus, and Caelan surrounded by darkness.

The pictures of the dragon gods in my mind glow a sickly abalone grey as the shadows around them writhe like they're alive. Morgana's empty eye sockets narrow, and her lips purse, like she's upset that I'm interrupting her. Razorus crosses his muscled arms over his chest and he rolls his golden eyes as if he's dealing with a petulant child. Caelan's red eyes pierce mine as he stands tall with his hands on his hips.

The dragon gods appear powerful and intimidating, but I can sense there's something lacking. Almost like they're shadows of their former selves. The gods have some residual powers due to their very nature, but my power is stronger. I possess the full power of the ancient dragon gods.

"Little dragon vessel, you've had your fun. Now it is time to hand over what doesn't belong to you." Morgana's bone chilling voice cuts through the silence.

I lift my chin in defiance and stay silent.

"Hand over our power, or we will bring an army of the dead to your door and destroy everything you hold dear. Starting with your lovers." Caelan growls.

"You do know that I currently possess your full power. All of it." I roll my eyes. "Is it really me who should be afraid?"

"So be it," Razorus replies.

"If you have the balls to try and kick me out of my castle. Bring it on," I inform the dragon gods and push the golden helmet off my head, ending the vision.

Drew's black eyes are wide. "Were you able to speak with the gods?"

I nod. "Let's join the army outside and shift. War is coming."

CHAPTER THIRTY-TWO

The bright orange sun dips below the western border as I stand on my balcony taking in the beauty of my castle and the area surrounding it. My wet hair is wrapped in a towel as I lean against the balcony and watch over five hundred metallic dragons roar into the sky. I search the area to my right and spot Levi and Jade blasting five of the large steampunk dragons with ice magic and freezing them in place, making the others roar in frustration. I figured that if Levi and Jade teamed up, they'd be a force to reckon with. They're both incredibly fast and brutal when they need to be.

The fact that Jace is encouraging them to freeze their giant metallic counterparts tells me that my mate is teaching the metal dragons to be defensive.

I've heard that the best offense is a great defense. If the metal dragons can rely on their dojo buddies, they'll be unstoppable. The dojo dragons approach the five frozen steampunk dragons and blast controlled flames at them, thawing them.

I suck in a deep breath of air and rub my palms on my clean stone washed jeans then push up the sleeves of my sapphire blue sweatshirt. I'm getting inpatient waiting on my allies. Brett said they all told him they'd be here by sun down, and it's quickly becoming twilight.

My hand reaches up and yanks the towel off my head. I throw it on the white wingback chair just inside the balcony door and shake out my long brown locks and brush my fingers through them. Jace and Levi recommended I take a shower after knocking twelve soldiers on their backs with a single blast of magic. I know we will need our army at one hundred percent before the war with the dragon gods. We might not have time for them to heal if I continue to take out my annoyance on my own soldiers.

I shake my head and roll my tense shoulders. I figure I can relax after I kick the dragon gods' asses and send them packing back to wherever they've been for the last millennium. For good.

A roar slices through the quiet sky, drawing my gaze to the eastern border and the five hundred or more black dots approaching. As they come closer, I notice a dark dragon with a golden stripe down its back. His scales glimmer green in the setting sun. Alongside the dark dragon is a silver one with a black stripe that starts at the crown of its head and goes all the way down its back to the tip of its tail.

The Palarnes are here.

"THE PALARNE ARMY IS APPROACHING FROM THE EAST, MY QUEEN," Ashgrave's voice booms.

I rush to my bathroom to put my hair up into a messy bun. I run out my bedroom door and stop dead in my tracks. The older woman from Poland is standing in front of my door with her hand lifted like she's about to knock. Lena's eyes are as wide as dinner plates and her skin is pale.

"I'm sorry, Lena," I place my hand on her shoulder to stop her from falling over. "Is everything okay with our expectant mother?"

Our resident midwife's mouth opens and closes quickly, like she's trying to force the words out of her mouth, but nothing's coming out. Lena's eyes drop to the floor, and when she raises them to look at me, she places a hand to her heart.

"I'm sorry, my queen," she confesses. "I didn't expect you to move that fast. You shocked me."

"Are you okay?" I open the door to my private bedroom behind me and hold out my hand, ushering her in to take a seat.

"I'm fine. Really." She shakes her head and stands as still as a statue. "I just wanted you to know that our new little blessing arrived about an hour ago."

"How are the mother and baby doing?" I ask, closing the door behind me.

"They are both doing excellent." A smile lights up her face and a twinkle appears in her eyes. "The little girl weighs three point five seven two kilograms or seven pounds fourteen ounces and is point five four six meters or twenty-one and a half of your inches long. The family of three is happy and resting now."

"Thank you for letting me know, Lena. I'll make sure to visit them when the war is over." I place my hand on her shoulder again. "Ashgrave should have asked you all to move to the rooms we've set up for you in the bottom level of the castle. Is everyone relocated there?"

"Yes, my queen." She stiffens her back and puffs out her chest. "That's where the baby was born."

"Good." A breath of air escapes my mouth. "I

need for you all to be safe, and Castle Ashgrave can protect you there."

"Thank you for thinking of our safety and comfort, mistress. We all came here because we knew you'd protect us." She gives me a wink. "We also knew that you'd care for us and our future."

"Thanks for saying that, Lena." I remove my hand from her shoulder. "But I need to go and meet with our allies now. I have our home to protect from some crazy, power-hungry dragon gods."

"Good luck, your highness." Lena turns toward the staircase down the hall. "We all know that if the war was based on heart, you would've already won it."

Without another word, she rushes down the hall and takes the stone stairs two at a time.

A heavy sigh escapes my lips, and I lean back against my closed bedroom door, dropping my gaze to the maroon and gold rug in the hallway. Lena said that if the war was based on heart, that I'd win—and I figure that's what this war should be about. Heart.

"THE NEW VAER BOSS AND MR. BLACK-WOOD, ALONG WITH THE DARRINGTON BOSS AND HIS ARMY ARE ALL APPROACHING THE WESTERN BORDER, MY QUEEN." My evil butler's booming voice makes my heart jump. "THE

FAIRFAX BOSS AND HER ARMY ARE APROACHING THE SOUTHERN BORDER, MISTRESS."

"Thank you, Ashgrave." I head toward the war room. "Have all the Bosses and their generals meet me in the war room. Please have my lords meet me there as well."

"RIGHT AWAY, MY QUEEN."

My mind wanders over the same nagging question—will Ashgrave remain loyal to me once Morgana comes back? I shake my head and continue toward the war room.

As I approach the open door, Harper's voice carries to me. "Irena, being a Boss agrees with you. Or, maybe it's being mated to Flynn that has your glowing green eyes even more brilliant."

"I'm going to kill my sister," Irena responds.

"Well, don't kill her yet. We need her to take out the dragon gods." Harper chuckles, knowing that I'm not in any real danger of losing my life to my sister.

I walk into the war room and place my hands on my hips. No one says a word, and all eyes are on me.

"The only beings dying today are the dragon gods." I pierce my sister with a deadly gaze. "Got it?"

"Oh my gods, Rory. I was only kidding." My sister

rolls her green eyes at me. "But do me a favor and keep the chatter of my love life to yourself."

"Fine!" I approach the comfy chair at the end of the table and take a seat and nod my head at my mate who's sitting to my left.

"Rory, Drew, and I have come up with a plan." My mate's chest puffs out as he sits up straight in his high backed chair and meets the gaze of everyone seated at the table.

"Tucker and Brett," he says as his neck swivels to the left. "You two will be in the jet. Tucker as the pilot, and Brett, you'll be firing the new anti-dragon gun."

"Hell yeah," Tucker pumps his fist in the air.

"Drew," my mate meets my fire dragon's dark gaze as he sits on my right side across the table from him. "You'll be at Rory's side. You're immune to her magic, so it's safe to say that you're also immune to anything the dragon gods can throw at you."

My fire dragon nods at Jace and grabs my hand.

"Levi, I need you and Jade to take one hundred of our large metallic dragons to Ash Town." Jace meets each of their eyes from across the table. "Levi, you have a direct link to Rory. We will need that if Ash Town gets overrun."

My ice dragon leans around Drew's shoulder to give me a wink as Jade nods in agreement with Jace.

"How about us?" Irena asks.

"I'll need you and Flynn's rebels to go to the east to make sure nothing crosses the boundary, big sis." I meet her glowing green eyes with mine. "We need to keep the dragon gods close once they show themselves. No matter what, don't let them leave Castle Ashgrave's boundaries."

"Isaac and Payton, you'll hold the southern boundary." I nod to the Palarne Boss who sits on the left side of the long table near the opposite end.

"Understood." Isaac slightly bows his head.

"Harper and Russell," my gaze meets Harper's big blue eyes. "I'll need you to hold the northern border."

"Got it." Harper nods from the right side of the opposite end of the table. "This is going to be fun."

"Milo," I search his emotionless face at the opposite end of the large table as a tall man with blond hair stands at attention behind him. "You and your army will be responsible for holding the western border."

"Now remember," I say as I meet the eyes of everyone at the table. "We don't know which direction they'll be coming from, but let them come."

"Let me get this right," Milo shouts from the high

backed chair at the opposite end of the table. "You want them to attack the castle?"

"We do." Jace nods.

"What about all of the people who live here?" Russell puts his hands on the table as he sits to Harper's left, sandwiched between his Boss and Flynn.

"They've all been relocated to the safest part of the castle." I place my hands on the table and stand up. "And Ashgrave is on our side."

I pray to whoever can hear that my murderous castle remains loyal to me—otherwise all of his residents are dead.

"THE DRAGON GODS ARE APPROACHING THE WESTERN BORDER. THEY WILL ARRIVE SHORTLY, MY QUEEN." Ashgrave's voice thunders, shaking the large black iron chandelier above our heads, and we all rush toward the door and down the stairs.

Tucker makes it to the large double wooden doors of the entryway first and throws them both open. Come on, Brett," he shouts over his shoulder. "Let's blow these dragon gods to kingdom come." His green eyes meet mine, and his trademark goofy grin spreads across his face. "Kick some god ass, babe." He and Brett rush out the door and head for the jet.

Irena and Flynn follow my weapons expert out the door. They both shift when they enter the courtyard, and Irena roars a command to Flynn's rebels and her army.

Milo and his silent guard are on my sister and her mate's heels. They shift, and the Darrington Boss roars an order to his army as one hundred of our giant metal dragons enter the courtyard.

The Darrington and Vaer armies take to the sky as Jace, Drew, and I leave the castle and enter the front courtyard.

Levi and Jade follow us out the door and shift. My ice dragon's blue eyes meet mine, and he bows his head toward me.

Stay safe, Rory, he sends through our bond as his faith in me washes over my heart and mind. *Keep my brothers safe, too.*

I will. Keep an eye on Jade for me. I send my love, faith, and respect for him through our bond before I close it.

Levi roars into the air, and the huge steampunk dragons take to the sky as Jade sends me her gratitude and respect through our magical link. She and my ice dragon flap their wings hard to be in front of the metallic procession headed for Ash Town.

Isaac and Payton enter the courtyard with

Harper and Russell following them. Isaac approaches me and extends his hand.

"Rory, you honor me by allowing my family to take part in this battle." The Palarne Boss shakes my hand. "We cannot allow the dragon gods of old to rule our planet. The results would be catastrophic."

Isaac walks around the large fountain in the center of the courtyard, approaching his younger brother, and he and Payton shift. Isaac roars and earsplitting order into the sky, and the Palarne Boss and his general take to the air, heading toward the southern border.

A high-pitched clearing of a throat has my gaze meeting my friend's baby blue one, and Harper wraps her arms around me. "If we win this war, we will all be free, Rory."

"Freedom from chaos, manipulation, and an untimely death is definitely worth fighting for," I whisper into her blonde hair.

Drew and Jace shift into their dragon forms as Harper and I talk. Jace roars an order as our combined army of steampunk and dojo soldiers take to the air, heading west to take on the dragon gods.

"Let's free the world, Rory." Harper drops her arms, steps back, and transforms into her lavender thunderbird.

Harper approaches Russell's black thunderbird and nudges his shoulder. He turns his head to look at her, and she gives him a wink.

Well, that's new. I wonder if Harper and Russell have decided to let their family know about their feelings for one another.

Russell's earth shaking roar pulls me from Happily Ever After thoughts for the Fairfax Boss and her general. Harper and Russell take to the sky, followed by their army, and they head north to contain the dragon gods.

Jace winks a huge dragon eye at me as he takes off to follow our army. Drew approaches me, and I shift into my beautiful diamond dragon form. We take to the sky to face off against the dragon gods.

The cool early evening air wraps itself around my large form and caresses my wings as my eyes take in the amazing shades of blues, pinks, and purples in front of us as we head into battle against the ancient dragon gods.

I know that I am more powerful than them, even with their powers combined. All I need to do is make sure to keep my powers focused on the lighter side of the darkness that fuels my magic. I have to use my heart in this battle.

A roar sounds out from up ahead as I fly through

a low-lying cloud, and it makes my bones hurt. Morgana!

As the last of the wisps of cloud cover my face, washing everything a white-grey color, I spot the gods as they descend from the tallest mountain in the west and my heart pangs with dread. The gods' army just went past Ash Town.

How are things over there, Levi? I ask through our bond as his heart beat settles into a steady rhythm.

Things were a little scary when the gods and their monstrous army came through, he answers. *But we're having the metal dragons surround the town while Jade and I fly patrols around it, and the villagers are all locked inside their homes with their windows barricaded in case they decide to double back.*

Let me know if you need any help. Milo is defending the western border, so I don't think they'll head back that way. I send him a wishful image of the blond guard ripping the wings off of Morgana's dark green diamond dragon while still in human form. If only it were that easy.

Not if they want to live, they won't. Levi chuckles through our bond as he sends me images of the Darrington Boss ripping Caelan's head off and closes our connection.

A large army is heading straight for us. Some are

dragons, flying in the air, and others are humans who are marching down the switchbacks of the western mountain. By the unnatural slate grey color of most of the humans, I can tell that they're undead. Over half of the dragons have the same sickly grey tinge to their skin, and most of them are spreading ashes with every flap of their wings. The dragon gods march behind the undead, using their bodies as a moving shield.

The gods' army is an abomination, and if I don't end this today, this corruption will spread and infect the world.

CHAPTER THIRTY-THREE

Jace roars an order to stop the enemy at all costs. He sends a beam of his bright blue electrical energy toward the front line of the rival army, turning three slate grey dragons to royal blue ash.

Within moments, the gods' dragon army surrounds us, and the dojo soldiers team up with giant metallic dragons. One dojo soldier to five of the large steampunk ones. They initiate an aerial dance. The five huge metal dragons turn around with their backs to each other and hover in place as the thunderbirds fly in and out of the makeshift circle. The large steampunk dragons fire at the enemy as they approach, and the sleek, fast, and maneuverable thunderbirds blast those who come too close to the metal giants. Our army is working as a team, and they're blasting enemies from the sky all around me.

The tip of my wing brushes Drew's. *It's time to end this. Let's find the dragon gods*, I tell him through our telepathic connection.

Now you're speaking my language, love. He tucks his wings and heads for the mountain trails.

I tuck my wings and follow my fire dragon as he approaches the undead army that's entering the valley below.

Drew blasts a group of zombie soldiers, turning them into marching candles. The group of fiery undead fall in a heap, burning the grass around them and turning to ash.

As I fly over the gods' human-like soldiers, I spot Caelan alone in a cave alcove. I silently land on the ledge above him and notice Caelan's sitting with his legs crossed. He's moving his fingers with his eyes closed, like he's playing an invisible piano or moving imaginary marionette puppets. The death god's top lip has perspiration forming on it, and some of his white hair is plastered to his forehead. He's the weakest of the three because he's using all of his strength to animate the "undead" fighters the way he reanimated Zurie.

I stretch my long neck over the edge of the ledge and snap my jaws at the death god. Caelan's eyes remain closed as twelve undead dragons drop to join me on the ledge, shaking the ground with their unsteady landing. The quaking ground has me stepping back from the ledge, giving up on snapping the death god in half with my strong jaws.

Two of the dragons roar into the sky, sending death and decay into the air, making me hide my snout in the crook of my wing. I turn and smash in both of their heads with my large tail, smearing their foul smelling ash on my beautiful diamond scales.

I focus my sapphire blue energy into a one-inch beam and send it through the skull of six of the remaining sickly grey dragons. They fall in a heap on top of each other.

There are only four more of the decaying dragons moving. They surround me, and I summon my chaos magic. I blast them with the cold wild magic and concentrate on pattern and organization. My magic grows warm and then hot as their bodies of ash turn into solid stone.

I shift to my human self and silently stalk toward the ledge that hangs over the death god. As I lean my head over the edge, I spy Caelan dripping in sweat and shaking as he continues to move his fingers in the air.

All of the shock and hurt from seeing the woman who trained me to be the fighter I am today bubbles to the surface. All of the hurt and anger of Zurie's death plan rushes into me.

I drop from the top of the ledge and land silently on the balls of my feet next to Caelan. I pool my magic into my fists and punch him in the side of the head, knocking him over. I straddle his chest and his red eyes pop wide open. I pummel the death god's head with my magic infused fists until his head collapses and flakes away in the wind of the January evening. To be sure the death god is really dead, I blast him with my magic and turn the rest of his body to maya-blue ash.

What the hell? My magic just changed to a lighter shade of blue. How did that happen?

Tucker's jet screams overhead, and I shift into my dragon form and enter the battle again. As I fly over the gruesome scene below me, I notice all of the undead soldiers are either turned to ash and blowing away into the evening sky, or are truly dead now. The gods' are not only down a god, they're down three-quarters of their army.

I hover and concentrate on the pull of each of my

men. Tucker is about three hundred feet to the west of me in his jet. Drew is fifty feet to my left in the valley, and I spot his massive red form burning the fallen undead with his blue-red flames. Jace and a few giant metal dragons are fending off some of the enemy dragons a hundred and fifty feet to my left. Levi's bright blue beam is over fifteen miles away, protecting Ash Town.

A voice cuts through the chaotic battle around me. "Help, Rory!"

Oh shit!

It's Irena.

I search the area below me and spot her in her human form, entangled in a dragon net, bleeding. I tuck my wings and dive, landing a few feet away from my injured sister.

Whoever did this to Irena is going to die, slowly and painfully.

CHAPTER THIRTY-FOUR

My gaze meets my sister's, and a drop of blood trails from her forehead down the side of her nose.

A giant metallic dragon crashes into the valley not far from me, and I lift my wing to protect my head and face from the gravel, grass, and pieces of metal that spray into the air. The ground buckles beneath my feet as the huge steampunk dragon explodes, sending shrapnel into the sky and causing the other metallic dragons to howl out in pain. Blue dust from the destroyed dragon slowly drifts through the air and covers my shimmering diamond scales. Some of it travels past me and blankets the nearby valley.

A sigh escapes my lips as I remember how the giant steampunk dragons were working well with the dojo soldiers earlier. I wonder what must have happened to the rest of the dragons in this one's group. I know that Ashgrave can make more massive metallic dragons, but his loss will still be felt.

I shift into my human form and run over to lift the heavy braided dragon net from Irena. She drops her gaze to the spikes keeping the trap locked into the ground. My feet carry me to the closest spike, and I yank it from the ground and head toward the one on my right.

"Are you okay?" I ask my sister.

"I will be once I'm out of here." She wipes the blood dripping from her nose with the back of her hand.

"How did you get caught in this humongous net, Irena?" I pull a spike from the ground and rush toward the next one without looking at my sister.

"I was shot out of the sky as I circled the eastern mountain. The one furthest from Ash Town." My sister points to another spike to her left.

"Where is Flynn and your army?" I yank the spike she pointed at from the ground with a grunt.

"Making sure no one from the gods' zombie

army can leave the eastern border and spread their decay to the rest of the world." Irena's chin touches her chest. "Are your men close?"

"Close enough." I pull the last spike loose from the ground. "Do you think we will need back up?"

She shakes her head and shrugs her shoulders as I pull the huge net off her. I run to Irena's side and kneel next to her, pushing her black hair out of her face. My sister's glowing green eyes morph into golden orbs, and her tanned skin changes to an almost translucent white. My sister's five foot nine inch hourglass form morphs into an over six foot tall man with a swimmer's build.

What the fuck?

Razorus! It was all an illusion.

Fan-freaking-tastic!

I put my hands on the ground and try to push myself up, but the trickster god places his hands on either side of my face and his golden eyes pierce mine as he forces his mind into mine.

He forces an image of Drew being frozen into a solid block of ice as he battles three blue ice dragons —and then shatters into a million tiny shards. The image shifts to Tucker flying his plane through a silver-blue cloud, electrical sparks shooting from the jet's engine as flames erupt from the huge anti-dragon gun sitting on top of it. The plane becomes enveloped in red and orange flames as it plummets into the green valley below, exploding on impact. The movie in my brain changes to an image of my mate's black thunderbird, sending blue electricity into a fire dragon, but then other thunderbirds corner him and blast him with their combined powers of electricity and flame. Jace roars out in pain and explodes, causing the nearby mountains, the valley below, and everyone in them to be covered with his royal blue ash.

I place my hands over Razorus's, and he sends me another image. This time it's of my sister. Irena is surrounded by Vaer dragons while Flynn lies motionless behind her. The orange fire dragons send blue-green flames into my sister's chest, smothering the blast of green ice she has aimed for them, and her chest erupts with flames. She lashes her bronze tail back and forth but can't free herself from the attack. Irena sends a painful howl into the night sky as she erupts into sickly grey ash.

My head drops to my chest as I try to fight the mental onslaught, but the trickster god keeps his grip on my head. Razorus sends an image of my ice dragon battling with two massive red fire dragons.

The red dragons dip and dive in the sky as they chase Levi through the mountains surrounding Ash Town. Levi is fast, really fast. He evades the fire dragons without a problem until a giant, orange fire dragon drops from the cover of a cloud and my ice dragon tucks his wings to dive toward the enormous western mountain top. One of the red dragons clips Levi's wing, and he spins head over heels, crashing into the side of the mountain and causing an avalanche.

My chest pangs with each loss the trickster god sends into my brain.

Levi's mind caresses mine. *Are you okay?*

What? How? My confusion leaks through our bond. *I thought you crashed and died?*

Nope. Just flying around keeping watch over Ash Town. He sends me soothing thoughts through our bond. *I sensed your loss and needed to check in with you.*

The only loss that's happening is the death of two more dragon gods. I send him my gratitude and love before closing our connection.

A massive bronze dragon lands, shaking the ground beneath our feet, and the trickster god stumbles backward, losing his grasp on my head.

I suck in deep breaths of cool mountain air and

struggle to my feet, wiping away the tears from my face.

My sister approaches me, placing her wing tip against my back. *Are you okay, little sister?*

I will be when this asshole is dead, I send to her through our telepathic connection. *It's time for Razorus to die. You blast him, and I'll teach him what the gods' power is truly capable of.*

This is gonna be fun, she says, removing her wing from my back and circling around to face off against the manipulative god, putting space between her and me.

Irena sends a blast of green ice magic into the ground near Razorus's feet, and he stumbles backward toward me. I place my hands on both sides of his head and he falls to his knees with his golden eyes wide. The trickster god struggles to free his head from my vise like grip as I focus my chaos magic into my palms and force my power into Razorus's skull. His eyes bulge in response to my magic flooding his brain.

My palms grow warm as I concentrate on order, peace, and truth. I send images of Caelan and how he was alone when I destroyed him, along with images of Jace and Drew working side-by-side as they train our army of thunderbirds and giant steampunk dragons, turning the soldiers' weaknesses into strengths. The trickster god whips his head backward to stop my mental attack, but I keep my hands locked around his skull, sending him thoughts of Levi and Tucker. My ice dragon and weapons expert were the first of my men to form a bond.

I want to show the trickster god that these bonds will never be broken, that our truth is greater than any lie he tries to assault us with. And most of all, I'm letting Razorus know that his time is up. He continues to fight against my iron grip as my hands glow a mayan blue, and they start to heat to an almost unbearable temperature. I gaze into his golden eyes as they turn an ice blue color, and his body shakes, erupting in ice blue ash.

The snap of a branch being stepped on has my eyes searching the copse of trees to my left as I brush the sparkling ice-blue ash from my hands. Morgana stands with a stoic expression on her face as her empty eye sockets narrow at me.

The goddess of chaos doesn't shed a tear for her dead brother as she pushes past a few of her downed dragons whose chests rattle as they take their last breaths. Morgana shifts into her familiar green dragon and rushes toward Castle Ashgrave.

Oh, hell no. My people are there!

That evil goddess isn't going to hurt my subjects or take my castle. I'll kill her if she tries. After all, I'm the one true queen of Castle Ashgrave. Not Morgana.

CHAPTER THIRTY-FIVE

I shift into my dragon form and fly toward my murderous castle with my sister hot on my golden striped tail.

Irena catches up to me and brushes the tip of her wing against mine. *Who in the hell is that green diamond dragon? And where the fuck are you going, Rory?*

To my castle, to stop Morgana, I tell her through our link. *Can you grab my men and our allies after you guys finish off what's left of the gods' army and meet me there?*

Will do, little sister. Go kick that crazy bitch's ass. Irena removes the tip of her wing, breaking the connection as she turns back toward the dwindling battle.

I land with a loud thud and quickly shift into my

human form as I rush through the open entry door of my castle. My feet come to a halt as I perk my ears to any sound that doesn't belong to my home. The grumble of someone talking under their breath comes from my throne room as I silently stalk toward the open door.

I approach the archway and peek inside. Morgana is sitting with both of her legs draped over one arm of my wooden throne.

"That girl has no taste. This throne should be made of gold and silver, not wood." Morgana snarls, and my bones chill. "Castle, change this throne to something more respectful." Her voice echoes in the large room.

"Ashgrave, ignore her," I say, approaching the center of the room with my eyes trained on Morgana's chin. There's something about peering into her empty eye sockets that turns my stomach.

"Stop confusing my castle, dragon vessel." Morgana places her feet on the stone floor in front of her and stands. "We all know that I am the one true queen, and I am to be obeyed."

I roll my eyes at the goddess of chaos and wonder how Ashgrave tolerated her attitude for eons. My murderous castle is smart and smiteful, but he is also kind.

"Who do you obey, castle?" The goddess of chaos asks Ashgrave with a sneer on her lips.

"MY QUEEN," my evil butler booms, rattling the heavy crystal chandelier that hangs over my head.

"Prove it," she orders. "Destroy the dragon vessel, you impotent fool."

This is it.

Who will Ashgrave be loyal to? Me? Or Morgana?

There's a pregnant silence, and I can't suck in enough air to fill my lungs. My heart stops beating in my chest as I think of metal hands raising through the stone floor of the Hall of Heroes, crushing all of the residents of Castle Ashgrave, and the giant metallic dragons turning on my allies and turning them to ash.

I imagine a huge metal hand plucking Tucker's jet from the air and the metallic hull of the plane screaming as the hand crushes the jet into dust. I suck in a breath of air and keep my face an emotionless mask as I think of Levi launching himself straight up into the air as one of Ashgrave's metallic hands attempts to catch him. My ice dragon could escape the first hand that reaches for him, but he'd be caught in one that extends from the top of the mountain. I push from my mind the very real threat of the metal hand crushing Levi into sapphire-cerulean dust.

The image of Drew being grabbed by a hand that appears beneath him and being pulled underground without a sound has my breath freezing in my chest. My mind floats to the bronze dragon that is my sister, and two metal hands catching her mid-air as she flies toward the remainder of the battle against the gods' army, crushing her into green snow. My heart aches at the thought of Flynn sending an earsplitting roar into the sky, drawing the attention of my mate—of Jace blasting the hands holding the green snow, and a giant metal hand reaching up and plucking him from the air, stopping his electrical beam. In my anxious vision, my mate turns his power to the hand holding him as the hand squeezes him, and the royal blue magic suddenly stops sparking.

My gaze drifts to Morgana, and a smirk tugs the corner of her lips like she can read the micro expressions on my face as well as Tucker can. "I have told you before that I am the one true queen."

"NO!" Ashgrave's voice retorts. "YOU ARE NOT THE ONE TRUE QUEEN OF ASHGRAVE. YOU MAY HAVE CREATED ME, BUT YOU HAVE NOT BEEN MY QUEEN FOR A LONG, LONG TIME,

MORGANA. THE ONE TRUE AND POWERFUL QUEEN OF ASHGRAVE—AND ALL MAGIC—IS RORY QUINN."

My heart beats solidly against my chest.

I really do love my evil butler. I can't imagine my life without him and his murderous nature.

The goddess of chaos growls and blast a hole in the stone floor near my feet. I do a backflip and land with my knees bent and my fists clenched in front of me. Winds appear out of nowhere, pulling at my hair and rattling the huge chandelier.

Morgana approaches me, surrounded by whipping winds. Sickly grey tentacles rise from her back, dancing and writhing like they're alive and have a mind of their own. I step away from the goddess of chaos as one of the wispy grey arms wraps itself around my waist and hoists me into the air near the hanging chandelier, upside down. As suddenly as the tentacle appeared, it disappears, and I fall from about fifteen feet in the air to the hard stone floor. A sickening crunch comes from my right shoulder as burning pain rushes through it, and my right arm hangs lifeless.

"Ha ha ha!" Morgana looks down her nose at me as I lie on the floor. "Today you will give me what is mine, little human."

I spring from the floor in one fluid motion as my left shoulder burns with an ungodly heat, healing itself.

I turn to face Morgana, being sure to keep out of reach of the tentacles that writhe around her like grey snakes. I place both palms out in front of me and focus on forming my battle axe. The curved handle of the axe forms in my hands, and I step forward and swing it at two of the grey dancing tentacles. My huge, magically charged battle axe slices four feet of the tip of two of them, sending the wiggling grey tops to the stone floor with a loud squish. The tentacles turn to grey ash, and a blood curdling scream erupts from Morgana. The sound sends ribbons of goosebumps marching across my skin.

"You will never stop being hunted." Morgana lashes at me with her remaining two tentacles, and I step backward out of their reach. "There will always be someone who will match your power and take you down," the goddess of chaos threatens.

"Really?" I ask as I allow my axe to disappear and concentrate my chaos magic into my hands. "I pity anyone stupid enough to put their life on the line like that. Especially when I hold all of the power of the dragon gods."

As I concentrate my chaos magic, I also call my death and trickster magic forth, combining all three. I focus my ice blue magic into my hands and rush toward Morgana, and place one hand on her chest while holding her in place with a strong hand on her back. Her empty sockets widen, and her jaw drops open as my palms warm up as I force peace, love, and heart into her body. She struggles against my grip as my hands become unbearably hot. They're so hot that I'm wondering if the white magic sparking from them are actually flames.

I picture the faces of my men, Tucker and his goofy grin, Levi and the way his eyes hold secrets for everyone but me, Drew and the way his large body demands to be followed, and Jace and the way our mate-bond completes us both. I focus all of the love I have for my men into the goddess of chaos. A white light shoots from Morgana's mouth as she turns to glimmering white ash in my grip.

CHAPTER THIRTY-SIX

I need to check on my lords and the battle outside.

As I turn for the door, I kick the pile of shimmering ash with my bare foot. I rush out of the open door and sprint for the courtyard to shift.

As I enter the courtyard, the sun brightens the eastern mountains, sending glittering rays of orange, red, and gold across the white marble fountain. Ashgrave remade it in my image after the battle with Kinsley. A sigh rushes from my lips as I'm reminded that my evil butler chose me over his creator.

I spy Irena, Tucker, Brett, Flynn, Jace, and Drew gathered in a circle with our army, the Vaer army, and the rest of our allies surrounding them on the other side of the stone wall, and I quickly make my way toward them.

Harper shifts back to her human form and rushes toward me, wrapping her arms around me. "You did it, Rory. You destroyed all three dragon gods."

"What about their army?" I ask the back of her head.

"They're gone." She puts her hands on my shoulders and leans me away from her.

"What do you mean, they're gone?" I quirk a questioning brow.

"She means, the undead humans and dragons exploded into ash the minute you destroyed Caelan." Milo gives me a huge smile.

"But they weren't all zombies. What happened to the dragons?" My lip quirks up into a smirk.

"After you ashed Razorus, love," Drew says, winking at me, "they were easier to take out. And once Morgana was destroyed, they began taking out each other."

"Shit!" I sigh.

The gods manipulated their army to fight for them, and now that they're all dead, the army literally fell apart. I shake my head, refusing to try and make sense of the gods' insanity.

"Three cheers for Queen Rory. The destroyer of gods!" Isaac shouts. "All hail Queen Rory!"

The armies all join together to cheer for me, and a thundering, "Queen Rory," fills the valleys surrounding Castle Ashgrave.

You're turning red, beautiful, Levi tells me through our connection. His love, support, and admiration flow into me.

How did everything go? I ask, reciprocating the flow of affection. *Are the villagers of Ash Town all right?*

I wouldn't have come back if they weren't, he jokes. *But seriously, Jade and I didn't have any excitement after the initial shock of the gods' zombie army.*

So I was busy killing gods and you and Jade were having fun running patrols? I joke, sending him a mental image of him and Jade running in a hamster wheel.

A scratchy dragon laugh comes from behind me, and I turn to meet Levi's ice blue gaze as Drew in his human form places his hand on my back.

You're so damn funny, Levi. I chuckle through our connection.

I think Drew needs your attention for a minute. I'm going to go see how the new toys worked for Tucker, he says as he sends admiration and contentment through our bond before breaking it.

I turn toward my fire dragon. He pulls me into his hard chest and heat pools between my legs. I take a deep breath to calm the desire flooding through me at being naked in Drew's arms.

"I always knew you were a queen," Drew whispers into my ear. "And I want to spend every moment of my life proving myself worthy of you."

Tears tingle in my eyes, but someone clearing their throat has me turning my head to spot my sister.

"Do you mind if we have some sister time, big fella?" She elbows my fire dragon in the ribs, and he unwraps me from his arms to protect himself from Irena's boney elbows.

"Sure, go ahead." He rolls his eyes and turns to follow Levi. "I'll have her for the rest of my life. What's a few minutes in the scheme of things?"

Irena rushes to my side and places her hand in mine, raising it above my head. All of the Vaer, Palarne, Fairfax, Darrington, and my armies send an outlandish applause out into the early morning sky.

My sister lowers our arms, and a massive orange dragon shifts into his human form, keeping his eyes lowered to the ground in front of him as he approaches us. The Vaer dragons and Flynn and his rebels shift also.

"Who's that?" I whisper to my sister.

"Tergarthen, the commander of my elite warriors," Irena responds, making sure to keep her voice low so that only I can hear her.

"Congratulations, Ms. Quinn, on an outstanding display of power." The commander drops to one knee in front of us, and the entire Vaer army and Flynn's rebels follow his lead.

"Well, thank you, Tergarthen," I reply.

"If it pleases you, mistress?" Tergarthen raises his eyes to my sister's. "We, the Vaer army, would like to declare again our devotion to Irena Quinn, Queen of the Vaer."

My jaw drops open, and my eyes go wide as my gaze wanders over the entire Vaer army. Flynn and every one of his rebels join the Vaer on bended knee with their chins to their chests as they bow to my sister.

Flynn stands and approaches my sister and me. He places Irena's hand in his, giving her a smile as bright as the sun, and her face turns deep red. She avoids looking down at his naked form by looking into my brown eyes with her glowing green ones.

"Rory… " Flynn catches my attention and I turn

my eyes away from my sister to meet his gaze. "I need to ask for your blessing?"

"Blessing for what?" I ask, rolling my eyes as everyone around me laughs. Even the giant steam punk dragons let out their sandpaper rubbing against sandpaper chuckles, and my face heats up, and I know my face is turning a shade of red to rival my sister's.

"Oh my gods! Are you serious?" My eyes bounce between their beaming faces. "Of course you have my blessing." I wrap my arms around both of their necks, not caring that we're all standing in front of thousands of dragon shifters, naked as the day we were born. "Just keep her happy, Flynn."

"I promise I'll spend the rest of my life trying, little sister," Flynn whispers in my ear.

I release my sister, the Vaer Boss, and her Andusk rebel leader fiancé, and step back to observe the massive allied army in front of me. They are all on one knee with their heads bowed. I swallow back the tears that want to leak from my eyes as Irena and Flynn step back and drop to one knee also. My eyes travel over all of the familiar heads in the group—Harper's long blonde locks, Payton and Isaac's black curls, Milo's dark chocolate brown mane, Jade's waist length tresses that touch the ground as she kneels, and Brett's mop of short black hair.

I've always felt like I was alone in life, and now I know I'm far from it. Rule 2 of the Spectres—trust no one.

I'm so happy I'm not a Spectre anymore.

My eyes wander over the crowd, and I spot Tucker's familiar dark-brown chin length shaggy mop, and next to him is Levi with his ear length light brown head. Drew's black short curly locks are sandwiched between my ice dragon and my mate's blond head. As if Jace can feel my gaze on him, his stormy grey eyes rise to meet mine. He gives me a wink and mouths "My queen."

A heavy weight is gently placed on my head, and I raise my hands to touch the item. My fingers slide over eight points that sit equal lengths apart, and stones as big as my thumb are imbedded in the top of each of those points. It's the crown from the treasury.

Ashgrave finally managed to place the crown on my head. A smile graces my face as I'm reminded that my evil butler chose me. He's loyal to me and our family. Castle Ashgrave is a true member of our family, and I love him.

"Please rise," I announce to the thousands of friends and family surrounding me.

My gaze drifts over my men, and I spot all of their mouths drop open at the sight of me in the crown and nothing else. Drew puts his arm around Jace's shoulder and bright smiles light up their faces. Tucker and Levi give each other a high-five as their eyes beam with love for me.

"Please stay, because not only will we be celebrating this victory, but also the new Vaer Boss—my sister, Irena." I suck in a deep breath and smile at my sister and Flynn. "And her engagement to her mate, Flynn Blackwell."

My sister raises her fist and shakes it at me, like she's upset that I told everyone about her and Flynn being mates. A smile lightens her face, and I know she's just joking. Knowing her, she's probably relieved to not have to hide her love for Flynn.

"We will also be celebrating the birth of the eighth dragon family—the Quinn family—my family. The family that resides at Castle Ashgrave." The cheers of the crowd become deafening.

I raise my arms in the air and the crowd goes silent. "The celebration will take place tomorrow at twilight in the ball room." Jace nods his head at me. "Rest well, friends," I say looking out over the

Palarne army. "And family," I say to the Vaer, Darrington, and Fairfax armies.

My eyes take in the way my lords' faces glows with happiness, and I know that I will never be happier than I am right now.

CHAPTER THIRTY-SEVEN

The sun casts orange, yellow, and golden beams of light through my large arched windows in my bedroom. I roll over in my comfy bed and trace the muscles in Jace's bicep. His arm is over his head with his hand covering his face as he lies on his back, and he's snoring softly.

I drop my hand and scoot over to my side of the bed and quietly place my feet on the floor. I think it's time to visit the newest member of our family.

Last night the residents of the castle moved back to their original rooms with the exception of the new parents. They were given the larger suite with two bedrooms, a private sitting room, bathroom, and balcony. The littlest member of the Quinn family lives down the hall from me and across the hall from Jade.

My toes curl in the white fur carpet beneath my feet as I remember Jade asking if she could share some of the baby items out of a few of her magazines with Ashgrave. I hope she and my evil butler didn't go overboard with baby gifts for the tiny girl. All I asked was to make sure the new parents had lots and lots of diapers and wipes.

I shake my head and chuckle to myself as I head to my closet to get dressed. I throw on a pair of white washed jeans, an ice blue sweater, and a pair of blue tennis shoes. I rush to my bathroom and quickly brush my teeth and run a brush through my long brown locks. As I look at myself in the mirror, a smile crosses my face.

There are no more dragon gods to worry about. All of my enemies have been destroyed, and my men and I can start a new life as a family—a true dragon family.

Today's going to be an amazing day.

I quietly make my way to my bedroom door and silently turn the knob, only to turn back to spy on my mate who is still in the same position that I left him in, softly snoring. I step out into the hallway and close the door behind me.

As I approach the door to the young parents' quarters, I observe the beauty of my castle. The way the sun glimmers off the golden threads in the drapes that frame the floor-to-ceiling windows. Iridescent rainbows glimmer over the walls and ceiling as the morning sunlight shines through the crystals of the chandeliers and sconces.

"The queen wants us to have all of this for our child?" A young woman asks as I approach the open door of the young parents' suite.

"SHE DEMANDS THE CHILD HAVE EVERY-THING SHE NEEDS," Ashgrave attempts to whisper, but fails. His loud voice shakes the sconces in the hall outside the suite.

I approach the door and spot huge stuffed dragons that resemble me and my men, a pink bassinet, piles of small pink, white, and purple clothes, and mountains of diapers and baby wipes. I cover my mouth with my hand to stop my laugh from escaping.

My evil butler went overboard.

"Good morning," I tell the blonde haired mother who is cradling a small pink blanket in her arms. A tall dark haired man puts his arms around her shoulder. The pink blanket moves, and a tiny hand pops out.

The young couples' eyes drop to the floor. "Good morning, my queen."

"I'm really not into formalities," I confess. "Especially within my own family."

Their eyes meet mine, and smiles grace both of their faces.

"I'm so happy that you count us as your family, my queen," the father tells me as he hugs his wife close. "My name is Peter DuBois." He kisses his pretty wife on the cheek. "And this is my wife, Claire." The young man who doesn't appear any older than I am, reaches his pinkie out toward the pink blanket, and a tiny hand reaches up and grabs it. "The tiniest member of our family is Blanche."

"Like Blanche DuBois in A Streetcar Named Desire?" I raise a questioning brow at the young couple.

"No. Like my great, great grandmother who was born in 1817." He winks at me. "It was a family name long before it was made famous by a play."

"Would you like to hold the baby, mistress?" Claire moves toward me, holding out the bundle in the pink blanket. "Here, hold her head like this," She tells me, placing my hand gently behind the baby's head.

My eyes take in the little girl in the blanket. She

has a tuft of red hair on the top of her head, crystal green eyes like her mother's, and the chubbiest cheeks I think I've ever seen.

"She's perfect." My eyes drift upward toward her parents' faces, and they're beaming with pride.

Little Blanche squirms and her mouth searches for food against my chest. "She's hungry." Claire reaches toward me, and I hand her back her baby girl.

"Thank you for letting me visit with her," I tell them. "She's adorable."

"Anytime you want to spend time with her, you're welcome to," Peter says with a grin.

"I'll probably take you up on that." I smile. "I haven't been around babies, so Blanche will be the first one."

Peter stands taller and puffs out his chest. "My que—"

I cut him off. "We're family. Please, call me Rory."

He nods his head while Claire puts a blanket over her shoulder, covering herself and the baby. "Rory, we would be honored if you would be Blanche's godmother. I know it's a lot to ask and you don't really know us, but…"

I just told this man that he's a member of my family. He and his pregnant wife came all the way here to give their baby a new life. I can't deny him this.

I place my hand on his shoulder. "I'd be honored. But which of my men will be the godfather?"

"All of them," Claire says from the chair she's nursing her daughter in. "Blanche will be the most fortunate girl in the world with all of you protecting her."

A chuckle escapes my lips. "I sure hope you never want her to date. My men are very protective."

"They will also spoil her rotten." Peter holds out his hand pointing to a corner of the room that's filled with over a hundred dolls of all shapes and sizes. "They all brought her over twenty-five dolls each last night."

I nod my head. "That does sound like them."

Claire puts Blanche against her chest, and the baby's little head presses against her mother's shoulder. Claire pats her back, and moments later, a loud burp echoes in the room.

"I think it's time for our little blessing to go down for a nap." Claire gets up from her chair and heads toward the door at the back of the room. "You're welcome to stay, Rory. I mean, it *is* your castle."

"I need to get things ready for the party tonight." I step toward the open door. "You will all be joining us, right? I can't have a celebration without my goddaughter and her parents."

"We'd be honored to celebrate with our family tonight," Peter says as I walk out the open door.

I head toward the stairway—I need my coffee. And a cup of my anti-pregnancy tea. One baby in the castle is enough.

Jade's voice travels to me as I approach the open door of the kitchen. "You need to ask Rory if you're serious about marrying me, Brett. She's our Boss, but besides that, she's like a big sister to me."

"Will that make you happy?" Brett asks Jade.

"Extremely," she tells him as I step inside the room that holds my caffeinated goodness.

"Am I interrupting?" I head toward the always-full coffee pot and reach into the cabinet above it to grab a cup.

"I have a question for you," Brett says as Jade's happiness and worry battle each other through our strange magical bond. "May I please have your blessing to marry Jade?"

I place my empty mug on the counter next to the coffee pot, and it instantly fills with my anti-pregnancy tea. I guess Ashgrave feels the same way about more than one baby in the castle at one time, and a smile crosses my face.

"It's about damn time." I turn around lifting my mug of steaming tea to my lips.

"Really?" Jade asks as she rushes toward me and wraps an arm around my waist, being careful not to spill any of my tea.

"Absolutely." I place my free arm around her slender shoulders and grin at her.

"I don't mean to change the subject, but are the treaties all ready for signing tonight, Brett?" My eyes meet his as Jade and I keep our arms around each other.

"They're all set, Boss." He nods at me. "This is the first time in history that a new dragon family was formed by a living goddess. Usually they're formed after centuries of civil war, or at least that's what the mural room shows."

"Seriously?" Jade and I ask at the same time.

Brett looks at Jade's face and then mine. "Seriously. You're a goddess who not only used one of the dragon gods' powers but all three *and* against the gods themselves." My public relations expert shakes his head and drops his gaze to the marble tile at his feet. "Rory, you defended the world against the gods, solidified your sister's seat of power, and have an unbreakable alliance with four of the most formidable dragon families there have ever been. No matter what, the Vaer, Palarne, Fairfax, Darrington, and Quinn will always be allies. Hell, if you think about it. Three of the four allies are actually family."

"Oh, shit. I never thought of it like that." I turn my head to search Jade's eyes.

She nods her head. "Not only that, Rory. You killed the dragon gods. All the Knights could do was trap them, but you actually took them out by using their own power against them. They're going to write books and songs, and maybe even movies about you."

"I sure hope not." I take another sip of my bitter tea. "All I want is to be left alone with my friends and family. I don't want to be famous, just loved for who I am."

"And you are truly loved, Rory." Jade squeezes my waist with her hand and her love for me rushes into me through our bond.

"Thanks, Jade. I love you too."

Now *this* is what I've needed my entire life—and I couldn't think of any other group of people I'd rather enjoy this life with.

D rums, flutes, horns, and mandolins fill the castle with glorious music as I stand on my balcony dressed in a black sequined gown with a sweetheart neckline and a slimming waist, accented by a wide, white sequined belt in the hour or so before twilight. I watch as the golden Andusk dragons land in the courtyard, and my giant steampunk dragons roar at them, forcing them to shift into their human forms. Two Vaer elite warriors and two Palarne soldiers show them to their assigned tent out in the courtyard. Inside the tent are clothes, food, and drink so they can be comfortable before the treaty signing and the party.

The Bane and Nabal representatives arrived a couple of hours ago. Aki asked to see his daughter, but Jade refused to talk with him. She doesn't hate her father, but she will never trust him. Thanks to Jade and our special bond, I know that she's happy and loved.

My bedroom door opens and I spy Tucker, Levi, Drew, and Jace walking in, dressed in black tuxedos with white cumberbuns looking dashing. I leave the sanctity of my balcony and join my lords in my bedroom.

"THEY ARE READY FOR YOU IN THE BALL-ROOM, MY QUEEN," Ashgrave's voice booms.

"Will you be joining us, Ashgrave?" I ask my murderous castle.

"I WOULD BE HONORED, MISTRESS," he replies and appears in the air next to me in his cat-sized metallic dragon form wearing a bow tie.

My bedroom door opens automatically.

"Guess it's time to get the party started, babe," Tucker says and places a kiss on the top of my head, making sure not to mess up the up do that's topped off with a small silver tiara that glitters with diamonds.

I refused to put the giant crown back on my head, but I compromised on the small tiara.

Drew taps the tip of the tiara and places a kiss on my cheek. "At least you're wearing something that represents your station, love."

Levi takes my hand in his. "Rory, you're stunning. Finally, the whole world can see you the way I see you." My ice dragon turns my hand over in his and gently kisses my palm.

Jace approaches me as Levi steps toward his brothers. My mate wraps me in his arms and gives me a heated kiss that makes me want to throw him on the bed and stay there all night.

"Rory, my queen… " Jace kisses my right collar-bone. "We are the luckiest men in the world. When we all started this adventure, we only knew that we all loved you." He kisses my left collarbone. "But now, we know that we're brothers, who will have each other's back for as long as we walk this world." My mate kisses the middle of my chest where my cleavage meets the dress. "We are a brotherhood that was formed at the dojo, and we thank you for bringing us together."

My eyes go misty. "Enough of this mushy stuff. We have treaties to sign and a party to get to." I turn from my men, and Ashgrave's little metallic body hovers closely behind me as I approach the stairs and walk down them, heading for the ballroom.

The joyous music envelopes the hallway as I approach the three sets of open doors of the massive ballroom. Tucker and Levi are close behind Ashgrave as I step inside the huge room full of people.

"ALL BOW TO THE ONE TRUE QUEEN OF ASHGRAVE, AND BOSS OF THE QUINN FAMILY, RORY QUINN." My evil butler's voice booms, shaking the monstrous chandeliers and making the music come to an abrupt halt.

Every gaze in the room lowers to the floor in deference to me as I approach the official treaty and the music starts filling the massive room again. My men move in, surrounding me from behind, and Ashgrave flies over the table.

"Please announce Irena as the new Vaer Boss when she arrives," I whisper to my evil butler, and he flutters one of his metal eyes closed and opens it quickly.

As I sign the treaty, I notice all of the families have already signed except me and my sister. I sign seven pages of the treaty that spells out the new rules. There will be no more stealing, smuggling, or drug trafficking. Humans and dragons are now considered equal and must work together to better the world economy.

"ALL HAIL THE NEW VAER BOSS, IRENA QUINN," my little metal dragon thunders, and I turn around to spot my sister walking into the ballroom that's decorated with white and green roses, dressed in an emerald green spaghetti strapped gown with a slit all the way up her left thigh, her black hair is straightened, and a small emerald tiara sits on top of her head. My mouth drops open as I watch her and Flynn approach me and my men.

"Close your mouth, little sister. It looks like you're trying to catch flies," Irena whispers and embraces me, hugging me so hard that I can't breathe. "Thanks for the announcement by the way." She releases me, and I suck in a deep breath.

"You ready to make it all official?" I hand her a pen and give her the pages I've already signed.

"You know they're calling you the Warrior Queen," my sister whispers as we sign the treaty that will change the world as we know it, for good.

"Who's calling me that?" I ask.

"Elizabeth, Aki, and Victor." She winks at me.

"I guess they're still a little butt-hurt about losing to me, huh?"

"You could say that again." Irena chuckles.

"Good!" I hand my sister the last page of the treaty and turn around to face my men.

Warrior Queen.

I love it. I'll continue to fight against injustice.

My eyes pan the ballroom, and I spot Peter, Claire, and little baby Blanche DuBois who are sitting at a table near the back of the packed room with Liam, the red headed nurse from the dojo, Aubrey, a strawberry blonde girl with chubby cheeks and freckles, and our friend Reggie. A huge smile crawls up my face at the sight of the people who will always have a special place in my heart.

I vow to take in refugees who need a place to be

safe, loved, and belong. Everyone needs a place to be known—even humans.

Levi's mind massages mine. *What's the matter?*

I want to fly, I tell him as my dragon roars in my head. *I'm a queen, and I need to be free.*

Then let's fly. Levi's love, admiration, and need to fly flood through our bond before he closes it.

I rush out the door with my men and Ashgrave hot on my tail. We get to the stairs and Tucker runs down them two at a time. Levi must have told him that I want to fly, and he's headed for his jet.

As I swing open the floor-to-ceiling windows at the end of the hallway, I jump out into the cool night air. I drop a few feet, and my strong wings carry me upward as I circle my castle.

As I glide over a small pond near the eastern wall that surrounds Castle Ashgrave, a weight settles over my body. I peer down into the pond, and the gold and white filigree dragon armor glimmers in the light of the setting sun. The armor is rightfully mine, and I'm reminded of that fact as the sense of right-ness floods my heart. I soar through the air with the wind being the only sound in my ears.

My little steampunk dragon, blue ice dragon, red fire dragon, and black thunderbird close in behind me as I approach the tallest spire of the castle. The black spire rises over one hundred feet at the center of my castle. I land on the top of the tower and watch as thousands of people flock to my land in celebration—in a desire to be near me and to support me.

The scream of a jet engine lets me know Tucker is on his way to join me and his brothers in celebration. Ashgrave, Levi, Jace, Drew, and Tucker fly in circles around me, and I send sparks of white energy into the sky and they explode like fireworks into the air. I allow a victory roar to erupt from my core, sending the people who are approaching into a fit of raucous applause. They see me for who I am.

I broke Zurie's chains and forged my own destiny, exposed Kinsley's lies for what they were and gave humanity the truth, and I delivered justice against tyrant gods who would destroy humans and dragonkind alike.

And, it feels damn good.

I'm the new Boss of the eighth family—the Queen of Dragons.

My men and I are finally forming a world much better than the one I grew up in, where peace and justice reigns.

I will always protect my men and my family with every fiber of my being, but in this moment I know that I'm responsible for more than just them—the downtrodden, the oppressed and weary—they all have a home here.

They all have a home with me here at Castle Ashgrave.

AUTHOR NOTES

Hey, babe!

This book was an invigorating rush that I couldn't stop typing.

I'm sure your heart pounded just like mine, experiencing the hair-raising action as Rory and her team not only face Kinsley Vaer—but the ancient dragon gods also. And, of course, there's the gratifying, fiery love scene between her and Tucker, which shows us just how sexy our loveable goofball can be.

Rory knows the end game is near. There's a deadly war coming, and she's going to be the one to finish it. But first, she needs the lords orb to strengthen her men and to bring Ashgrave to his full power.

Kinsley Vaer makes a pact with the dragon gods —triggering the gods and aiming them in Rory's direction. Rory uses all of her magic and wit to fend off the goddess of chaos, the god of deception, and the death god and his army of undead. But will it be enough?

Rory still questions Ashgrave's loyalty, especially with Morgana free. But she's not giving up her evil butler without a fight. He's become an important part of her family.

She knows that she needs to fight harder than she's ever fought before to take out Kinsley and the dragon gods—to change the world for the better and ensure peace and justice reign.

In *Reign of Dragons,* for the first time in her life, she defied her master.

In *Fate of Dragons*, Rory learned how to give up a bit of her control. How to compromise.

In Blood of Dragons, she learned what it means to have a family. To trust, to let down her guard to her inner circle, and grow as a person.

In *Age of Dragons,* Rory finally accepted who she is: a dragon, a warrior, and someone worthy of being loved.

In *Fall of Dragons*, she realizes she's not prey—

she's a hunter, one who doesn't need the shadows to survive.

In *Death of Dragons,* Rory steps up as a role model, she learned to live not just for her close-knit family, but for others as well.

In *Queen of Dragons,* she takes up the mantle of queen, learning that it's those around her—her family that enables her to carry the burden of protecting others.

In this book, Rory takes on a selfish, power-hungry Kinsley Vaer, who frees the dragon gods.

Our beautiful badass heroine is faced with the hardest battle she's ever faced, but she doesn't do it alone—her men are by her side every step of the way.

Once again, Tucker has me chuckling at his one-liners and goofy grin, and panting with his sexy green eyes and shoulder length mess of dark brown hair as he and Rory peel the wall paper with their hot sex scene. Our weapons expert has a heart of gold and loves to watch Rory smile, but he can take out a fly at fifty yards with a single shot. He's the perfect deadly combination.

Drew's admiration of Rory and support for her new station are hot as hell as he encourages her just when she seems to need it most.

Jace steps into his role as general of Rory's army. He trains the army of giant metallic dragons and dojo soldiers to work together because there is no room for weakness. Queen Rory's army will be unstoppable.

Oh, and we can't forget our hot as hell ice dragon. Levi and Rory grow even closer when the lords orb is found, and their bond becomes undeniable. Our heroine's silent protector finally finds his voice—with Rory, at least.

This is the last chapter in the Dragon Dojo Brotherhood. I love the way Rory's story has come full circle and how she's grown into her own power. Though it's hard to say goodbye, I am so damn proud of Rory and her men, and this is the perfect ending to their journey—one of triumph, loyalty, and love.

I couldn't play in this world so much if you didn't love reading it. So, from the bottom of my heart, *thank you*. Thank you a million times over. If I ever get to meet you in person, I'm going to give you an Irena sized hug.

You are a true gift to me.

If you haven't already, make sure to **join the exclusive, fans-only Facebook group to get the latest release news & updates**.

Until next time, babe!
Keep on being your beautiful, badass self.
-Olivia

PS. Amazon won't tell you when the next Dragon Dojo Brotherhood book will come out, but there are several ways you can stay informed.

1) **Soar on over to the Facebook group, Olivia's secret club for cool ladies,** so we can hang out! I designed it *especially* for badass babes like you. Consider this as your invite! We talk about kickass heroines, gorgeous men, our favorite fantasy romances, and... did I mention pictures of *gorgeous men?*

2) **Follow me directly on Amazon.** To do this, **head to my profile** and click the Follow button beneath my picture. That will prompt Amazon to notify you when I release a new book. You'll just need to check your emails.

3) **You can join my mailing list by going to** https://wispvine.com/newsletter/olivia-ash-email-signup/. This lets me slide into your inbox and basically

means we become best friends. Yep, I'm pretty sure that's how it works.

Doing one of these or **all three** (for best results) is the best way to make sure you get an update every time a new volume of the *Dragon Dojo Brotherhood* series is released. Talk to you soon!

BOOKS BY OLIVIA ASH

Dragon Dojo Brotherhood

Reign of Dragons

Fate of Dragons

Blood of Dragons

Age of Dragons

Fall of Dragons

Death of Dragons

Queen of Dragons

A Legend Among Dragons

Blackbriar Academy

The Trials of Blackbriar Academy

The Shadows of Blackbriar Academy

The Hex of Blackbriar Academy

The Blood Oath of Blackbriar Academy

The Battle of Blackbriar Academy

The Nighthelm Guardian Series

City of the Sleeping Gods

City of Fractured Souls

City of the Enchanted Queen

Demon Queen Saga

Princes of the Underworld

Wars of the Underworld

Sentinel Saga

By Dahlia Leigh and Olivia Ash

The Shadow Shifter

ABOUT THE AUTHOR

OLIVIA ASH

Olivia Ash spends her time dreaming up the perfect men to challenge, love, and protect her strong heroines (who actually don't need protecting at all). Her stories are meant to take you on a journey into the world of the characters and make you want to stay there.

Reviews are the best way to show Olivia that you care about her stories and want other people discover them. If you enjoyed this novel, please consider leaving a review at Amazon. Every review helps the author and she appreciates the time you take to write them.